The Gypsy Trail

The Gypsy Trail

Nicole Leigh West

LODESTONE
BOOKS

Winchester, UK
Washington, USA

First published by Lodestone Books, 2014
Lodestone Books is an imprint of John Hunt Publishing Ltd., Laurel House, Station Approach,
Alresford, Hants, SO24 9JH, UK
office1@jhpbooks.net
www.johnhuntpublishing.com

For distributor details and how to order please visit the 'Ordering' section on our website.

Text copyright: Nicole Leigh West 2013

ISBN: 978 1 78279 691 6

A CIP catalogue record for this book is available from the British Library.

Design: Stuart Davies

Printed in the USA by Edwards Brothers Malloy

We operate a distinctive and ethical publishing philosophy in all
areas of our business, from our global network of authors to
production and worldwide distribution.

CONTENTS

Acknowledgements

Thanks to Shelley, Desney, Vince, my family and fairy friends for their magical contributions to *The Gypsy Trail* adventure.

Chapter One

Ghost Hollow

The smell of stale sweat lingered as Claudia rolled on her back and pushed the sheet away. She inhaled, searching for the cool, antiseptic touch of morning air. Her fingers twitched as she touched her thighs and she opened her eyes to look at her legs.

One...two...three...four...five...ten. Ten bruises — violent handprints locked in blue. She tried to imagine what it was like to grip someone's flesh so hard that bruises formed. *Impossible.* She couldn't even squash the spiders that lived in her wardrobe, even though they held her clothes hostage with sticky webs.

She glanced away, towards the window and the grey sky crying misty tears. Rooftop gargoyles loomed over the grass, their shadows released by the rising sun. Ready for flight, batlike wings stretched towards the valley and open beaks whispered of escape.

Tears slipped down her neck as her feet touched the floor. Turning to face the mirror, she rubbed at purple smudges under her eyes. Her hair was a dark mass of knots and she imagined Margaret's voice echoing down the halls. "For heaven's sakes, Claudia, brush your hair!"

She groaned and raked her hands through the tangles, just as the smell of bacon rose from the kitchen below. Her nose lifted and her stomach rumbled, competing with the pain of her throbbing legs. She took a deep breath and looked in the mirror again.

At least the tangled hair hid her red, puffy eyes.

"Good morning, Miss Claudia," Margaret said, as Claudia ran into the dining room. Dust motes floated by the wooden panels on the walls, glinting in the light from the bay window, and her shoulders relaxed.

"Good morning, Margaret." She sat on an oversized antique chair and dangled her feet, trying to scrape the floor with a big toe.

Margaret put a bowl of porridge on the table and fussed about, placing the spoon and napkin just so. Claudia stifled a groan. Of course the bacon wasn't for her, Margaret would probably eat all of it. Rubbing wrinkled, chubby hands on her apron, the housekeeper hurried back to the kitchen, back to the delicious, sizzling pan of breakfast heaven.

"Oh well, you must eat this too." She pretended to scoop porridge into two imaginary bowls. Snow-White and Rose-Red nibbled on the gluggy oats, talking to each other in their musical language.

Gibberish really. Considering they only lived in her head. *Didn't they?*

They weren't real friends like other teenagers had anyway, but they smiled at her and ate with her at the lonely table and sometimes they slept in her bed, like two little kittens at her feet. They even looked like her, with straight, black eyebrows and large, almond-shaped eyes like Arabian princesses.

Except, theirs were green and hers were ugly old brown.

She wasn't jealous of their green eyes, not really. After all, she'd be so lonely without them. *Stuck in a tiny town in the Czech Republic. Has anyone even heard of Lednice? Doubtful. Maybe it's just a secret dumping ground for unwanted children.* She rested her forehead on the cool surface of the table. She sensed decay in her bones. *Is it possible to rot at the age of fifteen?* The old people in the old house invaded her cells until she felt ancient and shrivelled.

She dragged her head up from the table and spotted old man gardener outside, raking the leaves into a pile next to his shiny ride-on lawn mower.

Just like he did every day.

Plucking an imaginary rake from the air — pink and purple with gold prongs rather than rusty metal — she swished back and forth, scattering the dust.

"Miss Claudia, you mustn't behave so." Margaret stood at the door, staring with round, faded blue eyes. "Go at once to the schoolroom. You know Mr Campbell is waiting." Two hair curlers poked through the housekeeper's floral headscarf, bouncing as she spoke.

Why didn't the miserable old woman just go back to England? Surely she wasn't trapped here as well; *she* was an adult. As Margaret turned to go, Claudia stifled a half snort, half giggle at the sight of the woman's large backside wobbling under her skirt, drawing the material further into the crevices with each step.

Her need to laugh didn't last long. She stood still for a moment to study the long walk down the corridor to the schoolroom. Stag heads lined the walls, their antlers casting harsh shadows. As always, she ran straight down the middle, scared they'd leap out at her, terrified by the fixed stare of their dead eyes.

At the end, she stopped, ready tears close to spilling down her nose at the thought of another sunless day in the glass-walled conservatory.

Mr Campbell glared at her and pointed to the singular desk in the room. His role of taskmaster was never more apparent than first thing in the morning. Claudia sat on the chair and leant her elbows on the desk, squashing the urge to put more distance between herself and her tutor.

"Why are you still in your nightgown, Claudia?"

"I didn't think to change it."

"Well, next time, *Miss Claudia*, please ensure you dress appropriately for school." He peered at her from the top of his reading glasses. His eyes were too close to his nose.

Claudia nodded, trying hard not to groan. *Why?* There was no one to dress for. *Stupid man.*

"We will begin with geography today." Mr Campbell put four heavy books on the table.

His monotonous voice drizzled into her ears. He was balding, with a narrow, mouse-like face and Claudia imagined him scurrying back to a neat and tidy mouse hole each day, to read the dictionary over a cup of sugarless, milk-less tea. She giggled at the thought and covered her mouth, growing tired of her own endlessly changing emotions. A loud yawn escaped.

"Please refrain from that behaviour, Claudia. Open your book to page nine. We'll continue from yesterday." Mr Campbell pursed his lips.

Perhaps he was so cross because he'd just returned home from one of his hunting trips, without the rabbits he liked Margaret to turn into stew. Claudia always imagined fluffy, white rabbits, bounding across the fields to visit each other's burrows when Margaret offered her that stew. She never ate it.

At least today was geography. She'd have precious moments with her window to the world; the small window that was Mr Campbell's computer. *Imagine exploring exotic places like France and Italy and Africa.* She knew Snow-White and Rose-Red would love to join her on a trip overseas. She looked up at her tutor, the urge to annoy him with useless questions always too hard to resist.

A flash of colour zipped through the grey outside.

"Oh!" Claudia clapped her hand over her mouth. Leaning forward to stare out the window, she saw a long row of trucks and wagons and horse trailers snake through the field below. The very same field she'd named 'ghost hollow' for its haunted emptiness.

"Who are they?" She jumped up to press her nose against the glass.

"Gypsies. Carnival people. They are none of your concern whatsoever."

Claudia let the word roll around in her mind. *Gypsies.*

"Good Lord, girl, close your mouth. They're wandering thieves and nothing more. They are certainly not worthy of your attention. This country has enough economic woes without vagabonds disturbing the peace. Let that be the end of the topic."

Claudia no longer heard him. *Gypsies! Could they really be here, at this very moment, planning to stay on the grounds?* She ran back through the hall and into the library with its wall-to-wall shelves. The wooden ladder was there, beckoning her nimble feet and she climbed to the top shelf where Margaret kept all the interesting books.

She'd read about travelling theatre companies before, dancers and musicians of gypsy blood, forever trekking across the land. *Where is that book?*

"Miss Claudia, I will only say this once. Get down from that ladder and come back to the schoolroom." Mr Campbell's voice rumbled beneath her. Margaret, hands clasping her heaving chest, rushed to help her down.

Claudia's tingling fingers grazed the smooth, leather bound books as she turned to face her jailers. She stepped down the ladder and stood in front of the angry pair, biting her thumbnail and lowering her head. Out of the corner of her eye, she noticed old man gardener sneak by, one sturdy finger held up to his mouth in a gesture of silence.

What's he doing inside the house?

As she was thoroughly reprimanded by two stern voices, a sympathetic smile crossed the gardener's face. Her hands flew to her cheeks and she bit her bottom lip to stop the smile she so wanted to return.

"Now now, you must not cry. Contain your emotions as befits your station, young lady," Margaret said, assuming her most pompous tone.

Claudia scratched her head. *So confusing.* Not Margaret's complete misinterpretation of her feelings — the housekeeper rarely understood her — but her reference to Claudia's 'station'.

What is my station anyway?

She knew she was wealthy, of course, what with all the boxes of clothes, shoes and jewellery arriving monthly from London. But everything was far too adult for her and stupidly impractical. She was happiest in her nightgowns.

Can't believe Margaret is still lecturing. The words had turned into a drone.

Just keep nodding.

"You, man, what are you doing inside?" Mr Campbell's voice interrupted her thoughts.

"Excuse me, sir, just reporting on them gypsies to the gatekeeper." Old man gardener kept his eyes fixed on the floor.

"On your way then."

"Why can't he come inside?" Claudia asked, desperate to talk to the man and, at the same time, scared to the core at the mention of the gatekeeper.

"He is a servant; it's not his place to be in here with you, as you well know. Now, back to your books, Miss Claudia. There has been enough kerfuffle for one day." Mr Campbell shooed her out of the library.

Kerfuffle? Surely the old tutor is quite mad. He and Margaret were servants also. *So why are they allowed in the house?* Claudia shook her head, shrugged and skipped up the hallway, savouring the rare excitement she felt brewing inside.

* * * *

Alfred Campbell watched Claudia leave and frowned at the dark, messy hair hanging down the girl's back. He vowed to have a word with the housekeeper for failing to uphold grooming standards. After all, they were paid well by their absent employers; they could not be seen to be negligent with their charge.

A hot rush of heat stained his neck as his student turned back, matching his stare. The intensity of her dark, oddly-shaped eyes, tilting up, as they did, on the outer corners like a cat, always caught him off guard. Surely she was half mad. Good Lord, anyone would be, living as she had from such a young age. No contact with other children, or with normal society.

He cleared his throat, pushing his chest forward to straighten his spine. All that mattered was giving his pupil an education worthy of his wages from Edward Spencer and keeping a job far away from London. He wondered if the rain would soon clear. His fingers itched to grasp the cool, smooth surface of his new, double-barrelled shotgun.

"Mr Campbell, may we invite the gypsies inside?"

Alfred Campbell rolled his eyes at the suggestion. "Of course not," he snapped, annoyed at the interruption to his hunting daydream.

He watched Claudia as she stole sneaky glances outside. He followed her gaze and scowled at the colourful wagons and the people rushing around, leading horses from trailers and unpacking large objects at the far end of the field.

"Whilst we can do nothing about the presence of these people, we can, and most certainly will, ignore them. Eyes back to your book." He tried to raise his eyebrows in his most commanding manner.

"They're staying on our land; surely we're allowed to speak with them?"

"We, or rather you, do not own this land."

"Well of course I don't. But…well, surely my parents gave them permission to stay?"

"Gypsies rarely ask for permission and, I can assure you, your parents will not be happy about their arrival. However, if you must know, they *are* allowed to be here. Well, this land has a cursed 'open field' policy anyway. Lord knows why, but it means the public can camp on the lower section by the lake." He folded his arms and turned his back to the window.

"Why haven't you told me this before?" Claudia's head cocked to one side, a gesture that infuriated Alfred Campbell by its simplicity.

He took a deep breath. "You haven't asked and it's has been quite a few years since they were last here."

"They've been before?" Claudia sat on the edge of her seat, leaning towards him.

"Yes, many times. But you were in the nursery section, in the front of the house, where we could more easily shield your young eyes from such odious distractions."

"Well, then." Claudia frowned. "Why would my parents mind, if it's legal?"

"Because they would. The whole community *minds*. Now, that's enough. Start your reading. Please."

"My parents don't even care to see *me*, so why would they care if I see the gypsies?"

Alfred Campbell was struck by her voice. She didn't seem to speak with anger or resentment; it was simply a statement of fact. If it were he… No. Must stay focused on the work. "At this rate you will not be finished in time for lunch. Head down, young lady."

His student did as he asked, her head held up by thin, delicate fingers resting on her chin. She seemed to focus on her study, though Lord only knew what really went on inside the mind of an overly curious, teenage girl, until Margaret summoned them to a lunch of corn meat and vegetables with white sauce.

He ensured Claudia's meal was served in the formal dining room before joining Margaret at the small table in the kitchen.

He whispered to the housekeeper, "You must force Claudia to dress in proper clothes. I'm sure it's never likely to happen, but if her parents arrived unexpectedly they would be mortified by her appearance."

"I've tried, but she won't let me near her in the morning anymore. When I ask her to dress herself, seeing as she won't allow me to help, she just smiles in that vague way of hers and ignores me." Margaret waved her cutlery around in circles as she spoke.

"Well, I don't know what must be done but it's simply not right. She's far too old now to be behaving in such a manner." Alfred Campbell sat straight in his chair, elbows pulled in, carefully carving his lunch into bite-sized pieces.

"I know. It's strange, the way she only wears those nightgowns. Perhaps she's become shy about her..." Margaret looked up at him and her cheeks reddened. "Her approaching adulthood."

"You must speak with her then. I can't broach such a subject with a young girl."

"It's not my place either. Her mother should be here to do that. It's one thing to look after a little girl..." Her voice trailed off as she wiped beads of sweat from her forehead. "It's hard, after all, at her age. Maybe we could be more lenient with her schedule? Let her roam outside a bit? Her parents will never know and she might start taking an interest in more normal things, like..."

Alfred Campbell paused, dropped his fork and began to rub both temples. "That is absolutely out of the question. I'll simply write a letter to Mr and Mrs Spencer addressing our concerns. They'll surely tell us what to do, or perhaps Mrs Spencer will come here herself to speak with her daughter."

"Huh, wishful thinking." Margaret's cutlery clattered onto her plate as she stood to clear the table.

"Any left for me then?" The gruff voice came from the door at the back of the kitchen.

Alfred Campbell narrowed his eyes and watched as Margaret turned to face the gatekeeper, her lip curling and her hand reaching to cover the small amount of cleavage peeking over her apron. The man leaned against the doorframe. A ring of keys hung from his belt, weighing his pants down at the side to reveal the white, bulging flesh of his stomach.

"Yes, yes, I'll bring it to you at the gatehouse, just as I do every day," Margaret said, not meeting the gatekeeper's steady leer.

The gatekeeper sniggered softly and Alfred Campbell lifted a hand in greeting, but, instead, flicked his fingers up in a sign of dismissal. After all, there was no need for the man to come to the kitchen. Margaret would never forget to take him his lunch. *The woman runs the household with military precision. Besides, the man would do well to try dieting.*

Alfred Campbell concentrated on finishing his own meal, chewing each piece of food at least twenty times. He dabbed the corners of his mouth with a napkin, and rose.

When he went to collect Claudia, he found her gazing at the wall of the formal dining room, nodding her head and tapping her feet on the ground to a silent tune. This was further proof to him that more discipline was needed, certainly not less.

"Time to resume our lessons," he interrupted her, not willing to acknowledge his fear, triggered by the intangible light shining in her eyes. The childlike wonder conjured distant memories…a smile just for him, full of love, making him feel alive, protective, human.

Claudia stood and followed him into the schoolroom, but not before he noticed the peculiar smile playing on her pink, Cupid's bow mouth.

* * * *

The afternoon would have been long and boring without fantasies of the mysterious people outside, sending twinges of excitement to the pit of Claudia's stomach.

That evening, she raced earlier than usual to her bedroom after supper. Margaret and Mr Campbell had already retired to the servant's quarters and she was, finally, free from their hawk-like eyes.

Her narrow window allowed glimpses of the wagons as they began to disappear under darkness. One lone figure seemed to face the chateau, standing very still with his hands in his pockets. Claudia closed her eyes and imagined him speaking to her. His voice would be deep and musical like the perfect, storybook gypsy, dancing and laughing and talking with her about all the mysteries of the world.

When she opened her eyes again, the gypsies in the clearing had faded away into night and a cold chill had crept into the room. Flicking on the light, she walked to the fireplace to prod the coals into life.

The familiar jingling of keys echoed in the silence. She paused, clenching the metal fire prod until her fingers shuddered. Down hallways and empty rooms, the sound grew louder as it came closer. She dropped the rod and dived under the covers of the bed.

When the gatekeeper opened the door, she rolled into a tight ball, pushing her body into the mattress. His fat fingers lurched towards her, tugging at the sheets from the bottom of the bed. Tonight, if she screamed, would the gypsies hear her? No one *else* ever did. She whimpered, hiding her face in the quilt.

A fat hand gripped her jaw. "Quiet, little girl, or you know what will happen." He grinned, his black eyes widening beneath swollen lids as he scanned her bare legs.

She clamped her mouth shut, gritting her teeth and squeezing her eyelids together so tightly she thought they might burst. Sweat and mothballs invaded her nose. His hands felt hot and damp and rough with calluses as he pawed at the soft skin of her thighs. Her body trembled, and she screamed silently in the dark behind her eyes.

In the morning, Margaret let Spotty in before she woke. Claudia was only allowed to play with Spotty three days a week and only if she completed all her schoolwork correctly. She laughed as the purring cat jumped on the bed to nuzzle its wet nose into her neck.

"Now, Miss Claudia, this morning you must bathe and dress and only then will I allow Spotty to spend the day with you."

"I have no need to dress up, Margaret, but I'll certainly have a bath."

"Mr Campbell doesn't appreciate your unkempt appearance, Miss; you're nearly a lady and must start behaving as such."

Claudia sighed. "I'll wear a riding outfit."

"What for?"

"Riding outfits are more comfortable than those stupid dresses."

"At least that will be an improvement on the nightgown. The bath is ready for you. I'll be downstairs with breakfast when you're finished."

Claudia walked to the bathtub in the adjoining room and climbed in. The warmth seeped into her injured skin and she rubbed at the soreness, staring at herself and willing the bruises away. A small amount of dark hair, down below, had started to grow a few months ago and she wished desperately for it to disappear. *Why had it grown?* Maybe that evil gatekeeper had transferred it to her most private parts from his awful, hairy arms.

She hopped out of the bath, dried herself and tugged a brush through her knotty hair. She glanced at the one photo she had of her parents, in a gold frame at the back of her dressing table. *What would it be like to have shiny, blonde hair, like my mother's?* She wished she'd inherited that, rather than her father's dark hair. He stood next to Grace in the picture, his chest puffed out, a full head shorter than her mother with only a smattering of the hair left on his head — and it wasn't even dark, just mousy brown. Grace and Edward Spencer. *My absent parents.*

She tugged harder on the knots, so hard her head jolted each time they gave way. Her scalp began to sting and the stinging seeped into her eyes. The dressing table blurred in front of her and she tasted salt on her lips. She dropped the brush on the floor and ran to the table to slam the picture face down on the gleaming wooden surface.

You can't make me cry. You're not even real.

Mr Campbell actually smiled when he saw her that morning.

"Good to see you dressed today, Claudia," he said.

Claudia beamed, liking the rare approval. "I have a very serious question today, Mr Campbell."

"Yes?"

"Why can't I go outside on my own?"

"We have discussed this, Claudia." He rolled his eyes. Rolling of the eyes *was* a regular facial expression in the chateau. "Your mother's most heartfelt wish is that you remain indoors and receive a proper up-bringing. That does not include venturing outdoors and turning into a ruffian. You're not a boy."

"So I'll never be able to run on the grass?" She turned her head to stare at the wide expanse of manicured lawn.

"You may *stroll* on the grass at appropriate times, running only leads to accidents, and we do have our monthly visits to the stables at the neighbouring property. You like viewing the horses, don't you? And you also have the greenhouse and a three-storey mansion. Really, you're a very lucky young lady; not everyone lives in such luxury, you know."

"No, I don't know and how will I ever know if I don't go anywhere?"

"Claudia, there are many dangers in the world, even here around the chateau. Not all people are like Margaret and I. We must ensure your only influences are those that benefit your education and upbringing."

Claudia had already met evil. She pressed her hands over both eyes. *Think of something else. Think of something else.* The greenhouse *was* a place of beauty with its rare plants and tinkling fountains. But, apart from a section at the back where the roof was open to let the sun in to warm rare plants from Africa, it was all indoors, stifled and trapped within walls. *Just like me.*

"Why then, don't we live in England if this is such a terrible place outside?" She had asked the question many times before.

Mr Campbell's neck stained red. "I'm not privy to that information, *as well you know,* but I presume it is a matter of ensuring you receive a proper education, away from the distractions other teenagers face. After all, your parents have the means to do it and, well, they are very, very busy." His lips clamped together and turned white.

Stop. Stop asking. Not worth going to bed hungry.

The hours dragged on until Mr Campbell finally left the schoolroom to bring in the morning tea. Claudia swivelled in her chair to gaze out at the gypsy camp. The trailers and trucks were just visible at the end of the field, but it was too far away. She could only imagine smiling faces and glittering headscarves and bells jingling from dancing feet.

Close by, the leaves rustled in the hedge by the rose garden. *Surely Spotty hasn't escaped the library?* He'd seemed so comfortable there after breakfast. She peered through the glass, waiting for the cat to bound out of the green with a grasshopper or a field mouse caught in his claws.

Her hand slapped over her mouth before a gasp could escape.

A man, with black hair and deep brown skin, leant on the hedge. He held a hand up in greeting and his white teeth glowed as he smiled. Trying to control her sudden shaking, she lifted her hand in reply. He nodded, almost bowing to her, before turning back to the camp. It was all over in less than a minute and Claudia's throat constricted as she tried to draw her next breath.

Too soon, she heard quick, light footsteps rush down the stag head hall. She looked back at her book, her face burning red and her heart beating so fast she thought it might jump out on to the floor.

Chapter Two

Little Lady of the Glass House

Claudia's teeth chattered as she watched fog float by the window in the sitting room. *Why does autumn so quickly give way to winter?* Her breath misted over the glass and she drew her name with her pointer finger in the condensation. Outside in the front garden, Spotty slinked through the hedges, stepping gingerly over the wet grass in his search for insects. Claudia laughed at his sly antics and wiped the mist away so she could better see him.

But, the clear glass only revealed the gatekeeper waddling into the scene and wrecking it. He looked at Claudia. For long seconds she forgot to breathe as he stared at her while crouching to call Spotty, his hand outstretched and his fingers wriggling like fat sausages. The cat stalked towards the fingers, sniffing them as his tail flicked back and forth.

No, Spotty, he has no food. Get away from him.

The cat's ears pricked, as if he heard her mental warning. Too late. The gatekeeper caught Spotty in both hands, holding the feline up in the air. Staring right into Claudia's eyes, he put one hand around Spotty's neck, squeezing hard. Claudia dropped to her knees, sliding her hands down the glass, blinking through a rush of tears as Spotty hissed and tried to scratch, his paws flailing uselessly in the air.

Suddenly, the gatekeeper let go.

Spotty fell on his side, dead still.

Her forehead hit the window as she pushed hard up against it. "Spotty! Please, please get up." Her words stopped short at the glass.

She refocused and could just see the rise and fall of Spotty's breath. In seconds, the cat twisted on to his feet and bolted into a dense garden bed.

She drew a deep, ragged breath. *He knows I love Spotty, he knows I won't tell. So why does he pretend to hurt him? Evil, vicious man.*

"You're up early today, Miss Claudia. What's all the yelling for that cat about?" Margaret suddenly stood behind her.

Why can't Margaret see what's happening under her very nose? Maybe she can. Then why doesn't she care enough to help me? Claudia turned back to the window and saw the gatekeeper point a finger full of warning at her, before it turned into a friendly wave for Margaret. *No, she can't see. He's too sly to ever get caught. Ever.*

Claudia sniffed back tears. "I was trying to get Spotty to look at me."

"He can't hear you through the glass, silly girl. I've come to tell you that Mr Campbell is off hunting today, so you won't have any lessons."

Oh no, disgusting rabbit stew for dinner, then. "Hunting is an awful hobby, I wouldn't do it, even if it meant I could be outside more."

"Yes, I have to say I agree with you there. I don't fancy boiling rabbits either, but Mr Campbell must have his...recreation time."

"What will I do?"

"You can read your schoolbooks like a good girl. You'll have to eat a cold lunch, so I've left it in the kitchen for you. I'm popping in to town for the groceries."

Claudia smiled, excited about a whole day to herself. She could do whatever she liked. She could dream about the gypsies at the bottom of her garden.

"Now wipe that look off your face, young lady, there won't be any sneaking out to the courtyard, not with gypsies on the land. Not to mention that gatekeeper on full alert for trespassers." Margaret paused, her eyebrows knitting together.

Claudia no longer listened. She'd only disobeyed once, a year ago when Mr Campbell had been away. Margaret and old man gardener had gone in to town to buy the new ride-on lawn mower and, hours after they'd left, she'd discovered the front door open; not just unlocked, but *open*.

She'd bolted outside to run around the courtyard, circling it until she was breathless and dizzy and collapsing with laughter. Her eyes had closed to catch her breath and, when she'd opened them again, she'd been staring straight at Margaret's cream, Birkenstock shoes.

Can't be blamed for that, they'd left the door open. "But I—"

"Uh uh. No excuses, thank you." Margaret toyed with her necklace, pulling the chain away from the folds of skin in her neck. The wrinkles on Margaret's face were so deep, she appeared to wear a permanent frown. Claudia imagined putting her hands on the old lady's face and stretching it into a smile.

"May I please have Spotty inside today?" she asked instead.

"Well, maybe just this once on a Monday. I'll have the gardener find him. Use the two-way radio in the kitchen to call for the gatekeeper in an emergency, you remember? But I won't be long."

"Yes, Margaret, thank you." *Not even if the house is burning down around me.*

Margaret strode away. Claudia waited for the squeak of the housekeeper's shoes to disappear, before she sat at the kitchen table to eat a thick slice of bread.

She hummed a tune she'd been composing in her head. Mr Campbell tried to teach her music, although he was actually tone deaf. Sometimes, he let her listen to snippets of classical music on the computer. Her favourite was '*Scheherazade*', by Nikolai Rimsky-Korsakov. Listening to it made her heart ache for reasons she couldn't understand.

Still not allowed to play the grand piano in the parlour though. 'It's just for adults,' he'd said, over and over again.

She brushed the crumbs off the table the minute they fell and told Snow-White and Rose-Red to do the same, humming out loud as she cleaned.

"That's a nice tune, Miss," old man gardener said, appearing in front of her with Spotty. The cat purred happily in his arms.

"Oh...thank you." She lowered her eyes to the floor and fought against the burning in her cheeks.

"Here's your cat then." He gently placed Spotty on the floor. Claudia bent to pat the black and white fur. "Why don't you go outside and play with him?"

"I'm not allowed," she said, her voice catching and coming out a mere whisper.

He looked at her with a deep frown. "Who says?"

"My parents told Margaret and Mr Campbell to only allow me outside when accompanied by them until I receive a proper education, as befits my station." Claudia parroted her teacher in her most proper tone,

Old man gardener's face reddened, Claudia couldn't tell if with anger or amusement.

"You certainly speak like you're educated, Miss," he said, rubbing his weathered cheek with a gnarled, brown hand.

"Thank you." *What other way is there to speak?* She mentally searched her limited conversation skills to keep him talking to her. "Do you like being a gardener?"

He scratched his chin and looked up at the ceiling. "I like to see things grow."

"Me too. But I don't get to very often. Except in the green-house."

"Well, that's a sad thing, Miss."

Claudia thought for a moment. "You may sit down. If you want to, of course."

"Thanks for asking, but I mustn't sit here with you," he replied with a kind smile. She bit her lip, trying to stop the disappointment from turning into tears.

"You could come outside with me."

Claudia paused, momentarily forgetting to breathe. "Really?"

He nodded in a hesitant, jerky way. "But you mustn't go out

near them front gardens, the gatekeeper stays watch there all day lately."

"I promise not to." She stood too quickly and the chair clattered behind her.

"Stay to the back of the house and you'll be safe enough. Those gypsies won't do you no harm."

Was he going to let her talk to the gypsies? Surely she was dreaming and would wake at any moment with a pile of school-books in front of her.

"Come on then, Miss, shut your mouth or the bugs'll get in. Let's go." He held one hand out and she clasped it tightly, staring up at him.

He unlocked the kitchen door — and there it was. The outside. The grass, the trees, the flowers and the cloudless blue sky, without her jailors to stop her from running. Bending to touch a sharp blade of grass, Claudia inhaled the scent of fresh dirt, closed her eyes and drifted with the soft breeze.

* * * *

The gardener rubbed his chest, pressing his hand over his heart as he watched Claudia's delight. *What're these silly folk thinking, shutting a child away from nature? Ah well, it ain't none of my business.* He'd ignored the folk of the big house for long enough and he'd continue to do so. Ignoring them was easier.

"You behave yourself and I'll come get you after my chores are done," he said, and she looked up at him, eyes as wide as saucers and glistening with ready tears.

Like a timid sparrow, she came to his side, stood on her tiptoes and kissed his wrinkled, sagging cheek. He put his hand to his face, touching the warmth left there.

Dear old Martha, God rest her soul, would have loved the little chit. Ah well, no use thinking about a wife long dead and buried back in Essex. Best to leave the memories there. As he watched, the girl twirled in circles on the grass before taking off on a mad run down the hill.

He chuckled to himself before walking to the garden shed to get his tools. *Surely letting the little lass out can't cause any harm.* She wouldn't tell those stuffy caretakers in the big house and his job was safe enough. Who else would want to work out on this lonely property, with no one but the beady eyed, gruff odd jobs men to chat to?

She was so pretty. All dark eyes and hair with ruby cheeks and lips to match. *Like those porcelain dolls Martha used to collect.* Not one for being locked indoors, that was for sure. She had the look of a forest imp, bursting to come out of its shell. He chuckled to himself again, happy to help make it happen. Happy for the contact with youth.

* * * *

Wind whistled by Claudia's cheeks and she was glad she'd put the riding suit on today; the jodhpurs were perfect for running. What should she do first? Climb the trees? Find insects in the grass? In all the excitement she'd left Spotty in the house. *Oh well, he'll curl up in a nice corner and sleep.* She was almost breathless at the thought of visiting the gypsies.

Do I dare? What if they don't like visitors?

She shrugged. Better to just wait and see what happened. Right now, birdsong captured her attention and she could see them in the trees, feathers glinting red in the branches. She reached out to a Redstart on a lower branch, recalling Mr Campbell's monotonous voice as he'd recited the names of the most common birds in the Czech Republic. It watched her closely, turning its little head from side to side, before jumping lightly, higher and higher, to sing from a safe distance.

"I wondered when you would venture outside, little lady of the glass house."

Claudia's knees jerked. The hairs on the back of her neck tingled as the deep voice overpowered the chattering birds.

She slowly turned around.

It was the dark-haired man. The gypsy with the brown, brown skin. He stood with his hands clasped behind his back, smiling a wide, friendly smile.

"I...I'm not allowed usually. To be outside that is." She lowered her eyes and focused on the man's bare feet.

"That's a very strange situation. Who makes up those rules?" As he spoke, small wrinkles appeared at the corners of his eyes.

"My parents and Margaret and Mr Campbell." She felt bolder now. His bare feet somehow made her feel comfortable and safe.

"How did you come to be outside today then, may I ask?" His smooth voice made his words sound like a melody and he gestured with his hands as he spoke.

"Mr Campbell is away and old man gardener let me. Oh, but please don't tell anyone, he'll be in awful trouble if they find out."

The gypsy's laugh was throaty and infectious. "Of course I would never tell your secrets. What is your name, if you would give me the honour of knowing it?"

"Claudia Spencer." She stood very, very straight, holding her chin high.

"My name is Dane, it's lovely to make your acquaintance, Claudia." He offered a tanned, squarish hand for her to shake. She did so and curtseyed at the same time.

Why did I curtsey? Stupid. Quick, say something. "You sound...um...English."

"Actually, I was born near here, in Slovenia, but I've spent most of my life in England." He smiled, white teeth glinting. He didn't look poor and malnourished as Mr Campbell had said the gypsies were.

"Would you like to come to the camp?"

"Oh yes!" Claudia jumped up and down, all thoughts of

decorum lost in her excitement.

"That's better." He grinned. "You have the most beautiful smile, Claudia."

She blushed as she followed him down to the valley below, drinking in every detail of his appearance. He wore black jeans and a loose, red shirt that rustled in the breeze. Spiry arms swung wide to match his quick stride and dark, grey splattered stubble covered his jaw and upper lip. His black hair curled around his ears, bouncing over his eyes in springy coils. He wasn't even as tall as old man gardener — and heroes were supposed to be tall — but he *was* dashing, just like one of the heroes in the romance novels Margaret hid in the kitchen cupboards.

She stared at the wagons as they came into view. They were long and oval shaped, painted in greens, reds and yellows with intricate flowers and fruits carved into the wooden frames. Frayed, transparent curtains fluttered in the breeze, held open to the sun by golden tassels, and musky, smoky smells seeped from the dark interiors.

Claudia felt a nervous twitch above her left eye as she struggled to keep up with the gypsy's pace. Strange people lounged on the steps of the wagons, chatting loudly as they peeled and chopped vegetables into bowls or played cards. Many looked up at her with curious expressions, most smiled as she passed. All were dressed in flowing, textured cloth, like they'd wrapped odd bits of material around themselves and tied the ends up with strings of bells and pieces of gold rope. *Just like a scene from a book.*

She breathed in the scent of fresh horse manure and some kind of spicy cooking that mixed with the damp earth. The sweet sound of a violin blended with laughter, and she noticed a group of teenagers chasing each other through the trees, leapfrogging and playfully tackling in the dried leaves. They looked like her, these people with dark, tangled hair and large, almond-shaped eyes.

Dane placed a firm hand on the small of her back. She jumped, cringing at the warmth of his skin through her shirt.

The gypsy frowned, bending down so that his head was level with her own. "No one here means you harm, little lady. I give you my word. Are you scared?"

She rubbed her nose and looked at her feet, shuffling from side to side. "Well, a little. But I'm not really sure why."

"This is all new for you, it's quite normal to feel nervous. Come, let's meet everyone. Perhaps, then, you can relax." Dane, with great care, offered her his hand.

This time, the heat of his skin felt safe and comforting as his fingers linked with hers.

"We're a mixed bunch here. Mainly travelling showmen, but we've picked up some strays along the way." His warmth made Claudia immediately want to know who the 'strays' were. "Do you know what the word 'gypsy' means?"

"Mr Campbell told me gypsies were wandering thieves." *Please disagree with the silly man. Please.*

He laughed. "Yes, some think so. Gypsy most certainly means 'wanderer', but we're not gypsies in the traditional sense. The Romani people are the true gypsies and, while Romani do live among us, our lives just mimic theirs to some extent."

"Because you don't live in a house?"

"You are a clever one! Mainly, yes."

"Well, how does that make you thieves? Do you steal chickens to eat?"

He laughed again, a low, husky sound that echoed through the trees. "No, we work for our food. Gypsies can be...well...unfairly treated. But, enough of that for now. Do you see everyone smiling at you?"

Claudia glanced around, struggling between shyness and an awkward need to be liked. She almost curtseyed each time anyone made eye contact with her.

Stop it. Mr Campbell said you only curtsey to royalty. But, these gypsies are all so...majestic.

They finally came to a small clearing, down near the very edge of the lake. Claudia, overcome by the water, ran until she came to an abrupt stop on the edge.

"Go ahead, put your hand in," Dane said from some distance behind her.

She turned and looked at him, aching to touch the silvery surface. He nodded, a curious smile playing on his lips, so she crouched down and put one finger in. It sent fine ripples out to the centre.

"How beautiful," she whispered, sensing Dane as he came to stand beside her. She pondered over the strange expression on his face — a fleeting frown as his lips formed words that never came. He offered a hand to help her up.

"Will you come and join us at the clearing? I'd like you to meet my lovely Oriana. You'll like her."

Claudia wiped her freezing finger on her shirt and followed Dane back to the clearing, already fascinated by the thought of 'my lovely Oriana'. This time she noticed a woman, dancing to a violin crescendo, a ballet of red, purple and gold cloth consuming her body as her arms made patterns in the air.

Claudia couldn't take her eyes from the woman's undulating hips and the bells tinkling on her waist. Light brown eyes met hers and crinkled with a smile, but the dancer didn't stop. The music peaked, then her hips slowed as her hands came to rest in graceful swirls by her sides.

Behind the dancer, a young man rested the violin on the ground as if it were made of glass. As he straightened to stand, he placed his hands on the dancer's shoulders, towering over her slender form.

His green eyes met Claudia's in a direct, questioning gaze. "Who is this ravishing creature, Dane?" he asked, a charming lopsided grin splitting his face.

"Hush, Brishan, you are far too young to speak so," the dancer said, turning to swat his hands away from her shoulders.

"This is Claudia, from the house," Dane said, glancing over his shoulder at the chateau. "Claudia, this is the love of my life, Oriana, and our nephew, Brishan."

Claudia began to curtsey and thought better of it. *Just in time.*

Oriana made it easy for her, catching her shoulders and bending to kiss her flaming cheeks. The scent of roses tickled her nose and the gypsy's soft cheek left a trail of warmth on her skin. Before she could breathe in, to relish it, to fall into the unexpected affection, she felt a sharp tug on the back of her jacket.

She turned as Brishan grasped her hands. He tugged on her arms, nearly unbalancing her and forcing her to run with him or fall over. The sound of Oriana's laughter followed them on the wind as they ran all the way to the end of the clearing. Brishan gripped her waist to lift her over the trench of a dried stream, before pulling her, higher and higher, towards the top of a steep hill.

"You look like a fairy. Are you?" he asked, bending over to catch his breath in huge gulps.

Claudia frowned. "I don't think so, but I've never seen one to know." Her heart pounded in her ears.

"Oh, we'll have to fix that."

Autumn had covered everything in gold and red. Trees swayed with the colour of fire on their branches and the ground glowed with fallen, orange leaves. The boy-man beside her appeared wild and dishevelled like the leaves themselves as they tumbled over the grass. She tried to squash the nerves somer-saulting in her stomach.

"We'd only need to grow you some wings and you could fly off to fairy land." Brishan winked.

"How old are you?" Claudia asked. *Much too old to believe in fairy tales.*

"Sixteen, almost seventeen. And you?"

"Fifteen. You're the first boy I've ever really met. I mean, I know old man gardener and Mr Campbell, my teacher. And the evil gatekeeper. But they're old. Not like you." Her words came out in a fast, jumbled mass.

"Well, I'm happy about that. I feel special." His smile tugged at one corner of his mouth. "So, who is this gatekeeper and why is her evil? Does he cook and eat girls like you for dinner?"

"Oh, he's just very mean." Claudia glanced at her arm, absently rubbing an old bruise. "Won't Dane come looking for you? What about your parents?" Her heart thudded, hard and painful in her chest.

"My parents are busy rehearsing for tonight's performance in town, they're actors, and Dane knows you are safe with me."

"Why should Dane care about me? I only just met him."

"Dane cares about everyone." Brishan shrugged and his black, wavy hair tangled over his neck. "Sorry to drag you away just then, I...simply had an uncontrollable urge to." He smiled again, looking deeply into her eyes as if he was trying to find something.

She didn't know what he was trying to find, but she did understand what he meant. Spontaneous urges filled her life. *If only I could act on more of them.* She felt her face stretch in a smile and found she couldn't contain the giggles bubbling in her throat.

His eyes sparkled at the sound of her laugher. "What's it like to live in such a palace?"

"Lonely. It's kind of like a pretty jail." Claudia's face twitched as the sad truth spilled from her mouth.

Brishan's eyes narrowed. "Lucky *we're* here then," he said, his voice now quiet and gentle. "I understand feeling trapped." For a long moment, he stared towards the horizon, his winged eyebrows drawn together in a frown.

Claudia looked down at her feet, swallowing hard to combat the sudden dryness in her throat. "Brishan is a funny name."

Although, the way it sounded rolling off her tongue, '*Brisharrn'*, was somehow musical, like the whooshing of water fountains in the green house.

He laughed. "It means 'born in the rain', but really, I was conceived in the rain." His smile was open and sort of impish.

Claudia dragged her eyes from his and focused on the ground again. "I think I should go back now, old man gardener will come for me soon and I don't want to get him in trouble."

"As you wish, my fairy," he said with a low, flourishing bow. This time, her laugh exploded, full and unheeded, blending with the rustle of dried leaves. Brishan, laughing also, swung his arm over her shoulders to escort her back down the hill.

Dane and Oriana stood with old man gardener in the clearing. The group laughed also and Claudia felt her heart swell at the sight of the old man's smile.

He's made my dreams come true today.

"Well then, Miss, had a good time did you?" he called out to her as Brishan pushed her back through the trees.

"Oh yes, thanks to you." She wanted so much to hug him but an inbred sense of propriety held her back. That and the fact that she never hugged anybody and really couldn't quite think of how to approach it.

"Glad to hear it, but we must get you back now."

Claudia sighed and nodded once, her head swivelling from one to the other as the old man and Dane seemed to share a silent communication.

"It's been an honour to meet you, Claudia." Dane dropped to one knee as if addressing a queen. Claudia's cheeks flamed but she laughed all the same. Brishan caught her hand up in his own and kissed it, looking into her eyes with a cheeky wink. She remembered to breathe, then turned to follow old man gardener back to the house, waving at Oriana and smiling at all the shouts of 'farewell' following her on the breeze.

She'd never seen the chateau from this angle, rising up from the hill like a regal monarch on a throne. From the front, it looked like a fairy-tale castle, in amongst the roses and hedges of the manicured gardens, with the cast-iron, oval green house extending from its side. Battlements, spires and gargoyles adorned the giant, rectangular structure, in what Mr Campbell called neo-gothic style.

Often, she'd wandered the rooms, trying to count the windows on all three stories — sometimes fifty, sometimes sixty. She usually lost count.

But from here, with two wings jutting out from the long, main residence and rows of imposing arched windows, it looked like a living, breathing giant, waiting to swallow her whole. The square courtyard in between the wings was covered in beige gravel, and she listened as it crunched under her riding boots, all the while fighting the urge to run back to the gypsies.

"Now you go on inside and pretend like you read your books all day." As old man gardener spoke, large rain drops splashed on his nose and thunder rolled in the distance.

"I will. Thank you again." Claudia's voice trembled.

He unlocked the kitchen door and peered into the dark room, pushing his hand over his thinning grey hair to flick the water off. "All clear; go in out of the rain, a storm's brewing out here. And don't worry, Miss, I'll help you do it again." He rubbed the top of her head and Claudia beamed up at him.

If Santa Claus was real, this is what he'd be like.

She floated into her bedroom and sat on the floor to wait while the late afternoon drifted by, ready to watch the camp disappear under night again. Over and over, she replayed the day, moment by delicious moment, until she felt drowsy and flushed with the anticipation of more.

"Claudia!" Margaret's voice boomed through the hallways. Breaking into an instant sweat, Claudia stood, too quickly, and steadied herself on the side of the bed, before rushing to the kitchen.

"There you are, child, why is your face so red?"

Claudia scanned her brain for a lie, something so foreign it didn't come easily. "I was in my bedroom and I heard you calling, so I ran downstairs." *Not a lie, after all.* She breathed easier.

"You mustn't run anymore, you are far too old for that." Margaret sniffed loudly. "Mr Campbell has been...detained. Something about the weather. His hunt was obviously *not* successful." Margaret shook her head, absently rubbing the marble bench top with a bright green cloth. "The man should have been born years earlier. That way, he could have gone off to war, like my dear departed father. Hunting's not so exciting when you're forced to do it and the prey are people. Ridiculous hobby." Margaret looked down at a ring that dangled from her necklace.

Had her 'dear departed' father given it to her? Claudia opened her mouth to ask, but her throat closed over and the words wouldn't come out.

"Mr Campbell said you ought to know what books to continue on with, in his absence, and that you must complete the assignment for science, before his return. Yes?"

"Of course I will. But when do you think he'll come back?"

"Heaven knows. Your teacher is a brilliant man, but his passion for hunting is beyond my comprehension. Go and wash, Miss Claudia and take that riding suit off. Ridiculous, really, when you have so many beautiful clothes to wear." The house-keeper bustled over to the stove, mumbling under her breath about wasted money.

That night, the gatekeeper did not come. Had a magical spell taken over the household? Was she released from her night-mares? Maybe he was down in the valley, hunting gypsies with one of Mr Campbell's shotguns. *Please stay away, stay away from all of us.* As she closed her eyes, her sleep was blessed by unicorns and fairies, touching her with magic wands and flying her all over the world to visit ancient castles and sparkling beaches.

Gypsy magic.

The moment light filtered in through the window, Claudia jumped out of bed and ran to her oversized, uselessly full cupboard. *Why on earth do my parents send so many outfits, when I'm hardly allowed outside?* Their reasoning was beyond her comprehension, but today it didn't matter. She ran a hand over a brand new, soft brown riding suit that had arrived last week, clenching the material in her fists to contain her excitement. She carefully brushed her hair, and then dressed and ran downstairs to the kitchen.

"Good morning, Miss Claudia. I did ask you not to run, I believe?" Margaret quirked a heavily pencilled eyebrow.

"I'm sorry, Margaret, but I'm very hungry today."

"Well, at least you're dressed." The housekeeper sighed. "I've decided that Spotty can come inside again to keep you company, *however*, I noticed he seemed quite neglected yesterday, asleep on a chair in the library. I hope that means you were busy reading?" She curled a tea towel in one hand and planted the other on her hip. "The gardener will bring him in after breakfast."

"Oh, thank you, Margaret!" Claudia clasped her hands together, committing the brief moment of kindness to memory.

"You be sure to finish your lessons though, I've put them out on your desk in the schoolroom. A cold lunch is ready for you; I noticed you didn't eat yesterday?"

Claudia's cheeks blazed red. "I think I forgot."

"You must not forget to eat, that's why you're so hungry today. I'll be in the guest wing all week with two ladies from town; up in that airless attic, polishing all that ridiculous silver that no one sees. Ah well, but it must be done, even if it's just going straight back into boxes for you to inherit someday. Please don't bother us, unless you must, hmm?"

"I won't bother you." Claudia spoke in a whisper, lowering her head and dropping her arms so they swung against her legs a few times.

Today, though, the feeling of rejection was brief. She watched Margaret leave, then shovelled the porridge into her mouth and gathered up the bread and cheese left in the fridge. When old man gardener came, she was standing next to the back door, tapping the wooden frame and chewing on her bottom lip.

"I see you're ready then, Miss?" He chuckled. "Margaret...erm...that housekeeper not here today then? What about Campbell?"

"Mr Campbell is hunting, and Margaret is going to be up in the attic all day."

"Good. Let's go then."

"Okay. Thank you for coming for me again. May I ask you a question?"

"You can." He turned to face her, nodding once.

"What's your name?"

"Why, it's Lennard, Miss. Lenny to my friends."

"Well then, Lenny, it is my biggest ever pleasure to know you." Claudia dipped low in her best attempt at a curtsey.

"And you, Miss." He chuckled again.

"Please, Lenny, can you call me Claudia?" She smiled, feeling hopeful.

"I'd like to, Miss, but it don't feel right." His eyes glistened: red and watery. "Right then, Miss, let's go."

This time she ran all the way to the camp. Dane stood smiling under a fig tree, leaning casually against the trunk, one hand waving at them. She hadn't factored in the momentum of running downhill and had to put her hands out towards his chest to stop.

"Good morning to you, little lady of the glass house. Not scared anymore, I take it?" he asked, in a mock stumble backwards.

"I'm just so happy to be back!" Her legs trembled as she struggled to cope with the surge of adrenalin capturing her bones.

"And we're happy to see you again," Oriana said as she peeked around the side of a wagon. Dane shared an odd look with his gypsy girlfriend, before calling for Brishan.

Maybe they don't want me here. Why would they want me, the strange girl from the house, hanging around?

"Have you eaten, Claudia? We're about to have a delicious snack," Oriana said.

"I had some porridge this morning, but I could eat more." Claudia nodded and Dane caught her hand to lead her over to the clearing by the lake.

Freshly baked bread coated with sticky, sweet jam beckoned her taste buds and Claudia relished the oddity of eating outdoors, sitting cross-legged on the cold, dewy grass.

"Tell me what you do with your days, Claudia. Considering you can't go outdoors, how do you entertain yourself?" Dane stared at her intently.

"Well, I study each day. I do science and maths and literature and geography and Mr Campbell tries to teach me music, but he can't sing." Claudia spoke quickly, keeping time with the butterflies in her stomach.

"We can help you with that, dear one, music is as important as water within this camp." Oriana smiled as she spoke and Claudia couldn't help but stare. The gypsy's chocolate brown eyes twinkled beneath impossibly long, thick lashes, her straight, delicate nose crinkled and her full, red-tinged lips stretched over perfectly straight teeth.

"I can see you're very intelligent, your eyes glow with it." Dane smiled.

Claudia tore her eyes away from Oriana's striking face to smile at Dane. "I'm good at English and I love geography, but I definitely don't like maths."

Just as her nerves calmed beneath Dane and Oriana's warm and welcoming words, Brishan trotted up on a muscular, black horse. His hands held the reins in a relaxed grip and Claudia gasped, frightened the animal would rear and kick her.

"Good morning, fairy. You look dressed for riding, jump on," he said, winking and gesturing to her with long, tanned fingers.

She knew she looked stupid, staring at him with her mouth open, but nerves rendered her senseless. *Speak, Claudia, just speak.* She looked at Dane and Oriana and they gazed back with open faces, no pressure in their eyes.

She took a deep breath. "These are my only comfortable clothes, everything else I have is, well, too good to wear." *How to tell them? Where would I start?* "I've only ever sat on a horse to be walked around a pen." She looked at Dane, rooted to the spot now as the butterflies inside surged into a frenzy.

"Forgive us, sweet one. We presumed, because of your clothes yesterday, that you were a horse fanatic. But it doesn't matter, Claudia," Dane said, nodding at her and putting his hands out to help her up. "We'll teach you." With that he lifted her, his lean arms gripping her waist, to place her in front of Brishan. There was no saddle, so she grasped the horse's mane, her fingers almost paralysed with her fear.

"Go slowly, Brishan, no showing off," Oriana instructed, giving Claudia's ankle a reassuring squeeze.

"Me? A show off? What on earth do you mean?" Brishan called back with an airy laugh, as he delicately repositioned her hands on the crest of the mane and kicked the horse into a trot towards the valley.

Claudia held on tight and squealed as they sped, faster and faster towards the open field, her fear disappearing with the onset of freedom. Brishan chuckled in her ear, the musical sound ringing through the rushing wind. She turned to face him, anxious to see his eyes, eager to gauge his expression. His long hair streamed behind him in a black, torrent of waves. The almond-shaped eyes crinkled with laughter, hiding the shocking green of his irises and his powerful arms glowed with a dark tan.

I'm on a horse, in the valley, with a boy. Oh my God. She opened her mouth to tell him how much she was enjoying the ride, just to make sure she wasn't dreaming. But his jaw clenched and his eyes narrowed as he stared, not at her, but straight ahead.

"Whoa!" His shout vibrated in her chest.

Claudia's neck strained as she swung to the front, just in time to see a woman standing directly in their path, her purple, voluminous cloak billowing in the breeze.

Brishan pulled frantically on the reins, but the horse reared and her body fell back with the momentum. He gripped her waist with one arm and the air left her lungs as her ribs were crushed beneath the strength of his hold.

Her breath came back in short, quick gasps.

Then she was falling, falling within the iron-tight circle of Brishan's arms; and all she knew was the wind roaring in her ears.

Chapter Three

Good Luck Tears

Claudia screamed. A woman leaned over her, breath strong with garlic. Tendrils of grey hair dangled from her head like slithering snakes. Her eyes were dark amber and her thin lips moved rapidly, murmuring some kind of chant.

"Welcome back, sweet one, everything is fine, you're not seriously hurt." Dane's face came into the picture, blocking out the woman's purple clad body.

Claudia struggled to sit as a succession of images flashed through her mind. "Oh, I remember. Is Brishan hurt? What about the horse?" she whispered through dry lips.

"Both horse and boy are fine. It's lucky Cosima was there, she's a strong healer." Dane smiled down at her, gently sweeping the back of his hand over her forehead.

"But…" Claudia didn't know what to say. This witch, and she surely must be a witch, had made them fall from the horse. She'd been standing right in front of them, blocking their path. *Hadn't she?*

How to tell Dane? Why hadn't Brishan told him?

"Hush now, just rest a moment. I see you have your friends with you."

"Friends…?"

"Why, the two dark haired beauties hovering over you." Dane laughed as if it were commonplace for others to be able see one's imaginary friends. She could see Snow-White and Rose-Red, quite clearly beside her. *But how can he?*

"I see your curious brain working overtime. Trust me, all is revealed to those who wait and those who rest. I'll come back for you in a short while. Let Cosima's medicine do its work first." Before he left, Dane brushed the hair from her face with a touch so comforting in its warmth that a sigh escaped her lips.

Claudia looked around, realising she was inside one of the wagons. The room glowed purple and blue from naked light bulbs and the bed enfolded her in rich, silky fabric. With timid fingers, she touched her head and noticed a tender, swollen bump towards the back.

The snake-haired woman had left with Dane and she was alone, except for Snow-White and Rose-Red, giggling into tiny hands and looking at her with mischief in their eyes. Claudia shook her head as she tried to sit up again. A smooth, red sheet slid from her body, revealing her nudity. At the same moment, someone knocked on the door. She gasped, quickly covering herself and running a trembling hand through her hair.

"Bet you got a good knock on the head." Brishan stood in the doorway, a forced smile highlighting his red-rimmed eyes.

"I can feel a bump. Are you...okay?"

"Better than you I expect, little fairy. But you'll soon recover. Oriana has found some clothes for you to wear." He walked to the bed and put a bundle at her side. "That riding outfit of yours just won't do for the festival, and besides, my mother is washing it. Seems you slid into a very muddy ditch."

"What festival?" *When will I wake up?*

"You'll see." Brishan's smile disappeared as he turned to stare out the window towards the horizon. He lowered his head and seemed to study his thumbnail before biting at the edges. "Stupid people leaving traps out in the middle of the valley. I can't imagine who would do something so thoughtless. Probably trying to catch wild deer or something."

"What traps?" *I'm either dreaming or completely stupid.*

"The trap we nearly ran in to, that's why we fell. I'm so sorry I didn't see it in time. I was too...well...let's just say...preoccupied." His lips turned up on one side, ever so slightly. "Poor Zeus had a hard time, but he did manage to jump over it, he's a good horse. I'm really sorry about your head." Brishan frowned and gazed at her without blinking.

"I know it wasn't your fault, it was the woman, Cosima. She blocked our path."

"What do you mean? She *was* out in the valley collecting herbs. Lucky, because she's a master healer, stopped all that blood pouring out of your head in a second."

"But—"

"Oh!" he said, slapping his forehead and nodding. "You saw her before we fell, right?"

"Yes," Claudia said with some force.

"It was a projection of herself. Hard to explain, but she has the second sight. She knew it was going to happen before it did."

"Oh."

"It's okay now, Claudia. Everything will be okay. Get dressed and come outside, I don't want you to miss out." He bowed, his smile fully returned as he backed out of the wagon.

Claudia put her hands to her head and squeezed, feeling like she no longer knew what her own name was. She picked up the bundle and unravelled it, gasping as glittery, blue fabric rimmed in gold tumbled out. The dress shimmered as it moved, and when she slipped it on, the sleeves engulfed her arms, swirling about in a dance of their own. A red tasselled headscarf topped with a gold floral wreath completed the outfit and for a few seconds Claudia simply stared down at the magnificent clothes and her petite frame in it.

"My lady. Might I say you look ready for a festival? What are you waiting for?" Dane was at the door, grinning and offering her his hand.

Music filled her ears and vibrated in her chest. Her face contorted into a mass of twitches and she clamped her teeth down on her lower lip to control them. She stepped out of the wagon with the help of Dane's outstretched hand and ran straight into Lenny.

His weathered old face lit up at the sight of her in the

costume. "I hear you've been in a bit of a scrape, Miss, everything all right now?"

For a moment, she wanted to run into his sinewy, brown arms and ask him to take her away from these strange people with their dark eyes and weird magic. *It's just my head, and the shock and the...don't be afraid. Nothing to be afraid of.* But the feeling remained.

"There there, Miss. You'll be fine. I'll stay here with you for a short while before we have to get back." Lenny seemed to read her mind and his kindness made her throat constrict. A single tear ran down her face.

"Tears are good luck you know." Brishan was at her side again, his lopsided grin transforming his elfin features. "It is said that once a tear enters the earth, it sparks a shoot that grows up to the sky to grant your deepest desires."

Gently, with his pointer finger, he stroked the path the tear had left on her cheek. His green eyes focused on hers and her breathing deepened. A sense of calm washed over her like a cool, refreshing breeze and she unclenched her fists, releasing the stiffness building in her spine.

"Feel better, little fairy?" Brishan's voice, low and melodious, sounded much older than his sixteen years. She felt vague and sleepy, but peaceful all of a sudden.

"Come then, there is dancing to be done." He clasped her hand and pulled her towards the clearing. She turned to make sure Lenny was following, and he was, his skinny, bowed legs carrying him as fast as they could.

Brishan led her towards a group of strangers and pushed her out in front of them, as if she were the prize catch of the day. "My parents," he whispered in her ear.

"So, this is the fairy." Brishan's mother, Selina, spoke in a voice coated with honey. She looked very much like Oriana, with thick waves of chocolate coloured hair and matching eyes, but she was shorter and older and more...motherly. Claudia took one step closer, angling her body towards the woman.

"Brishan thinks he's finally met a fey creature." Brishan's father, Eamon, towered over Selina, his tight red curls falling into his green eyes. "Watch out, he might capture you in a bottle to keep under his bed." Eamon winked and Claudia couldn't help but smile at the man's cheerful face.

"Are you Oriana's sister?" Claudia turned back to Selina, her voice a mere whisper as she glanced down at the grass. *How lucky they are. Imagine having a sister!*

"Do we look so much alike?" Selina asked, glancing over her shoulder. Claudia noticed Dane and Oriana approaching, smiles playing on their faces.

"What awful things does my sister say about me?" Oriana raised her black, perfectly arched eyebrows

"Oh nothing, dear sister, Claudia was just observing our likeness," Selina said, dark eyes glinting.

"Well, yes, apart from my superior intellect." Oriana laughed and knelt down to hold Claudia's hands. "How are you, sweet one? Does your head still hurt?" She spoke with such concern that Claudia felt a lump in her throat again.

"It's a little sore, but not too bad."

"You're very brave. Cosima will soon give you more medicine and it will heal completely. Do not be frightened of her, I promise you, she means you no harm."

Without thinking, Claudia threw her arms around Oriana, trying to convey the emotions coursing through her: trust, thankfulness, delight. Oriana simply patted her back and whispered soothing words in her ear.

Is this what it's like to have a mother?

"Would you like to see our show?" Oriana pulled back and smoothed Claudia's hair from her face.

"Oh yes!"

"Go and sit with Brishan then, we're about to start."

A low, throbbing, drumbeat announced the start of the

rehearsal. As Claudia sat, transfixed, the story of a poor gypsy girl falling in love with an unattainable prince unfolded within the haunting music. Oriana, playing the lead, danced with a desperate passion as she tried to seduce her prince. Dane, the prince, plucked exquisite melodies from a lute within the glow of an imaginary fire, all the while staring in adoration at the gypsy dancer.

The spell was broken only by applause, exploding and filling the air with rapture. Dazed, Claudia closed her eyes and pressed her palms over her heart, seeking to contain the magic within. Then, she felt warm hands slide over her shoulders, gripping her under the arms to lift her to her feet. Brishan turned her to face him as the sound of tinkling bells and echoing cymbals caressed her ears. Dancers swirled into the clearing, claiming the space with vibrant movement, their energy forcing her feet to tap out a song of their own on the spongy ground.

Dane and Oriana drew them into a dancing circle and Claudia squealed as they spun faster and faster on the grass. Oriana's smiling face grew blurry in front of her and their clasped hands became slippery with sweat. Her chest heaved as she struggled to draw breath and she collapsed on the ground, laughing amid the heat of dancing bodies.

Afterwards, time held no meaning as Claudia melted into a world she'd never known existed. She felt like a balloon, too full and ready to burst with the excitement of being with the gypsies. Dane smiled and laughed at her answers to his onslaught of questions. Oriana constantly fussed over her — gentle, thoughtful, playful — filling her with a warmth even the sun couldn't match, and Brishan...the way his eyes sought hers through the crowd, the way they sparked in time with his teasing banter; Brishan's attention filled her body with an uncomfortable, mysterious heat.

After an impromptu, solo performance of something he called

an Irish jig, dedicated to his father, Brishan placed a violin in her hands. "Here, I'll teach you."

"Okay." She held it against her chest, as she'd seen him do, and placed the bow over the strings.

Brishan shifted behind her, wrapping his arms around hers and placing her hand correctly on the violin's neck. She inhaled the scent of sandalwood and rain. He leant forward, over her shoulder, his cheek grazing hers and his warm breath on her neck. Tingles raced the length of her spine.

She flinched as the orange glow of afternoon sun disappeared in the shadow of the woman standing in front of her.

"Time to look at the wound again, child."

Not only does she look like a witch, she sounds like one would too. I should just talk to her, try and be a bit friendly at least.

Claudia smiled, forming random words in her head. But the witch did not smile back; she simply crooked a finger and turned away. Reluctantly, Claudia put the violin down to follow, taking comfort in the soothing pressure of Brishan's hand as he squeezed hers.

Cosima led her towards a wagon, its interior drenched in purple. A potent, chemical-like smell curled among stacked, glass jars. A snake twisted inside one, floating dead in yellow liquid. Mushrooms forced the lids from other jars and dried herbs dangled from the roof. The witch handed Claudia her freshly washed riding suit and turned her back as she changed.

"Sit, sit, your two friends will sit by you." Cosima pointed towards a low bench covered in a paisley patterned cloth.

Claudia glanced at Snow-White and Rose-Red, giggling as usual and looking at her with cheerful goodwill. "How…why can you see my imaginary friends?" Her words rasped through a dry throat and she held her breath for the answer.

"They are not imaginary, child. You have been gifted with them; probably at birth."

"So, they *are* real?" Claudia gasped, unable to hide her astonishment.

"In a spiritual sense, yes. They are Companion spirits, given to those ordained to follow a life path cursed with much loneliness. The alignment of the stars in your birth chart would have foretold this."

Loneliness was certainly nothing new, so this much made sense, but her confusion still grew at an alarming rate. "Margaret and Mr Campbell, my carers, can't see them, I'm sure of it."

"Why, of course not, child. Our blood does not course through their veins, as it does yours."

Cosima dabbed some foul smelling, green ointment on Claudia's head and a rush of heat flooded the area. She crinkled her nose, wanting to tell the witch that only boring old English blood ran in her veins, despite her wishes for different parentage.

"You would do well to remember that Companions are only play things, child. They can keep you company and make you laugh and, if your own will is very strong, you may send them to those with our blood as spiritual messengers. But they cannot interfere in your life nor help you in moments of danger. Companions can be a curse as you grow old and no longer cherish their constant giggles."

Claudia couldn't respond. Her eyes fluttered and her head grew light as the warm goo infiltrated her wound.

"That's enough information for now, Cosima, thank you." Dane appeared at the entrance and came to sit beside her. Snow-White and Rose-Red flew off the seat in a fit of tinkling laughter. Cosima bowed her head and left the wagon.

"How do you feel, sweet one?" His voice came to her as if from a long, droughty tunnel.

"Funny. Strange funny, but better."

"Don't concern yourself too much with Cosima's truths, soon you will come to understand our mysteries. "

"I thought I made them up. Snow-White and Rose-Red, I mean. I thought they were in my head and I don't really believe in magic anymore."

"Magic is not always about wands and tricks and wizards. It's many things, like how we use our spiritual eye, your third eye, when it opens. But, you're tired, sweetheart, we can talk about this another time. Sleep now, Lenny will come to take you home soon. All will be well, I promise."

Claudia's eyes were closing against her will as thousands of questions tumbled about her mind: unanswered and strange beyond all reasoning. The low voice of the gypsy soothed her as he spoke calm words of affection to quiet her thoughts. She sank, deeper and deeper, into sleep.

With a start, she woke to find herself in her own room — and Margaret at the door, staring at her like she was the mess left over from last night's dinner.

"Miss Claudia, you were asleep in your clothes yesterday afternoon when I came to give you dinner, and now I find you still here!"

Claudia sat up and rubbed her eyes, feeling deliciously rested and full of anticipation. Until panic set in.

"Are you listening? Just because we've not been able to supervise you constantly, does not mean you can lapse into laziness." Margaret shook her head with so much force that Claudia tensed, waiting for the woman's hair curlers to fly right off her head like mini torpedos.

"I'm...I'm sorry, Margaret, I was tired yesterday." *How is it possible she hasn't discovered what we did? And how on earth did Lenny get me into bed?*

'You must bathe immediately and come down to breakfast."

"Yes, Margaret."

"I'm expecting Mr Campbell to be home within the week, so your lessons will surely resume in a few days. Then perhaps your boredom will be relieved and you'll be able to remain awake at the appropriate times!" Margaret huffed and puffed as she strode away up the hall.

Claudia felt her heart constrict just thinking of the loss of her new found freedom. She couldn't go back to empty, joyless days with Mr Campbell. For the first time in her life, she felt she belonged somewhere. Really belonged. She absolutely would not allow herself to wake from the gypsy dream that had taken over her life in two, magical days.

But, how could she continue to see them? *Sneak out a night?* Surely Lenny would help her; the old gardener clearly had a few tricks up his sleeve. But what could they do about the gatekeeper, roaming the halls at night? She cringed at the thought of him and pushed his image to the dark recesses of her mind.

She'd neglected poor Spotty over the past two days. This morning, she would take him some treats after breakfast; Margaret would no doubt have Lenny bring the cat in again to ease her guilt at leaving her alone. If only the old housekeeper knew what was happening under her very nose, she'd surely explode. Claudia giggled at the thought.

She padded downstairs in pretty brown ankle boots and a white dress with a matching jacket, one of many in her overflowing cupboard. It swirled around her legs and she liked the feel of the lining underneath, rustling as she walked. Claudia caught a glimpse of her reflection in the long, oval mirror in the hall and stopped for a second, in awe of her own transformation.

Her hair floated softly over her shoulders in thick, black waves, her cheeks were rosy within the glow of her pale skin and her lips looked dewy in the morning light. Brishan's face flashed through her mind, with his cheeky grin and smiling eyes, teasing as they searched her own. She touched her bottom lip, then bit down gently on it to watch it colour red.

Heavy footsteps approached, then stopped abruptly behind her. "My, my, aren't we prettied up today then? Hoping to see me were you? Missing me over the last few nights?" The gatekeeper's eyes scanned her body as he licked his fleshy lips.

One fat hand clenched and unclenched, stretching towards her face and the smell of grease and metal made her want to gag.

She froze. Running would only enrage him and provoke further scrutiny. But staying in his presence was so disturbing she felt bile actually rise in her throat.

"Been having to keep an eye on those vagabonds outside each night, haven't I? Keeping me busy making sure they don't come anywhere near the front of the house. But don't worry, girly, I'll be back."

"Claudia!" Margaret hollered from the kitchen.

She ran towards the housekeeper, cowering under the sound of her tormentor's sniggering laughter.

"My goodness! Well I never!" Margaret, both hands flying to her cheeks, stared at Claudia's dress. "At last you've come to your senses and might I say you look quite the young lady. Mr Campbell will be pleased."

"Thank you, Margaret." Claudia blushed with pleasure, happy now with her decision to appear more grown up for her gypsy friends and overawed at the compliment.

"You do look pale though. Are you feeling ill?"

"I'm…just hungry, Margaret." Although her hands still trembled.

"See you at tea time then," Margaret said, glancing twice over her shoulder at Claudia as she made her way to the attic.

It wasn't long before Lenny came with Spotty curled happily into his chest. She now noticed the muscles in his skinny arms and the sturdiness of his bowed legs. There were many elders at the gypsy camp and, by comparison, she realised Lenny must only be sixty or so.

"I hope you didn't wake up too uncomfortable this morning, Miss, I did the best I could."

"Oh, Lenny! I'm surprised you could carry me," Claudia said without thinking, and immediately wished the words back.

Lenny chuckled. "There's still some strength left in these old bones yet."

She smiled at him and resisted the urge to throw her arms around him. Instead, she stood to take Spotty, cuddling the purring creature on her chest. Trails of black fur covered her white dress, wrecking her unusually spotless appearance.

But it doesn't matter. Every moment I get to spend with the gypsies is what matters. And every moment might be my last.

No. She almost dropped the cat with the onset of emotion. Indirectly, the gypsies kept the gatekeeper away…for now. She looked into Lenny's eyes, desperate to tell him of her predicament, knowing he'd help her any way he could. But, as she opened her mouth to speak, Spotty rubbed his head against her cheek, dribbling as he purred and looked at her with half closed, sleepy eyes.

Gorgeous Spotty. Won't risk you. Can't. You're all I have.

Just stop the thoughts.

She breathed in and stood tall, smiling at Lenny as he led her down to the gypsy camp, to people greeting her with smiles and warmth and the promise of another exciting day. One last shake of the head completed her familiar thought-ridding ritual.

Today, as always, the sounds of the camp reached her ears before she could see it properly, loud and vibrant as families worked at morning chores: singing, laughing and yelling out to each other from the open wagon doors. Lenny spotted Dane with a small group by the lake's edge, so they continued to stroll down the valley. Claudia's spirits rose higher and higher as they approached.

Dane stood to greet them, smiling but holding a finger to his lips. "Good morning, friends. Brishan is in the middle of a lesson. Claudia, you might find it interesting," he whispered, motioning for her to sit beside him on the fringes of the group. Lenny patted her arm and gave them a silent wave as he headed back to the chateau.

Brishan sat cross-legged, his palms resting upwards on his

knees, middle fingers and thumbs touching. His eyes were closed and Claudia stared at the beauty of his face, structured so finely with an angular jaw, straight, elegant nose and prominent cheekbones. His skin glowed in the morning light and he sat unnaturally still, like a tanned Roman marble sculpture. She turned to look at Dane, questions filling her mind.

Dane smiled and bent to whisper in her ear. "Brishan is learning to be a master healer, like Cosima. He has the natural ability, but now he must harness that and turn it into something real, something he can use for the rest of his life, to heal people."

Claudia recalled the feeling of calm that had come with Brishan's touch, when he'd wiped a tear from her face after the horse riding accident.

What kind of magic is this?

She gazed at the group. Cosima meditated opposite Brishan and two elderly men filled the gaps. They all chanted words she didn't recognise and touched their foreheads, just above their noses.

"This"—Dane put two fingers on her forehead—"is your third eye. When you need help to focus, spiritually, concentrating on your third eye will help."

She gasped as heat from his fingers penetrated her skin. Dane grinned and turned back to watch the strange lesson, catching one of her hands in his own and squeezing it tight.

It was a struggle to remain still as her body fought to squirm and run and jump with the freedom and new information her mind received. She hugged herself with her free arm to keep the feelings safe.

A moment later, Brishan opened his eyes and stared right at her, as if he'd known she was there, the bright green of his irises glowing like emerald jewels in the sun's rays. She drew a deep breath and held it.

"Good morning, fairy." His voice seemed to speak to her ears alone and the stillness of his face shattered under the onslaught of his smile. Suddenly, he was on his feet, a moving, nimble creature with flowing hair and boundless energy. He ran behind her and lifted her up, twirling her in a mad spin, laughing as the skirt of her white dress flared about her legs. The laughter of those around them floated by her ears and she found herself giggling uncontrollably as her head grew dizzier and dizzier.

Gently, he lowered her to the ground and she collapsed sideways, her stomach cramping with laughter. Brishan flopped down beside her, pushing her hair out of her face and grinning so that his eyes were barely visible within the black lashes framing them. Claudia caught her breath, eyeing the brown hand that brushed tendrils of hair from her cheeks.

"I'm sorry I wasn't finished in time to greet you." The smile left his face as he spoke.

"Why would you be sorry? If my lessons were that interesting, I'd never want to stop."

Brishan's lips pressed together and he inhaled, quickly and deeply. "Interesting yes, but not when they take over your life, sometimes I just want to—"

"Come, you two, let's eat." Dane stood above, offering both hands to help them up. Claudia dragged her eyes from Brishan's and jumped up to join everyone at a makeshift wooden table set under an old oak tree. The usual fare of freshly baked bread and jam sat among cured meats, gourmet cheeses and peeled fruits shining with droplets of juice. Brishan's smile had returned and she decided to forget his strange comments — for now.

"Word has finally spread in town...we did so well last night. The little community theatre was a full house!" Oriana said in greeting as Claudia squeezed in beside her. "We can't think of anything better to spend our hard earned cash on than a delicious feast, and today, we feast all day!"

Claudia laughed, infected by the happiness surrounding her. Brishan and Dane sat opposite, tucking into the steaming bread. She looked down the table at twenty or so laughing, singing, feasting people and pinched herself, hard, on the arm.

Dane raised an inquisitive brow. "You're not dreaming, precious one."

Her mouth dropped open. *Surely he's reading my mind.* "I hope not."

Brishan grinned, still chewing on a piece of prosciutto. "Don't worry, fairy, I think I'm dreaming every time I look at you. And I never want to wake up."

Oriana laughed and pulled her in tight for a hug as Claudia's cheeks flamed redder than the strawberry jam on her bread.

"Miss, Miss!" The voice reached them above the noise of the feast. Claudia turned to see Lenny running towards them, his little bowed legs moving so fast she feared he'd fall over.

She stood to meet him halfway, but froze when the familiar, obese silhouette of the gatekeeper appeared at the top of the hill.

'Claudia, quick, put this on." Oriana wrenched a silky scarf from her own head and put it over Claudia's. "Go now, sit by Dane and keep your face down."

Claudia slid the scarf over her eyes and rushed to Dane's side. He pulled her down in between himself and Brishan, keeping a firm hold on her waist.

"Oh, thank the Lord I reached you first. Miss Claudia... Dane..." Lenny doubled over, fighting to catch his breath. "The gatekeeper's coming, with three men from town. They want to talk to you."

"It's okay, Lenny. Thank you, we'll take it from here. Go back to your work and come for Claudia when they've gone," Dane said as Oriana helped the gardener to stand straight again.

Dane squeezed Claudia's hand before standing to greet the party of men, now almost upon them. "Good morning, gentlemen, what can we do for you?"

"It's not a good morning for us when we find criminals in our town," the tallest of the group said, his bald head shining in the sun.

"We camp on open land, and we break no laws in doing so."
Dane stood perfectly straight and his voice boomed; deep, low,
controlled.

"The law you speak of will be overturned as soon as it's
passed in parliament. We're here simply to give you warning of
that and to ensure you remove yourselves immediately."

"If it's not yet passed, we have every right to be here," Eamon
said from the far end of the table, his green eyes, a mirror image
of Brishan's, flashing beneath his red hair.

"Not for long you don't. The owners have written to express
their displeasure and a warrant will soon be issued for your
arrest. This land is privately owned and it is *their* right to remove
unwanted…trash."

Claudia drew a quick breath and felt Brishan's hand clamp
down hard on her own. She heard the gatekeeper's vile laugh mix
with those of the other men and her heart pounded loudly in her
chest.

"I see you have this under control, I'll be on my way then."
The gatekeeper spoke to the men through his laughter and,
glimpsing up from under her scarf, Claudia saw him waddle
back up the hill.

"May I ask what kind of law enforcement agency you work
for?" Dane's voice now held a touch of controlled fury and
Claudia cringed, pressing her shoulder into Brishan's.

The tall man laughed. "One that ensures the community is
purged of trash, when needed."

How dare he. Claudia stood; unfamiliar, white hot anger
surging with strength through her veins. *This is my land and these
men have no right to say such things.*

"It is *you*, who has no right to be here." Where the strong, even
voice came from, she had no idea, but she felt it leave her throat
before thought or reason entered her mind.

"Claudia, please, sit down," Oriana stage-whispered.

"Ah, the famous gypsy spirit, in the body of a girl-child," the tall man said, stalking towards her with a smirk twisting his face. "Is this who fights your battles, then?" He turned back to look at Dane, before leaning down so that his nose almost touched hers and his foul breath burned her cheeks.

She felt a strong grip on her shoulder as Brishan stood and pushed her behind him, firmly keeping hold of her arm.

"Come any closer to her and you will not be leaving with your head on your shoulders." His voice was little more than a husky growl, but the force behind his words oozed menace.

The tall man stepped back, almost falling in his haste to remove himself from Brishan's glare.

"I think perhaps it's time for you to leave." Dane signalled to the road beyond with his hand, as the other men of the gypsy camp began to walk towards the trio.

"This is not the last time you'll see us, if you choose to stay," the tall man called, from a safe distance up the hill.

Dane, Brishan and Eamon remained in a straight, still line, watching until they heard the powerful engine of a car roar into life and fade into the distance. Claudia, still standing, felt tears drip down her nose. She sniffed, loudly. Dane turned and stared at her for a long moment, his eyes glassy as they searched her own.

He opened his arms and walked towards her. She flung the scarf from her head and rushed into his chest, squashing her face on his shoulder and hiccupping in her desperate need to stop her tears.

"You, precious one, are so brave. Reckless. But very brave," he said into her ear as he smothered her cheek in kisses. "You have no need to defend us, although I admire you for it. I won't have you put in any danger for befriending us."

She pulled her head out from under Dane's arm and glanced over his shoulder. Brishan faced her, arms folded across his chest, lips in a straight, thin line. *He's angry with me. I shouldn't have interfered.*

"I'm so sorry," she whispered into Dane's ear, while looking directly at Brishan.

"Never be sorry for standing up for yourself, or for what you believe in. It's a rare gift, such bravery. We may have to make you an honorary gypsy." Dane chuckled and led her back to the table, where everyone had recommenced eating and talking amongst themselves, although more quietly than before.

The day passed under a grey cloud, despite their best efforts to ignore the storm threatening to erupt around them. Claudia helped Oriana with normal chores, washing and preparing food and rounding up the children for baths and naps along with the other women. The wagons were equipped with compact toilets and showers and portable generators for heat. The fully self-contained world on wheels consumed every fibre of her being until the morning's episode faded when compared to her new world.

Every so often, Brishan appeared at her side, strangely quiet but always smiling and playfully caressing her face, in between his lessons and rehearsals. Dane had disappeared into the forest beyond the valley, riding away on Zeus, smiling at her as he galloped off. Oriana said he went to commune with the trees and Claudia had laughed, not knowing what that meant, but liking the sound of it.

Too soon, Lenny came, the poor man still shaken from the morning's episode and looking like he wanted to hug her. She threw caution to the wind and wrapped her arms around his skinny frame, laughing when she felt him tentatively hug her back.

Dane returned and they stood in a line, Dane, Oriana and Brishan, waving at her as she trudged home, her heart heavy with yearning for them before they were even out of sight.

Two days later, as Lenny and Claudia made their way to camp, she could see, from a distance, clothes and blankets being pummelled by chattering women and rubbish, propelled from inside the mobile homes, clattering into large metal bins. *Is this a gypsy version of housekeeping?*

Mr Campbell was due back the next day and, though she blessed each day of his absence, she now broke out in a cold sweat whenever she thought about what his return would mean. *Helping the gypsies with the work will get my mind off it...*

On the steps of his wagon, Dane polished his long, black show boots. "Good morning, friends, how are you both today?" He smiled, winking at the same time and Claudia felt her cheeks warm with pleasure.

She smiled back. "What's everyone doing? You all look so busy."

Briefly, Dane glanced at Lenny before reaching for her hand. She sat down beside him on the wooden step and let him wrap his arm around her shoulder. His fingers smelled of shoe polish and their calloused tips stroked her arm.

"Sweet one, you know we've all grown very fond of you, don't you?"

Claudia nodded, feeling the now familiar happiness filling her heart.

"You have much to learn from us and the day will come when that will be possible."

Again, Claudia nodded. *What have I done to deserve such a wonderful speech?* Out of the corner of her eye, she saw Brishan sprinting towards them.

"Wow! Today you truly are a fairy princess!" Through great gulps of air, Brishan tried to whistle as his eyes scanned her body.

Claudia's stomach churned and she couldn't resist smiling at the compliment. She'd been trying on all the dresses in her cupboard and today she wore a red one that highlighted her dark hair.

"Have you told her yet?" Brishan glanced at Dane, his jaw clenching as his hands raked through his tousled, black hair.

"Told me what?"

"Claudia, sweet one, to tell you this hurts me as much as it may hurt you, for reasons you don't yet know." Dane breathed in deeply. "Do you remember when I told you the meaning of 'gypsy'? We are wanderers. We must travel to earn our living...and we've put you in danger here. We must leave Claudia...and we must leave tonight."

Chapter Four

Moon Shadows

The blood swirling in the bath water looked like thin, fractured red ribbons. Claudia stared at it as her face grew cold with sweat. The hideous substance had been on her bed sheets too. Her private parts were leaking and there was nothing she could do to stop it.

"Are you finished with that bath yet, Miss Claudia? You've been in there for an hour." Margaret stood outside the door for the second time, her yelling muffled by the heavy wood. The housekeeper obviously wanted to start her day and probably wouldn't leave her alone until she'd given her breakfast.

What to do? What to do? I can't...I don't want her in here. Stupid. Just ask her. Can't deal with this anymore on my own.

"Margaret...could you...could you come in? Please." Claudia cringed at the thought of Margaret seeing her in the bath, but her throat was closing and tears threatened to destroy her vision completely. Besides, her body felt so leaden now it wouldn't move, even when she tried.

"What is it? Heavens above, you're getting slower as you get older. You should be getting more organised, I've never..." Margaret stopped still when she saw the deep red water. "What have you done child, cut yourself?" The housekeeper shrieked, picking Claudia up under her arms and hauling her out of the tub.

"No, Margaret, it's...it's coming from..." Claudia glanced down and Margaret's eyes followed.

"Oh good Lord have mercy on me. So it's finally come. Don't cry about it, child, it happens to all of us. Dear me, I can't be calling you child anymore then, can I? Didn't you read that book I gave you? The one your mother sent?"

"Yes." Claudia gnawed at her bottom lip to keep the building hysteria at bay.

"Well, you're growing up, just like the book said. Here, towel yourself off. Your mother has sent you things to deal with this. You remember when I showed you? Must be two years ago now. You're definitely a late bloomer." The housekeeper washed and dried her hands, then searched inside the glass-walled cabinet above the basin.

Claudia hadn't really understood the book about human growth and reproduction and remembered growing bored with it before she'd finished. She'd had thousands of questions, all of which Margaret and Mr Campbell had simply refused to answer. She'd had no idea the impact on herself would be so brutal.

Margaret handed her a box with pretty pink flowers drawn over its shiny white surface. "Put one of these on, inside your underwear. When it needs changing, just wrap it in toilet paper and put it in the bin." Margaret sounded very business-like now, despite her red cheeks.

Claudia's hands fumbled with the plastic coating on the box. Margaret still stared at her and the housekeeper's eyes glistened: suspiciously red. One of her wrinkly hands reached towards Claudia's face, but dropped quickly to its regular resting place on her chest to fiddle with the necklace there. Claudia bit her lip again and drew a shaky breath, her body moving closer to Margaret's — but the housekeeper had already turned away.

She sniffed and wiped her nose with the back of her hand, then opened the box to reveal rectangular pieces of something like cotton, covered in gauze. *They look like fat paper planes.* Her tears found their way down her chest, trickling over her stomach.

Claudia stiffened her shoulders, drew a deep breath and shuddered as she peeled the plastic strip from the back of a pad. *I can do this. It's not so hard...* Even the words inside her head trembled and faded within her fear.

But, after a few attempts, she had the pad in place. She

dressed herself and tried to leave the bathroom so Margaret could come back in and clean. The awful thing between her legs rubbed against her thighs and felt so bulky and awkward she didn't know how she'd be able to walk around all day.

"You may spend the day in the library, Miss Claudia. I'll inform Mr Campbell that you're unwell."

"But—"

"It'll be all right, Claudia. We all go through it. Chin up now." Margaret pursed her lips, raising her arms again as if to draw Claudia in for a hug.

Claudia held her breath, desperate for contact, for comfort. But, already, the housekeeper had lowered her head, moving out of the room, mumbling about meeting in the kitchen for breakfast.

The tears blurred her vision again and she fought the temptation to lie down in bed to sleep and block out the traumatic morning. How long would it continue, this horrible intruder attacking her body? She did her best to walk downstairs without appearing as if she had the 'thing' hidden between her legs.

Her sixteenth birthday was almost upon her and presents had started to arrive from London. Each day more and more boxes piled high in the hallway, all addressed to her. She could only imagine the jewellery, shoes and dresses; all useless objects bought to fake a love that didn't exist.

And now, no love existed at all. Not without the gypsies. Oh, Lenny visited, when he could, and still took her down to the lake in secret, late in the afternoon while Margaret and Mr Campbell were busy in their own quarters before tea. Daily, almost every minute, her mind travelled back to that awful morning, six months ago, when the gypsies had prepared to leave. Back to her tears and the pained expression on Dane's face. To Brishan's jaw, tightly clenched like the white knuckled fists at his side, and to Oriana's tearful hugs. They had promised to return soon, promised on the very souls of their ancestors. *Whatever that meant.*

Every day, she stared out the schoolroom window, hoping to see the first wagons arrive, pining for a glimpse of Brishan's emerald eyes.

Still, much had changed.

The mirror in the hall showed a different girl from the child Claudia had been mere months ago. Now, she always wore new clothes from her abundant collection. Today, she'd chosen an ankle length, dusky pink skirt that swished around her legs as she walked. A tight, white knitted top hugged the breasts that had appeared, Claudia felt, out of nowhere, and her hair, which Margaret had recently cut, rested mid-back in cascading black waves.

Her parents had finally sent orders that Claudia was to take proper horse riding lessons and learn to play social sports; badminton and croquet so far. Claudia only cared that she was finally allowed outside more often. So, a horse was purchased for her sole use and Mr Campbell was charged with teaching her how to ride. The horse was a white Kladruber, a very rare horse and much too large for Claudia. Mr Campbell said the breed was virtually a national treasure in the Czech Republic, so that's why her father had requested the purchase of one. The poor thing was an investment.

Each Saturday, Pavle, a groomsman from the stables at a nearby property would walk the horse to the front of the chateau, and Claudia was led round in a circle while Mr Campbell shouted out instructions pertaining to her own posture and head position. The novelty wore off quickly. Claudia only ached to gallop across the hills towards freedom.

She was permitted time in the sun to read each day, Spotty curled up neatly at her feet. She was even allowed to stroll around the border of the chateau, providing she stayed close to the household gardens and didn't go towards the road at the front, or the valley at the back. Mr Campbell and Margaret still watched her closely, although their passion for containing her lessened.

But, there would be no horse riding today. Her terrible infliction had even forced Margaret to cancel her other lessons. Perhaps Mr Campbell thought 'growing up' was contagious. She hoped it didn't last much longer; her lower stomach cramped, as if protesting the loss of the dirty coloured blood and breakfast tasted bland, even though Margaret treated her to bacon and eggs. At least Snow-White and Rose-Red snuggled into her sides, watching as she ate, their little legs floating up in the air and their giggles ringing out like wind chimes.

"What should we do today?" Claudia looked at them both, willing them to talk. Silence.

"Perhaps we could catch a plane to…let's think…Morocco. Yes, we can eat in the outdoor markets and buy lanterns and maybe take a camel ride in the dessert." Just like in the pictures of her new book, the one Margaret had bought for her with pages full of travel photos.

More silence.

She bit her lip. Her chest tightened and she breathed in through her nose while one, stupid tear landed on the corner of her mouth. She tasted its saltiness with the tip of her tongue and, head down, wandered into the library.

That night, she changed the dirty 'thing' between her legs and put it in the rubbish for Margaret to get rid of. She couldn't believe the blood that still flowed out of her and when she crawled into bed, she had to lie flat on her back to keep the pad in position. Margaret would be angry if she soiled the sheets again.

Sleep wouldn't come, but the gatekeeper did. He pushed open her bedroom door and smirked, his eyes narrow and his pace slow and laboured. Her voice froze in her throat and she stiffened her body to stop the instinct to fight. She glanced at Spotty, asleep in the corner, unaware of the terrible danger he was in. The gatekeeper followed her gaze and focused on the cat for long, silent seconds, before kicking him roughly out the door.

Claudia caught the sheet tight under her chin as the gatekeeper crawled onto the bed, weighing it down and tearing the sheet away to expose the top of her white nightgown. Tears splashed over her nose as his fleshy fingers fumbled with the buttons. Sobs escaped as her newly formed breasts were exposed to the cool night air. It was a new game and he liked to play weekly, at least.

He kneaded her breasts as she'd seen Margaret manipulate dough for bread. Tonight they were extra sensitive and pain shot through her when the fat fingers grazed her nipples. His moves were seared into her brain and as he started to lift her nightgown, she squeezed her legs together tightly, not knowing what he'd do when he saw the disgusting pad.

"What's this? You know what happens if you resist me, girly," he hissed, pulling her thighs apart with force. Claudia clamped her hands over her face. Long moments passed and the sound of his breath rattling in his throat was the only sound in the world.

"So, it has come," he said at last.

She peered through her fingers and saw his hands reach for each other, rubbing together until the fat knuckles cracked.

"Now the fun can really begin. But not tonight; soon when you're finished and fully turned into a woman." He hauled himself back off the bed to return to the servant's quarters, still rubbing his hands as if he'd been handed a grand prize.

Claudia rolled over on her side, curling into the foetal position, forgetting about the mess she might make of the sheets. Her whole body shook with rasping sobs. She almost wished Spotty would die so the gatekeeper couldn't threaten her any longer. *No, can't think such things. Evil.* Spotty was all she had, the only living being that showed her any love or affection, apart from Lenny. Her confusion turned into frustration and it all added to the terrifying, reoccurring nightmare she was trapped in.

Morning came and Claudia could barely get out of bed. A thumping headache matched the cramping in her stomach. Her back ached and she wanted to cry just thinking about the boring day ahead — the 1st of June and her sixteenth birthday. Even Snow-White and Rose-Red, peeping over the covers with round, green eyes, couldn't coax a smile from her. She stumbled down to the kitchen, hoping breakfast would ease the cramping.

The back door slammed shut and Claudia turned as she heard hurried footsteps.

"You'll never believe it, Miss."

"Believe what, Lenny?" Claudia stared at the gardener, noticing his flushed face and his thin lips curving in a wide smile.

"They're back! And on your birthday!"

"What?" Her heart thudded in her chest and she raced to the windows in the schoolroom.

Wagons and trucks and horses made their way into the field below. *Impossible.* But the cold glass against her nose proved she was awake and not dreaming the blissful image.

Her hand flew to her messy hair; she looked down at the crumpled nightgown and rubbed her blotchy face. *And,* apart from her appearance, if Mr Campbell couldn't even stand to be in her presence because of her 'infliction', she wasn't going to subject the gypsies to it. *I must stay out of their sight until the blood is gone.* The thought created a lump in her throat, so huge, swallowing was impossible.

"Lenny!" she called as she walked back to the kitchen.

The gardener and Margaret stood side by side, their hands almost touching. Claudia stopped dead. Margaret stepped away from Lenny, her hand almost slapping his as she moved.

"Well? Why did you call for the gardener? I suppose you want that cat of yours. I thought he was already inside," she said in a voice more sharp than usual, even by her gruff standards. Her face looked swollen and tired beneath the pink curlers in her hair, but her eyes shone and sparkled beneath the heavy lids.

"Um, he must have escaped outside."

"Well then, man, fetch the cat," Margaret snapped at Lenny. He nodded and winked at Claudia on the way out.

"I'll take him up to my room today, Margaret," Claudia said. *Why is Margaret letting Lenny into the kitchen?*

She wondered if Mr Campbell knew. The strict teacher had always forbidden Claudia to talk to the other servants and she and Lenny had spent months now hiding their new found friendship.

"Yes, you're better off there I suppose, in your condition," Margaret said, before busying herself with the breakfast dishes. "And, happy birthday, Claudia, I'll bake you a cake for desert tonight."

As if cake will make everything okay. Why should I be ignored, when Margaret herself surely suffers the 'condition'? Don't all women? A not so Happy Birthday to me.

For three more days Claudia stayed in her bedroom, only coming out for meals. She could see the gypsy camp from her window, and she felt their energy flowing through her veins. It tugged on her heart, constantly pulling her thoughts towards them. She ached to run into Dane's arms, to gaze into Brishan's eyes, to feel the warmth of Oriana's kind words. But nerves now mixed with the painful cramps. What if the gypsies had changed? What if they no longer wanted to see her?

What if, what if, what if?

The blood had finally dried up; she'd seen no signs of it on waking at least, and she felt almost normal again, sitting at breakfast the next day. Normal, with a singing soul and a churning stomach

"I have some good news, Miss," Lenny said, his face poking around the back door.

Claudia felt her heart race. "What is it, Lenny?"

"I've been wanting to tell you for days now, but Margaret said to leave you be." He looked at the floor as his voice faltered. "Your friends at the camp have been asking for you, Miss. Everyday. They're mighty keen to see you."

Claudia let herself smile for the first time in days. "How will we do it this time, Lenny? How will we sneak down there?"

The weathered face widened into a happy grin. "I've come to an arrangement with Margaret." He glanced at the floor, fidgeting with an old silver watch on his wrist.

"What do you mean?" Claudia frowned.

"After your lessons this afternoon, you're allowed to visit the gypsies, taking me with you of course. Margaret will keep our secret."

"How can this be?" Claudia's jaw dropped.

"Best you don't know for now, Miss." Lenny chuckled under his breath. "Just enjoy the freedom. I'll come get you at three-thirty."

Claudia leapt up from her chair and threw herself at the gardener, smothering his cheek in kisses. He laughed and, when he hugged her gently in return, Claudia felt herself melting into the embrace.

"I don't care how it came about, I'm just so happy it did!"

"As I am, Miss. But be sure you don't mention it to Margaret, she likes to keep up appearances. Know what I mean?" He tapped his nose as he left to do his chores.

Claudia didn't know what he meant, but it didn't matter. *Nothing matters, not now they're back for me.* She ran down the stag head hall, and the dead eyes lining the wall were invisible to her.

The day's lessons dragged on torturously. She tried her best not to stare out the window towards the bustling camp and Mr Campbell seemed pleased with her apparent concentration, after so long a break.

Three o'clock arrived and Claudia raced to her room to change. She would wear one of her birthday presents — a knee length, red dress with ruffles that fell over her shoulders, just like she'd seen on flamenco dancers in her books.

She brushed her hair until the ebony waves shone and raced downstairs to look in the hallway mirror. Her waist looked small beneath the shoulder ruffle and she spanned her hands around it. *Brishan's fingers would meet together if he did this.* Her skin glowed bronze from her time in the sun, highlighting the black of her brows and eyelashes. Excitement made her hands shake and her spine tingled with nerves as she stepped towards the kitchen.

Lenny waited with his elbow pointed towards her. She gripped it, squeezing hard, and followed him through the afternoon shadows engulfing the chateau, down to the valley below. A small group of people, frozen like the statues in the garden, stood on the fringes of the camp.

She stopped, unnerved by their very stillness.

Her heart missed a beat as one figure broke free.

Before she could think, she was encircled in Dane's strong, spiry arms. She breathed in the scent of him — grass mixed with spices — and looked up at his face. A few extra lines seemed to crinkle as he smiled.

"Claudia, my little lady of the glass house. Let me look at you, it's been much too long. Do you know how much we've missed you?" Dane frowned as he scanned her body. "Lenny said you were sick?"

"Oh…I just felt unwell. But I'm much better now." Claudia looked down at her feet, hating the heat creeping over her cheeks.

When she looked up again, a tall, muscular man stood behind Dane, his black hair blowing in the breeze, framing startling green eyes. Claudia's stomach flip-flopped as the longed for, lopsided grin transformed Brishan's face. He stared into her eyes, unblinking, eyebrows raised, and beckoned with his hand.

Seconds later, his arms replaced Dane's. She sank into his tight embrace, almost fearful of her thudding heart, but savouring the goose bumps trailing down her arms.

"You're no longer a little fairy, you've grown into a beautiful temptress," he whispered into her ear, causing shivers to run from her legs to the top of her head. "I've been waiting for this moment, just to see you again." He pulled back to catch her face in his hands, a slight frown forming as he slid his palms gently, slowly, over her arms to snake about her waist.

She fought the trembling that threatened to turn her legs to jelly. "You've grown also." *What did I just say? Stupid.* The muscles in his arms tensed beneath his brown skin as he pulled her close, so close her hip bones pressed into his thighs.

His frown turned into a deep crevice as his eyes flicked between her face and the horizon over her head. "I just didn't think…"

"What?" Claudia instinctively stepped back.

His mouth opened to respond, but instead she felt his hands slip reluctantly from her waist as Oriana and Brishan's own parents, Eamon and Selina, swooped in to hug her.

It was all the same. The wagons, the dancers, the screaming laughter, even a feast set out in her honour. Deliciously, gloriously the same, like a dream, frozen in time, simply waiting for her to fall into it again. As they gathered in the clearing, all feelings of loss and heartache disappeared under the glow of the sunny afternoon and their love.

The slight pressure of Brishan's thigh against her own kept her heart racing and she found herself holding her breath each time he moved, his very touch waking every nerve ending beneath her skin. Every so often, he would wink at her, or squeeze her hand playfully, staring into her eyes before dropping his own to study her lips, raising them quickly again to catch her gaze on his.

Yet, the frown would reappear whenever he watched the dancers. Especially two teenage girls; hips swirling to the drumbeats by a fire in a rusty black cauldron. They glanced at Brishan from under their black lashes and stared at her whenever they thought she wasn't looking. Each time she felt their attention, prickles crept over her neck, keeping time with the goose bumps. One girl, in particular, with light hazel eyes, smiled whenever Brishan looked her way. A smile that disappeared as quick as it came, and never reached her eyes.

Suddenly, Oriana was rubbing her shoulder, startling her out of her thoughts. "Tell me why you were sick, sweet one, Dane and I would like Cosima to look you over."

Claudia wasn't keen to see the witch-like healer again and felt a flush of embarrassment, with Brishan sitting so close. Oriana seemed to sense her discomfort.

"Come down to the lake with me." Oriana smiled and offered a hand to help her up.

Momentarily silent, they sat side by side and stared at the gently rippling water.

"I think I might know what ailed you. I can sense you've changed," Oriana said.

Claudia's heart leapt. *Could the awful blood have such a lasting effect?*

"Oh, my darling, please don't look so petrified. You've become a woman, haven't you?"

"I don't know. It was just...blood." Claudia stared at her feet, embarrassed to look into Oriana's eyes, afraid of the disgust she might find there.

"It is reason for celebration, darling! It's your ancient connection to the moon and Mother Earth, come into its own." Oriana's eyes glittered as she extended both arms towards the sky, as if thanking Mother Earth.

A celebration? No, she doesn't understand.

"No. It's dirty and gross and Mr Campbell didn't even want to give me lessons while I had it. He didn't want to be in the same room as me." Claudia thought about the gatekeeper, and how the blood had even kept *him* away.

Oriana's chocolate brown eyes widened and she frowned, bitting her bottom lip until it glowed dark pink. With a sigh, she caught Claudia's shoulders between her arms, hugging her tightly. "Do you know why you bleed, Claudia?"

"It's the reproductive system."

"Yes, but do you understand what that means?" Oriana asked, her tone softening.

"No." Warm tears ran down her cheeks and she swiped at them with the backs of her hands.

"Oh, sweet one. Be happy! It means you can give birth! It's Mother Earth's greatest gift to women."

"Really?"

"Yes! Just as the moon has cycles; new, waxing, full and waning, so do women. The moon's phase's move through your body, readying, filling and emptying your uterus. Menstruation is a time of great psychic wisdom and power for women."

"What's a uterus?"

Oriana laughed and nodded. "If ever you feel bad about anything, you must tell yourself it's probably because of ignorance. All things can be explained, just as this can. Never live in fear simply because you don't have all the facts. Promise?"

"I promise."

For long, exquisite moments, Claudia gaped in awe at the information spilling from the older woman's lips. Sex, birth, death, the inner workings of males and females, sperm; all words Claudia had never known. Her mind swelled with the empowerment brought by knowledge and her heart filled with the connection she felt to the gypsy woman giving it to her.

"There you are, my lovely ladies. What have you two been

whispering and laughing about for so long?" Dane appeared behind them and Claudia jerked in surprise, losing her balance as she scrambled to her feet.

Oriana winked at her before turning to Dane. "Oh, just secret women's business, but you needn't worry, we were about to come back to the party."

"Good, I'm missing you both and I want nothing more than to talk to Claudia, surely it's my turn now?" Dane beamed at Claudia, then kissed Oriana full on the mouth.

Linking arms with them both, he led them back to the clearing, bombarding Claudia with questions. She tried to listen and answer carefully, distracted by the knowing glances Oriana and Dane shared. *What are they thinking?*

She was thinking it would be the best thing on earth if they were her parents; life would have been so different. *How lucky Brishan is to belong here.*

Back at the clearing, Lenny stood next to Brishan, deep in conversation. Brishan bestowed a smile on her, so stunning, that she found herself catching her breath in one, muted gasp.

"Lenny has kindly said he'll let me walk you home. Just as far as the tall trees in the garden, so I can't be seen, of course." He caught her hand up in his own and Claudia gazed at her fingers entwined with his.

"Brishan!"

The high-pitched voice was unfamiliar. Claudia turned towards the sound and her gaze met that of the teenage girl with the glowing hazel eyes. The girl stood by the fire, her purple painted nails glistening as she beckoned to Brishan with a long, graceful finger. The glowing embers framed the dark scowl twisting her face.

Claudia spun to face Brishan. He had lowered his head, and an odd twitch pulsated at the corner of his mouth. His fingers tapped a violent tune on his thigh and his body was rigid and straight.

He drew a deep breath. "I'll be back in a moment to walk you home, if you're willing to wait for me. Please say you are."

Claudia nodded before any thought entered her mind.

Brishan dragged his eyes from hers to face the gardener. "Lenny, I promise I'll see her home safely, you can go if you like."

Lenny simply smiled and squeezed Claudia's shoulder, before turning to walk up the hill. Dane emerged from the twilight shadows, wearing a deep frown as his head tilted towards the girl at the fire. Brishan stared intently at his uncle for a long moment. Claudia shuffled her feet and started to pick at the skin around her thumbnails.

"Just be honest. It's all you can do," Dane said, placing his hand on Brishan's shoulder.

Brishan lowered his head again, thrust his hands in the pockets of his jeans and strode towards the fire.

Claudia stared at Dane, desperate for explanations and fearful of the hazel-eyed girl for reasons she couldn't understand. Dane still watched Brishan, and so she turned again, in time to see Brishan take the girl's hand and lead her into the trees. Swift anger pooled in her stomach. *I must not cry, not now, not when the gypsies have finally returned.*

Dane touched the tip of her nose with his pointer finger. "This is not for you to worry about, precious one. Brishan has…fires he has to put out. Brishan will always battle fires, as he learns to accept his path."

"I don't understand."

"I know, nor do you have to just now." Dane looked over her head, as if deep in thought. "I don't think he expected…after all there's never any way of knowing…" He placed his hands on her shoulders, holding her at arm's length. "We left you a curious, bright, spectacularly gifted teenager and now we find you fully grown into a beautiful young woman. You've made quite the transformation, sweet one." He smiled, tweaking her nose with his thumb and forefinger.

Claudia breathed deep, trying to still her barrelling stomach. For endless moments, they stood in silence, Dane's soft touch on her arm coaxing the worry away with peaceful energy.

Leaves rustled on the ground as footsteps approached.

"Ahh, you see? Here he comes, to walk you home. Think no more about this, I promise all will be well." Dane hugged her as Brishan returned, the green eyes already seeking hers, penetrating her soul as he closed the distance between them.

They walked, ever so slowly, towards the chateau and his fingers drew circles inside her palm. They stopped behind the trunk of a giant, old oak tree. Dappled, pink twilight covered the ground and the air was quiet and still, so still that all she heard was the roar inside her chest.

Brishan turned her to face him, gently tugging on her arms. His fingers searched her face, caressed the smooth skin of her neck. She closed her eyes and felt her lids flutter as his warm breath tickled her cheeks. Feather light, he kissed the tip of her nose, and all thoughts disappeared as shivers trailed her spine.

A thumb ran over her mouth, putting slight pressure on her lips. She parted them in surprise and, with a stifled groan, he pressed his lips to hers. Gasping at the emotions flooding through her, she remained motionless until she heard Brishan inhale — sharp, quick, loud — as his mouth began to move slowly on hers.

She melted into the soft, wet movement, trembling as Brishan's hands explored her back, her shoulders, his fingers delicately weaving into her hair and ever so slowly gliding over her arms. Claudia's palms pressed into his muscular back as he lowered her, softly, to the ground.

The sound of leaves crunching beneath them filled her ears as their bodies melded into the grass. He lay beside her, hand cradling her face, staring at her with a smile playing on his lips. Claudia wondered if any jewel was brighter, or clearer than his forest green eyes.

"Can I kiss you again?" One peaked, black eyebrow quirked. His smile stretched — dazzling, tender, teasing.

Can't breathe anymore. Can't talk. Instead, she simply closed her eyes and nodded, magnetised by the closeness of him. The cool, evening breeze caressed her legs, her arms, her face, as she felt his warm lips close over hers once again. Her hands reached for his neck, her fingers pushed through the thick, black hair. Her breath came in short, quick bursts, faster and faster until she clung to his shoulders, trying to anchor herself against the surge of unfamiliar feelings.

He moaned and the sound vibrated through her lips as the tip of his tongue touched hers. She gasped, struggling to sit, to escape the building pressure.

He pulled away, frowning and smoothing her forehead with his hand. "Did I hurt you?"

"No. No, Brishan, of course not. I'm just...it's just that..." She wanted the ground to open and swallow her whole, until she could make up something to say. Anything but the truth of the gatekeeper's drooling lips flashing before her eyes as Brishan's tongue had touched hers.

"My sweet fairy," he murmured under his breath. "I know you haven't done this before, please don't be embarrassed, it's all new for you."

Relief at Brishan's misinterpretation rushed through her and she sat up, tentatively touching his shoulder. "It was just...a shock." *Not a complete lie, at least.*

"Claudia, I didn't know a girl like you existed. The first moment I saw you, running down to the lake, with that look of wonder on your angel face." He sat up, a slight frown tugging at his eyebrows as if he was trying to find the right words. "I thought all my dreams had come true. I waited that day, as patiently as I could, dying to, well..." He laughed softly. "I couldn't help it. I had to drag you away from the others, just for a moment, to see if you were real."

Claudia smiled, all thoughts of the gatekeeper disappearing beneath his green gaze. She thought back to the moment they'd met. "And I was thinking you must be far too old to believe in fairies."

"Ah, see, I've proven you wrong. You are a fairy. My fairy. And I challenge anyone to prove otherwise!" With that he pulled her to her feet, catching her in a tight hug. She pressed her face into his chest and felt her whole body soften and relax into his embrace.

Night had fallen. She could see the outline of the chateau in the distance, beckoning with cold tendrils, wrapping firmly around her neck, even within the warmth of Brishan's arms.

Chapter Five

Shattered Silence

The cool water lapping at her skin didn't quench the fire inside her body. Brishan's now familiar hands caressed her legs, her stomach, her back as he lifted her towards the centre of the lake.

It had become their favourite place, the magical body of water at the bottom of the valley. Here, they were left in peace, away from the knowing glances of the older gypsies. The first time Claudia had swum in the lake, three weeks ago now, she'd thought nothing on earth could equal such pleasure; apart from Brishan's hands and soft mouth playing on her neck.

Today, Sunday, they'd eaten an afternoon snack of freshly baked bread and cheese she'd brought from Margaret's kitchen, before running to immerse themselves in the silvery depths. It was so cold it took their breath away, despite the heat of the summer sun.

Claudia wore her only swimsuit, another ridiculous present from her mother, while Brishan swam shirtless in his black shorts. She never tired of gazing at the muscles rippling through his stomach. His biceps clenched when he carried her in the water, and she loved to feel his back as his powerful legs kicked to keep them afloat.

"You need to learn how to swim, it's dangerous not to know."

"Okay, teach me." She smiled. She liked the challenge.

"Mm, I can think of more enjoyable things to teach you right now."

"Such as?" Claudia caught her breath as his fingers trailed down her spine.

"Such as, what it feels like to be naked in the water." Brishan raised his eyebrows and a slow smile spread across his face.

"Is that what you used to do with your *other* girlfriend?"

Claudia joked, but felt a curious, gnawing resentment in the pit of her stomach at she thought of the hazel-eyed girl.

"Does that still bother you?" His smile was gone in an instant.

"No." *Yes.*

"Has Misha been bothering you?"

"No, I barely see her. In fact, I think she hides whenever I'm at camp."

"Oh, I know she does. I was actually hoping she could get to know you, as I do. Well, not *quite* as I know you." His lips curled in another smile before he looked closely at her, eyes suddenly full of concern. "Claudia, we've spoken of this. Misha and I...we've known each other since we were in nappies and we...we experimented, that's all."

She lowered her eyes and began to play with the straps of her swimsuit, picking hard at the stitching. "I guess."

"Misha and I are friends; she is not my fairy queen." Again, he smiled. "Now, back to our lesson for today."

Claudia giggled despite herself. "What if someone sees us?"

"No one will come down here, they know it's *our* time."

"Okay, but only if you promise not to look." *I can experiment, just like the hazel-eyed Misha.*

Brishan laughed. "What's the fun if I can't look?"

Claudia frowned.

"Okay, I promise." Brishan pushed her towards the shallow side of the lake so she could touch the bottom. Claudia bent so her entire body was in the water and quickly removed her swimsuit, laughing through her nerves.

Brishan grinned and struggled out of his shorts, throwing them on top of hers on the grassy bank. "How do you feel?" The smile was gone from his face.

She suppressed a shiver. "Cold."

"Walk out further, so you can stand up straight."

She waded in, amazed at the power of the water caressing her limbs without the distraction of clothes in between. Claudia was very close to Brishan now. His eyes narrowed and his jaw clenched as he stared at her bared shoulders. Ever so slowly, his hand surfaced to stroke her collarbone with a feathery touch, from one end to the other.

Claudia closed her eyes and sighed. A mellow breeze lifted her hair and strands tickled her cheeks. She swayed back and forth on legs that wanted to float and her arms spread over the surface of the lake, fingers skimming the surface.

His palms now covered her chest, moving to mould themselves around her shoulders and down the back of her arms. Fingertips grazed the sides of her stomach and made circular pathways from the small of her back to her neck.

A whole hand came to rest on her breast.

Claudia screamed, the sound cutting through the valley and shattering the silence. Fear and images of the gatekeeper exploded through her mind in lightening quick flashes. Her nipple, hard and stiff, protested the feeling of a hand resting there, and she cringed in anticipation of pain.

"Claudia? What is it sweetheart?" Brishan's broken voice betrayed his panic. She covered her face with both hands and tried to sink into the silence of the lake. He caught her, picking her up as if she were a baby, and carried her to shore. There, he placed her down in the sun on the grass and covered her quickly with her clothes, whispering soothing words in her ear and gently smoothing wet hair from her face.

"Claudia!" Dane's voice echoed among the trees as he crashed through them, standing above her in seconds.

Claudia felt a deep cold in her bones and could only stare up at him, scared and confused. Dane bent down and gently began to dress her, looking into her eyes the whole time with kindness. She stretched a trembling hand toward his cheek and he held it there with his own, strong and solid and safe.

Come now, little one, we must get you warm again," Dane said, before lifting her and cradling her body into his chest.

The sun streamed down with heat as Dane lowered her on a blanket. Oriana appeared and began to fuss over her, drying her hair and rubbing her arms. Brishan disappeared and returned with a mug of steaming tea. He held it up to her lips and she took small sips, feeling its hot spiciness soothe her throat and warm her insides.

"What on earth happened?" Claudia heard Dane whisper to Brishan. She watched as Brishan's cheeks coloured deep red and she ached to reassure him, but her vocal cords seemed dry and inactive.

"I...we were swimming naked and I..."

"It's okay, Brishan, just tell us, so we know how to help her," Oriana said, looking from Dane to Brishan with a deep frown.

"I touched her...here." Brishan pointed to his own chest. "And she screamed, as if in pain." Brishan's voice was so filled with distress that Claudia wanted to hold him; tell him it wasn't his fault. Yet she couldn't...wanted only the safety of Dane's presence.

"Claudia, precious, are you hurt?" Dane asked, rubbing her arms with quick, warming strokes.

Claudia shook her head. How to explain the torture of the gatekeeper? Brishan would never hurt her, inherently she knew. But those parts of her, the private parts of her, had only been touched by the gatekeeper. She wanted to die with shame and tears began to stream, unchecked, down her cheeks.

"I think we should ask Lenny to take her home, Dane, I'll speak with her tomorrow, when she's had a chance to calm down." Oriana's soothing voice broke through the turmoil in Claudia's head and she glanced at the older woman, hoping Oriana could see how grateful she was. She needed to go home to her bed, to think, to breathe and recover

Huddled under the covers that night, dry and warm, Claudia hugged Spotty and tried to stop the flow of tears. She didn't get a chance to wipe her eyes before the familiar sound of keys clattered through the halls. She sat up, trying to press her back into the wall as if she might disappear inside it. *Why isn't he at the security post?* She'd thought she was safe from the gatekeeper, now that the gypsies were back.

She'd thought wrong.

The gatekeeper pushed open her bedroom door. He stalked her; she'd seen Spotty hunt mice the same way...slowly, deliberately, quietly. She started to cry as he sat on the bed. The mattress dipped under his weight and her body rolled into him as he tugged the sheet down. Sobs ripped through her chest, tearing at her throat.

For the first time during one of the gatekeeper's visits, she sensed Snow-White and Rose-Red; she heard their fluttering and the musical chime of their unintelligible voices ringing loudly. She let her mind scream out, telling them to hurry — find Dane, find Brishan, bring help. Anything to save her from the hell she was about to endure.

The sheet was gone, discarded on the floor. She felt cool air on her breasts as they were bared open to the nightmarish figure towering over her. He pushed his mouth onto hers, attacking her face and blocking her airways. Fat hands probed at her underwear, roughly tugging until it tore completely, leaving her naked and vulnerable to his wild, violent gaze.

She closed her legs against the onslaught, but her thigh muscles were no match for his strong hands, pulling her legs apart, ripping his own trousers off and pointing his ugly, swollen 'thing' towards her. She wished she didn't know the things Oriana had told her, for now she knew what was coming. Strangely, she wondered why he hadn't gone this far before.

Oh my God.

He'd been waiting, waiting for her youth to blossom into womanhood. Womanhood that was now being torn apart.

Claudia knew what he'd do if she screamed — he'd kill her beloved pet, or possibly...*me*. Yet a long, howling yell escaped her mouth as the hard member poked and prodded, trying to force its way in. A hand clamped down on her face, smelling of grease, forcing her mouth to close and her teeth to shudder. She bit down on her tongue, tasting the metallic sting of blood as she fought to breathe through her nose.

Fierce pain burned in her groin as he pushed harder, tearing her skin as her opening gave way.

The door to her bedroom swung open with violent force.

Dane stormed in, eyes wild with fury, screaming her name, hurling himself at the gatekeeper and dragging him away from Claudia. She gasped to catch her breath as the gypsy threw the obese man to the ground and wound his strong hands around the fat neck.

The gatekeeper's eyes bulged as he struggled to breathe. Dane squeezed harder, wringing the life out of the man beneath him. Claudia dragged herself from the bed, nightgown hanging in tatters around her ankles, trying to reach out to Dane, anxious to save him from his own anger.

No, let Dane kill him.

For one moment, Dane turned, reaching out to touch her face. "Are you all right, Claudia?" His voice was unrecognisably harsh, but quiet and low.

Claudia just stared at him.

The sharp click of a switch sounded abnormally loud in her head and light flooded the room.

"Stop right there, you! The police have been called. If you move, I will shoot."

Claudia's knees buckled as she heard the voice of her teacher. Mr Campbell stood at the door, shotgun aimed at Dane's head. The gypsy slowly lifted his hands from the gatekeeper's neck and a raw, rattling gasp for air escaped the monster's throat.

Margaret stood behind the teacher, her hands grasping her heaving chest. Running footsteps down the hall signalled the arrival of Lenny and they all stood at the door, the three lonely adults of the house, staring at the scene in her bedroom. Claudia grabbed the remnants of her nightgown to her body and stood, feeling her body rise, tall and straight.

An overwhelming sense of calm rushed through her aching limbs and she faced the stunned audience, courage coursing through her blood.

"Lower your gun." Her voice sounded low and guttural as she stared at her teacher. Mr Campbell's mouth opened with a ready retort that didn't come.

"The monster on the ground is the person the police will take away. Dane...Dane just...saved me." She looked towards the gypsy and he ran to her, gathering her in his arms. He led her gently to the bed and cradled her head on his chest, smoothing her hair and rocking her body as she sobbed. Claudia gave in to the tears, watching as they spread onto the gypsy's red shirt.

"Remove your hands from her this minute." Mr Campbell moved towards the bed, his arm straight and stiff with the gun still firmly clenched in his hand.

Lenny gripped Mr Campbell's elbow, pushing him away from the bed. "Give me the weapon, you stupid old fool, or point it at that bastard on the floor." His lips quivered as he spoke and his eyes flicked to Claudia. "Come on, lass, let's get you out of here."

"How dare you, man! The gatekeeper can hardly be blamed for doing his job, and as for this...thief..." his eyes came to rest on Dane "...he must be held accountable for his trespassing. Yes, yes, Margaret, get the girl out of here, but you"—Mr Campbell's eyes fixed on Lenny—"explain yourself this instant."

"Good Lord have mercy on us all." Margaret, moving from the doorway as if startled from a dream, shuffled to the bed. "Miss Claudia...oh you poor child...you poor, poor child." Margaret caught Claudia's cheeks in her hands, tugging her from Dane's embrace, muttering and sobbing, her head moving from side to side.

"Someone...explain...this...instant." Mr Campbell's monotone voice sliced through Margaret's hysterics.

"Don't you see? Don't you see what's been happening all this time, under our very noses? I knew something was off about him, always creeping around the halls, leering at me when he thought I wasn't looking…oh good God…I'm so sorry…I can't believe…" Margaret gripped Claudia's hands, holding tight as she slumped to the ground.

Claudia watched as Lenny bent down to pat the housekeeper's shoulder. She realised that Dane had been wrapping her in a soft, warm sheet while Margaret spoke. He steered her towards the bathroom, his voice low and commanding, speaking to the housekeeper he'd never met.

"Margaret, Claudia will need a doctor. From what I hear about you, I know you'll be able to organise this for me. Yes?" The gypsy's hypnotic voice calmed Margaret's hysteria and she stood up, sniffling and nodding her head. "Lenny, please, would you be so kind as to go downstairs and wait for the police?" Dane turned to fix a steady gaze on Mr Campbell. "You must be Claudia's tutor?"

Mr Campbell nodded, his head jerking in two swift movements.

"The gun isn't necessary, but thank you for wanting to protect Claudia. I know you mean well." Dane's voice faltered only when he looked back at the gatekeeper. "The man is unconscious and will remain so until the police arrive."

"How do you know? Who are you? Do you honestly mean to tell me…" Mr Campbell's eyes widened as he scanned the gatekeeper's motionless form.

"I understand your confusion. Claudia has been visiting us, during our stay on the land. We mean her no harm, and right now I'm only concerned about her, so please, put the gun away, we've seen enough violence." Dane held his hand out towards the teacher, palm up, as if taming a wild horse.

Mr Campbell looked from Dane, to Lenny, to Margaret. The

housekeeper nodded, confirming the truth of Dane's words. All colour left the tutor's face. "All of you leave this room. Now. *I* will guard him until the police arrive."

Margaret quickly gathered clothes for Claudia and ushered her into the bathroom. Claudia was numb. Numb and thoughtless as she was dressed. She could barely feel Dane's arms as he carried her out again, down the hall to the servant's quarters, into Margaret's room. Soon, someone else arrived, a man speaking with a thick, sharp Czech accent. He pushed a needle into her forearm. *What did he say? Something about pain?* There was no pain, when there should have been.

Bang.

A sound, so explosive, she felt her teeth shudder. Dane's hand suddenly left her forehead and in its place was icy cold air. Footsteps echoed up the hall, running, someone was yelling. Then the hand was back. Dane's hand, hot on her forehead, stroking her growing panic into silence.

Morning dawned and, for a moment, her thoughts lingered on Brishan, swimming in the lake...drops of water sliding down his naked chest.

What would it be like, to wake up with him in my bed? My bed...

Her stomach clenched and she sat up, gasping for air. Her surroundings were unfamiliar, dark and quiet and the walls were closing in, making it hard to breathe.

"Claudia, you're safe; safe with us. Shh..." Oriana's soft voice entered her mind and she turned to find the gypsy lying beside her, in the strange bed.

Dane walked over from the other side of the wagon, to sit beside her, a placating hand reaching for her own. "Relax, precious one. We will not leave your side. I promise."

She breathed deeply and allowed herself to be led back onto the soft pillows, closing her eyes against memories and drifting towards the soothing spell of familiar voices.

Moments or maybe hours later, she heard the door to the wagon open and Lenny's face peered down at her, tears welling in the old man's eyes. "Morning, Miss," he said, his voice cracked and dry.

"Hello, Lenny."

A single tear ran down the weathered features. "I'm so sorry, Miss, had I known…" he broke down, sinking onto the floor with his face in his hands.

She dragged herself up and knelt on the floor beside him, pulling his skinny frame into her own and squeezing him with all the pity she felt for him and for herself. They rocked back and forth and Lenny patted her back, rhythmically, like she was a newborn baby being rocked to sleep.

Finally, he looked deep into her eyes. "How long had it been going on for, Miss?"

She looked at the eyes of loved ones staring at her and braced herself. "As long as I can remember, a few years after I came here from England…I think." *And it must be all my fault.*

"Well he won't do you no more harm, Miss, he's dead. Dead as a door nail and that crazy teacher with him." Every part of Lenny's body shook, his face distorted by anger.

Dane swore under his breath and when Claudia looked at him, his jaw clenched and his lips tightened. "Lenny, please, this is not the time. Claudia needs rest before the police interviews this afternoon."

"They're dead?" *Just like the rabbits. Breathing no more, all life gone from their bodies. I'm glad the gatekeeper's dead.* But quick, hot tears traced her cheeks. Mr Campbell's mousy face, his lips set in a straight, hard line, flashed by her mind's eye. *Oh God, what's happened?* She couldn't bear to ask the question. Not now.

Poor Lenny couldn't contain another round of sobs. Only Oriana remained quiet and calm.

"Could I ask you both to leave us, please?" The gypsy woman said, her quiet authority radiating towards the two men.

Surprisingly, they obeyed at once, both bowing their heads and leaving them alone in the dark, cool interior of the wagon.

"You must tell me all of it, dear one. You must free your mind of these events so it can recover. Then you can move on. I promise we'll help you, we know how to get you through this, sweetheart. Trust me."

Claudia felt bewitched by the husky voice and soothing words. A torrent of words flowed out of her, describing the fear-ridden nights, the confusion, the loneliness. Oriana cried when she cried, yelled when she yelled, fell silent when it was too much to remember.

And then it was over. The story told, the barriers broken. Claudia's tears no longer rushed down her face and her swollen, red eyes began to clear. The witch, Cosima, had come into the wagon, unannounced and unnoticed. Sweet smelling ointment was slathered onto her limbs, all over her body. The two gypsy women chanted in high tones, Snow-White and Rose-Red cuddled into her sides and she fell into a deep, dreamless sleep.

When she woke, a pink hue coloured the air around her. Roses perfumed the air and she breathed deep of their sweetness before sitting up. She lay in a pile of blue silk and a canopy of vines sheltered her from the soft breeze. She turned to see the lake glittering in the late afternoon sunlight. Three familiar faces smiled down at her and she felt strong fingers gripping her arm.

"So, my fairy queen has awoken from her slumber." Brishan's eyes glistened as they reflected the sun's beams, but the green sank into dark smudges and his fingers clenched her arm too tight.

She smiled back. "Brishan." She sighed, and he nestled in beside her on the silk and pulled her into his arms. The warmth from his skin seeped into her bones and she rubbed her nose on his hard chest. Brishan seemed to tremble as he held her, almost crushing her with the strength of his hug.

"You must eat, sweetheart," Dane said, gesturing to Oriana, who was walking over with a platter piled high with food. The soft strains of a violin played on the air and Claudia wondered, briefly, if she'd been spirited away to fairyland.

No, she could see Eamon and Selina, not far in the distance, plucking on their instruments, looking over at her and their son with sad smiles on their faces. The sound of children's laughter came from the camp and she knew she was in the real world, just a better one than she'd ever known.

She ate and drank sweet fruit juice from a fancy silver cup, sitting within the circle of Brishan's arms, squirming each time his grip became too tight. Dane handed her delicious strawberries from the platter and Oriana smiled at her with something like relief.

"Feel better?" The gypsy woman asked, raising a delicate eyebrow.

"Amazingly." Claudia felt a jolt of happiness when she realised she really did feel better. One hundred percent. "What kind of magic have you played on me?" She laughed, and easily squashed the questions threatening to spill from her mind to her mouth.

"Nothing but the magic of family," Dane said, lowering his eyes and reaching out to touch her hand.

"I wish." Claudia sighed.

"It is one wish I can grant you," Dane said.

Claudia frowned at him.

He looked at her then, his black eyes moist and narrow. "Claudia...I know your mother. She and I grew up together in England."

Claudia sank further into Brishan's arms, a deep sense of foreboding racing up her spine.

"Your mother and I were in love, for a brief moment in time. Our love produced a child. You, Claudia... You are that child."

Chapter Six

Into the Flames

She stood, too quickly, and stumbled over her own feet. *Run, run Claudia*. Her legs stretched out in front of her, carrying her up the hill where she'd first met Brishan. Carrying her far, far away into the valley, into the forest beyond, past tree trunks that sliced her arms and scratched her face, over piles of fallen twigs and, finally, onto a bed of leaves, crunching under foot, under her head, as she lay face down, in their soft, yielding midst.

Her heart pounded, too loud for her ears to endure. It sounded like rushing water, threatening to engulf her, drown her, kill her in a pit of lies. Did this mean her whole life had been a lie? *God, what does this mean?* She swallowed hard, her throat raw and aching.

One of the gypsies stood above her; she could hear his breath, but he didn't speak, not for precious, silent moments. How odd, to suddenly long for silence when all she'd ever craved was release from its suffocating stillness.

"Claudia." When he spoke finally, his voice blended with the breeze, whispering through the leaves beneath her head. Like rain. Brishan's voice.

"Did you know?" Her voice was muffled by the leaves and barely audible, even to her own ears.

She heard his deep, ragged sigh. "Yes."

Claudia found it hard to breathe. She could smell the earth beneath her, fresh and cool, and she heard insects rustling in the dry foliage. But still, she couldn't breathe. The roar in her head was deafening.

She sat straight up, flinging her head back, desperate for air to enter her lungs. Her hands clung to her chest, feeling the sharp rise and fall. Brishan was moving her, pushing her head between her legs, pressing her back, whispering unknown words into her ear.

And then *he* was there. Her father. *My father?*

Dane sat before her and lifted a hand to her face.

"Don't touch me," Claudia rasped, her throat burning with the effort.

"Claudia..."

"No. You can't. You can't tell me this. I have a father. He's short...and fat...and he doesn't care if I live or die...but..." She gasped to catch her breath, clawing at the air and trying to make sense of her scrambled thoughts.

"I know this is hard for you. But that's why we didn't tell you before. We needed you to know us first, to love us. I've always hoped...I thought you might have...sensed the truth."

Claudia met his gaze. She saw deep understanding in the brown eyes, understanding and tears set to fall from the dark lashes. And truth. She felt it through the panic and fear as it washed over her in peaceful waves. Her breathing slowed and a spark of hope ignited in the dark recesses of her emotions.

"I'm dreaming," she whispered.

A fleeting smile crossed Dane's face. "No, sweet one, you're not. This is real, as real as can be. You belong with us."

"Somehow, I feel like I've always known...at least, I've hoped and wished for it." Claudia's neck burned with familiar embarrassment and she fiddled with the leaves in her hair.

"Claudia, please forgive me for not helping you sooner. If I'd known you were in trouble..." Dane lowered his head, hiding his eyes from her by focusing on his hands. "If we'd taught you how to reach us, you might have suffered less, but I didn't think you were ready. I made a grave mistake."

Yes...your mistake. You could have...should have...told me. Claudia's fists curled and she slammed them into the ground, over and over until she felt the skin on her knuckles split. Dane caught her wrists, forced her to stop and when she looked at him again, a single tear glistened on his cheek.

Claudia shook her head, wrapping her arms around her own body. "It's my fault. I should have trusted you; I should have trusted my own instincts."

"You did, my brave, sweet daughter, when you sent for us." Dane frowned suddenly, catching her chin between his fingers so that it was impossible for her to avoid his gaze. "Tell me, please tell me, that you know *you're* not responsible for what the gatekeeper did. Tell me, I want to hear you say it."

She heard Brishan's sharp intake of breath as his hands paused on her back. She hadn't realized he'd been stroking her, massaging the pain from her body.

She thought about saying yes. *Yes! It is my fault.* She'd let it happen, her fear had paralysed her strength, immobilised her will. But deep, deep down in the depths of her soul, she knew this to be a lie; she knew because the words caught in her throat, she knew because the man sitting in front of her...*my father*...resonated with truth.

"No. No, I don't think it was my fault. Not now. But...I've doubted...in the past." Her voice cracked and she lowered her head into Dane's lap, feeling his tears drip on her cheek and blend with her own. His hand massaged her forehead, pressing between her eyebrows and over her temples.

For a long moment, they were still as Claudia's heart rate returned to normal and her crying stopped. Brishan began to hum, his low, melodic voice drifting with the wind.

"Oh my gosh!" Claudia sat up straight, pushing Brishan's hands from her back.

"What?" The two men turned to her in surprise.

"Does this mean," she stared at Brishan, not wanting to speak the unthinkable. "We are related!"

"Not by blood, sweetheart. Not even by law. Brishan is Oriana's nephew by blood, and Oriana and I are not formally married. We don't need marriage to prove our love. Our spirits connect us." Claudia detected a faint hint of amusement in his tone. "Do you really think we'd let the two of you...well...let's just say you can rest easy, sweet one."

Brishan was grinning madly, now sitting at her side in the leaves, obviously relishing this proof of her affection for him. She punched him in the arm, once again fighting the flush creeping up her cheeks. He pulled her back on to the leafy canopy, tickling her stomach until she screamed with laughter and begged him to stop.

And the sun crept in to her heart, wiping away the doubt and holding her in its warm glow.

There seemed no need for further explanations that day, as they walked back to the camp and her silken haven. She felt calm and...like she belonged. Gypsy blood ran through her veins. *I'm a real gypsy... I'm a real gypsy.* She started to skip as she repeated it to herself over and over again.

Margaret and Lenny arrived at the camp, just as the sun was setting. Lenny's arm rested casually over Margaret's shoulders and Claudia struggled to contain an amused smile. *Surely Margaret and Lenny couldn't be...?*

"Miss Claudia, I come to offer my sincerest apologies." Margaret's eyes focused on the blue silk surrounding Claudia and her new found family. She kept saying the word over and over in her mind; *family.*

Claudia felt gracious towards all human beings at that moment, even the grumpy housekeeper. She smiled. "Why?"

"For my neglect of you, which led to such unforgivable events." Her voice was strong and gruff as usual, but the housekeeper's eyes watered and her hands, clasped together at her waist, trembled against each other.

Claudia was silent for a moment, remembering the lack of affection and understanding. But it wasn't Margaret's fault. She felt Dane kneel behind her and place a strong hand on her shoulder. The feeling of utter safety and strength from that one touch sliced through her self-pity. She faced Margaret and stood, tall and proud.

"It is not your fault, Margaret. It is only the gatekeeper's and he's gone."

"Oh, Miss..." Margaret said, before her voice cracked and disappeared. She turned and hid her face in Lenny's neck, her body shaking with silent tears.

"Well done. I'm proud of you," Dane whispered in her ear.

"I hate to spoil the day for you, Miss, what with all the...the happenings. But the police are back and they want to talk to you. And to you, Dane. Just statements and the like. Me and Margaret have already spoken with them." Lenny fidgeted with his ear as he spoke, looking from Claudia to Dane and back. "Don't you worry, Miss, they're very nice, one lady and a man."

The last thing she wanted to do was revisit last night in her memory. But, she must. And Dane was here, right by her side. And he wasn't going anywhere. She turned to Margaret. "Could you...could you tell me exactly what happened? I mean, before I speak with them?"

Margaret took a deep breath, dabbing at her eyes with the sleeve of her dress. "Oh Claudia, I had an inkling that Alfred Campbell was half out of his wits, what with all that hunting. But, as the story goes, and I only have this from your parents mind you, way back when they first hired him; after all he never spoke to me about anything personal. Where was I? Oh yes, well, Alfred had a daughter about your age now, back in England, and she was murdered in their very own house, while he slept and..."

Lenny, rocking back and forth on his legs, spoke before Margaret could finish. "The reason she's telling you this, lass, is that your teacher shot that gatekeeper. Shot him dead, then turned the gun on himself."

"Shh. Let me finish, Lenny! He might have been crazy, but

Claudia and I *have* lived with him for most of her life, and too much of my own. The poor man deserves some understanding, God rest his soul." Margaret glared at Lenny until the gardener stood still in passive silence.

"Most importantly, Claudia, I think he must have lived with awful guilt, not being able to save his own daughter and all. What the gatekeeper did to you," she faltered, her hand gripping her necklace as she shook her head from side to side. "That lovely female officer at the house told us the gatekeeper had a police record. For years they'd looked for him, but he'd changed his name over and over, moved from country to country...well, anyway, I think seeing you...like that...with that monster, tipped poor Alfred Campbell over the edge."

Claudia looked down at her hands, a pang of guilt competing with the exhilaration she'd felt only moments ago. How unhappy Mr Campbell must have been. *Unhappy and normal and filled with regrets...just like everyone else.* She looked up, her gaze flicking automatically to her father.

Dane searched her face, his own portraying love and under-standing. "Lenny, Margaret, thanks for coming for us. We'll be at the house soon. Right now, I'd like to watch the sunset with my daughter." Dane put his arm around Claudia's shoulders and led her towards the lake, just as the sun released its last rays over the velvety, silver water.

In the days that followed, Lenny became the 'man of the house', hiring another gatekeeper, a gardener to replace himself and a kitchen maid to help Margaret. Claudia loved to watch him give instructions in his blunt, friendly way. His eyes sparkled in a way they had not before. Pride, thought Claudia; that's what pride looks like.

He refused to stay in the main wing, but she heard his footsteps each night, sneaking up the stairs to join Margaret in her new room across the hall from her own. She started school again under the watchful eyes of Oriana and Dane, completing exams left by Mr Campbell. But their lessons, so enthusiastically and lovingly given, now filled her soul in a way Mr Campbell's never did.

The gypsies continued to wow audiences with their magical shows each night in neighbouring towns and Claudia joined them sometimes, playing the cymbals or helping the costumiers. There was so much life outside the chateau.

After shows, the performers would come to the chateau, pulling boxes of old clothes and costumes from the attic: their impromptu performances enlivening the halls with screams of laughter.

And time stood still each evening, when Brishan kissed her goodnight before going back to camp. For Claudia, life before was forgotten as autumn turned into winter and the lake at the bottom of the valley slowly began to freeze.

"Claudia, I've received an email from your mother." Margaret came into the parlour one afternoon, a hint of the old sharpness colouring her tone. Claudia looked up from the piano, her eyes falling on the marble fireplace, now alive with flames making patterns on the red velvet-covered walls.

Her fingers stopped mid-note. Silence followed the house-keeper's words and Dane, sitting beside her on the piano stool, placed a firm hand on her shoulder.

"Only the angels in heaven would believe it, but she's coming to visit. Within the week." Margaret's eyes flicked to Dane and the crease between her brows threatened to engulf her whole face.

Claudia looked at her father.

He frowned and rubbed his chin with his thumb and pointer finger. "How much does she know of our situation here, Margaret?"

"Nothing. I hope I've not done wrong, but I felt it best that she wasn't informed of recent happenings. I've only told her the gatekeeper was in trouble with the law, in order to explain why we needed to hire new staff."

"I think you've done the right thing, Margaret, her husband wouldn't approve of any of us right now." Dane raised a pointed brow at the housekeeper and her hands flew to her cheeks.

"I'm not judging you, Margaret, we're all happy here as we are. But we knew it was going to come to an end." Dane stood and held his hand out to Claudia. "We have to face the inevitable, sweet one, and for that, there are things you need to know."

Somewhere, in the back of her head, Claudia had been waiting for this moment. The untold story lurking behind all the fun and hilarity and newfound warmth of family, could not, after all, remain hidden forever. *But I wish it would.*

Dane led her down to the camp to his wagon. He pulled out an old, wooden chest, its ornately carved latches rusty and stiff. "These are letters from your mother, to me. You can read them, Claudia, and decide for yourself how you wish to think of us."

Claudia gasped. "How long have you been getting letters from her?" Claudia herself had only received four or five a year for as long as she could remember; and then they were full of nothing but frivolous society gossip she'd never understood.

"Some from the year you were born and one a few years ago, finally telling me where to find you. My father always kept a post office box, in London. Really, it's the only permanent address we were ever capable of. I didn't check it for months, possibly over a year even, and that was the year of your birth. You can't imagine how devastated I was Claudia, finding out about you and not being able to see you right away."

"But...I don't understand any of this."

"I know. I know. It's complicated, as life is, at times. All we can do is try and get through the hard times — and look forward to the good ones."

Dane hugged her, then held her at arm's length, searching her eyes, giving her encouragement through his gaze alone.

He left her alone in the wagon, and her hands trembled as she opened the first letter.

September 29th, 1994

Dane,

Our daughter, Claudia Jane Spencer, was born on the 1st of June at two o'clock in the morning. She entered the world with her dark eyes open, quiet and curious. I shan't bore you now with the details of my pregnancy, or my marriage. I know how much, just this news alone, will shock you.

Suffice it to say I am not entirely miserable, I am fed, clothed and housed as befits my upbringing and as soon as I am recovered, I will enter society as the wife of a well-respected politician. I will be showered with money and fame. That is, if the constant political turmoil doesn't destroy us all.

I have news you will not like. Edward hated Claudia on sight. Had she been fair, she may have passed for our daughter. But she is not. She is as dark as you are dark, with huge black eyes and a head full of marvellous black hair already.

He is furious and will not hold her; in fact, he barely even looks at her. We were hoping she would look like his child and be accepted as such. Now I know the reason I wasn't allowed out of the country house in Yorkshire. He was waiting and keeping his options open. I almost admire his deceiving ways, he is so very clever.

When she is of an age deemed old enough by him, she will be sent away to a family property, out of the country. Edward will provide for her food and clothing and education, with my father's money. But she cannot be part of our lives, as our child. Edward's career would suffer for it and we must not risk the loss of his popularity with the public.

It is worse than that, Dane. I am not to tell you of her whereabouts. She will be kept inside until she is grown old enough to seek employment of her own, away from the eyes of London society, away from you. We will then accept her as a distant relative and ensure a decent life for her.

Edward is full of rage. He would kill you with his bare hands if he saw you, and despite his hatred for the daughter that should have been his, he will not have her further tarnished by being in your presence, ever.

I once loved you, Dane, but I was a child. A silly, bored child too neglected and ignored by those around me to resist your gypsy charms. I used to love watching you run from your tiny wagon at the back of the estate, excited from a night of musical shows, wanting to share it with me.

Your family gave us laughter and loyalty. Your father gave my father faith in the human race. My family saved yours from poverty, then, you and I killed their relationship. The birth of Claudia has killed him. Tarnished his bloodline. Now she too, is to be ignored.

I know you must think me cold, awful even in my acceptance of this. But I am what I am and you knew that also. You fell in love with someone not of your kind. Do not blame me entirely for the conse-quences. I write this letter simply as a courtesy, I know how you must have worried. I hope it finds you somewhere on your travels throughout the world.

Sincerely,
Grace Spencer

Claudia clenched the yellowed piece of paper so tightly her knuckles turned white. She couldn't bear to read the other one postmarked the same year. *How could she do this to me? To Dane?* Picking it up in both hands, she tore it to shreds, watching the words float towards the floor, never to be read again. She opened the latest one, crispy white and folded neatly.

December 4th, 2004

Dane,

You must never write me at the manor or anywhere again. The luck with which I've intercepted your letter is truly exceptional. Had Edward found it, I would have been made to pay dearly for your desperation.

His temper has only increased with time and you are, in his mind, his archenemy. Not only did he have to compete with you, a mere servant, for my attention as a child, he now must deal with a child you fathered. He would shoot you on sight. Or hire someone to do so. Do not take this lightly; he has the power and connections to have you killed. He is a dangerous man.

Please bear that in mind, for I have decided to tell you where your daughter is. I have not laid eyes on her myself for many years and I find myself growing sentimental. Please do not ever tell her of her parentage; it will not help her when she must come to re-join society with our wealthy associations and their old-fashioned views on class and parentage. It will be hard enough for her when she learns the truth of what must be done. But, I suspect she already feels like an orphan, the lie should not be too terrible for her to tell.

We must do everything we can to marry her into a decent family or obtain appropriate employment for her and if you are to see her, you must abide by this also. You cannot provide her with anything. Do not risk her future to appease your own feelings. I certainly have not.

She is in the Czech Republic, a small town called Lednice, at one of my grandfather's estates. You must understand that she has been kept inside and sheltered from the world, least she turn out like me; unable to resist temptation. I will not inform the caretakers there of you. You must approach the situation as you see fit.

If you do not heed my warnings, however, you are risking your very life.

Sincerely,
Grace Spencer.

Claudia swiped at the tears and squeezed her eyes shut to stop the hurt. It had been so long since she'd seen her mother; the revelations in the letters shouldn't surprise or bother her. *They wouldn't, they can't.* She'd found her family and it didn't include the cold hearted woman in far way England. It never had.

Clank.

Outside, metal crashed against metal, very near the wagon, very loud. The letter dropped from her hands, floating to the ground like a white dove's feather, oddly contradicting the words on the page.

"Claudia!" Brishan screamed her name. Claudia leapt from the seat, her hand resting over her pounding heart, and flung the door open to a world now dark with the onset of night.

The air rushed by her face as black clad men ran towards the middle of the camp. She pressed herself into the shadows of the doorway, breathless as more hooded men hurtled through the trees on horseback, emptying cans of foul smelling liquid all over the grass. The hiss of matches striking sounded unnaturally loud and flames sparked near the wheels of the caravans.

Brishan barrelled into the wall; as if his legs had been moving so fast he couldn't stop them without doing so. He doubled over, gasping for air and staring up at her, eyes wild and frantic as he scanned either side of the wagon. His hands gripped her waist and lifted her high. Suddenly her hair covered her face, the strands sticking to her mouth as he threw her over his shoulder and started to run.

She pummelled her fists over his back. "No! Brishan, put me down! What's going on? I have to help. I'm not going to the house unless you tell me where Dane is." Her heart clenched at the thought of what her father had been through, of what Grace's letters meant. And now this — his camp under attack. *I will not lose him now.*

"Claudia, listen to me, don't you think he'd just want you safe inside? It would kill him if anything happened to you. Shut up and calm yourself."

His harsh tone shocked her into stillness. She fought against the twinge of hurt, his insensitive words pricking her like barbed wire. *But he's right. What can I do? Fight the intruders with my own puny hands?* She heard the gypsy women screaming, screaming as they followed Brishan's crazy pace towards the chateau, screaming for their children to hurry, screaming back at the men frantically putting out fires with blankets.

The screams even echoed far into the valley as families escaped through the trees with rearing horses.

Margaret and Lenny, along with the new, burly gatekeeper, waited by the kitchen door. Brishan lowered her to the ground and told them all to hurry inside. Lenny gripped Claudia's arm, in readiness for a fight, but the urge to fight was gone as quickly as it had come, replaced by a fear so strong she felt her legs turn to led. Taking short, sharp breaths, she watched Brishan sprint back to the camp. Flames seemed to rear up around him and she slumped to the ground, clutching her stomach.

"There's nothing we can do now, Miss, we've called the authorities. You know those gypsies are the strongest bunch of people I've ever come across. I know they'll be all right. I know it. Your father's not going to leave you after all these years of trying to find you; not without a fight." Lenny knelt beside her, gnarled old fingers timidly patting her shoulder.

Claudia looked up at him, immediately ashamed of her outburst. "You're right, Lenny. I am not helping them by turning into a sobbing mess."

"That's more like it, Miss. Now, come into the kitchen. Me and Margaret are making food. When this is over, I dare say there'll be many mouths to feed."

Lenny wasn't wrong. Hours after the police left, and the fire had died down because there was nothing left to burn, Claudia heard shuffling footsteps outside. One by one, family by family, gypsies were ushered into the house, given warm drinks and food, and placed by the fire to recover.

Claudia helped as many people as she could, running between hungry mouths and the back door, anxiously waiting to see the familiar shapes of Dane, Brishan and Oriana.

She tapped her hand against the doorframe until her fingers bruised. *Where are they?*

Two soot-covered children ran up to her, gripping her legs and yelling out for their mother. She took them inside by the fire, anxiously searching the faces there, waiting for one of the distraught women to show that she knew the lost babies. They couldn't have been more than four years old. She sank to the ground, pulling the warm little bodies into her own.

She must have fallen asleep; it was silent now as she lay alongside exhausted bodies strewn across the floor. The children, now perched on her lap, breathed softly and the fire had burnt itself down to crackling embers.

She placed their little heads on a rug and walked quietly to the kitchen door. The smell of fire singed her nose and smoke lingered in the air, its thick tendrils weaving towards the sky. Silhouetted against the ruined campsite, Brishan and Dane rested their heads on their knees, facing each other and talking in low, mumbled tones. Claudia ran to them, stumbling on her feet, knocking over a misplaced, ceramic bowl so that it rolled along the cement with a deafening clang.

Dane turned, his head swivelling almost too quick on his neck. Soot covered his cheeks and long tear marks wove through the blackness. Brishan stood, stretching his body as if it would barely obey the instruction to walk. He knelt at her feet, grasping her hips and pushing his face into her stomach. She wove her hands into his long, matted hair and stared over his head at her father.

"She's gone, Claudia. Oriana. She's gone." Dane's voice, husky and deep, sliced through the thick air.

Claudia felt her chest constrict. "But...but Selina and Eamon are inside, they said she was with you," Claudia said, standing dumbly now with her mouth open.

"She was. Until I started putting out fires. Seconds, Claudia, I only took my eyes from her for seconds." Dane stared absently towards the forest. "I can only think...someone..." His voice cracked and he put his head to his knees.

Brishan stood, looking into her eyes, brushing her hair from her face. "We think she's been taken by the raiders. There were rumours, in town, of groups searching the borders, kidnapping women to sell into prostitution in Russia and Germany. And then, there are always those whose aim in life is to rid society of the Romany — and there are many of the old blood among us." Brishan's voice, hard and cold, was at odds with the tears streaming down his face.

"Oh my God. But why? I don't understand." Claudia rushed to Dane's side, reaching for his hand.

He pulled it away sharply. "It's the way of humanity sometimes, Claudia, discriminating against those they don't understand. This is not the first time we've been targeted and it won't be the last. I'm sorry, Claudia, sorry this has happened to you. To all of us." He caught her hand in his own, his face softening with the touch. "I have to find Oriana. Can you take me to your horse? Now, even in the dark? Many of the attackers came by horseback, through the forests. Cars are too easily traced." He seemed to speak to himself for a moment, but when he looked back at her, pure agony poured from his eyes. "I need to follow their path."

Claudia felt desperate to help, but desperate to make him stay, safe with her, at the same time. She took a deep breath, knowing instinctively what she must do and what she might sacrifice in doing it. The neighbouring property wasn't far away, she was sure she could find it in the dark. They could sneak into the stable and take the horse. *Of course they could.*

She swallowed hard. "Yes."

They ran through the night, side by side, breath mingling

with the cold air in puffs of white. Brishan held her hand, pulling her with him, helping her when she stumbled. The paddocks were obstacle courses of felled trees, ditches and sharp rocks, reaching out to stab her shins and pierce her shoes. She focused on the shoes, forcing the panic away, concentrating on her steps so she didn't slow them down.

The neighbouring mansion and stables were silent and dark. They edged around the wooden building, towards the great Kladruber, calm and peaceful in his stall. Dane stared at the horse, the one she'd sat on for months as she was led in quiet circles around the garden. He whispered in its ear, leading it out with tenderness as Brishan came forward with a rope halter and lead rein. They began to retrace their steps to the chateau, the Kladruber showing the whites of his eyes and prancing with his head held high.

"Shh. There, there, my powerful friend." Dane stopped, speaking again in soft, smooth tones. He rubbed the indentations above the horse's eyes with his thumbs and, in moments, the large eyes stilled, the Roman nose-shaped head lowered, and they could walk again.

Claudia rushed ahead, into the kitchen, gathering supplies for Dane; some clean clothes and any food she could shove into a backpack. Holding her breath now, she hurried outside. Dane stood in the moonlight, horse by his side. The acrid smell of burning rubber filled the air, there were still tyres alight. Claudia fought back tears and handed him the bag, wanting to beg him to stay, but knowing his heart shattered with each second lost.

Dane stared at her, buzzing with energy now as he prepared for the journey. "I promise I'll be back, sweet one. Be strong. Believe that all will be well." He looked down, tugging on the rein to steady the eager Kladruber. "I saw some of the men ride down into the valley, towards Mikulov. I'll search there first, in the surrounding properties. If I'm too late, I'll find their trail and hunt them down, whatever country they've taken her to." Again, he seemed to speak to himself.

He touched her cheek. "I truly didn't think the need to leave you again would come. But there'll be lessons for us all to learn, there always is." He hugged her to him, so tightly her ribs threatened to break.

Finally, he released her, holding her at arm's length and letting her see the pain in his eyes. For the first time, Claudia noticed the deep crevice between his brows, the lines crossing his forehead and the grey stubble scattered over his jaw. He spoke no more words, but pulled Brishan to him, gripping him around the shoulders, before turning towards the horse. The Kladruber waited, snorting and swishing his tail.

Dane mounted without sound. He didn't look back as he raced towards the forest.

Brishan, holding her hand again, tugged her inside. Selina and Eamon stood by the door, the Irish man holding his wife as she sobbed. Brishan lifted Claudia's hand to his mouth to kiss her fingers, letting them go one by one as he moved closer to his parents. They enfolded him in their arms, relieved tears mixing with their panic. Claudia was out of her depth, trying so desperately to help but feeling too inexperienced to know how, almost collapsing with the pain of watching Dane ride away.

She heard a man clear his throat. Lenny stood in front of her, tears pooling in his eyes. Claudia covered her mouth with both hands...she didn't dare shout out.

Lenny's scrawny arms encircled her, camphor ointment from somewhere beneath his flannelette shirt hit her nose and she sank into his comforting embrace.

He stroked her hair and led her out to the front garden, to the swinging chair near the lavender bush, just as the sun peeked over the horizon. After a short while, Brishan took his place and the old man walked inside, head bowed with tiredness, ready to feed the lost and lonely people waking from a real nightmare.

Soft fur caressed her shoulders as Brishan wrapped them both in a coat. They curled inside, Snow-White and Rose-Red settling beside them on a sprig of lavender. They looked into each other's eyes. They looked until they found the silent nothingness of sleep.

Much later, something woke her up; her eyes blinked uncontrollably in the strong sunlight. Brishan's body still warmed her, encased beneath the fur coat.

"I warned you, Grace. I told you she'd be nothing but trouble."

The voice was low and pompous and...strange. Her eyes snapped open. It belonged to a short, stout man, standing above them. A woman stood next to him, blonde hair glinting in the sun and red lips pursed together so tightly they were turning pale through the paint.

"Claudia, wake up this instant and look at me. What on earth is going on here? Why do you stare so? It's me, your mother."

Chapter Seven

The Promise of a Hug

Brishan jumped up and the air swirled, cold and harsh. Claudia blinked over and over, trying to focus. Her arms ached as she pushed herself up from the chair, ignoring the knot in her stomach.

She pushed her hand through the hair tangling about her face and pressed her palms over her dress to try to smooth the wrinkles.

"What do you have to say for yourself, young lady?" This from the portly man, presumably Edward. A man so vile, so full of hatred that he'd sent her away from her own mother. She took a deep, shaky breath.

"Excuse me, Sir, Madam," Brishan said, keeping his eyes on the ground. "Last night we were attacked. Our camp was destroyed and these kind people have taken us in." Brishan's eyes flicked sideways, meeting Claudia's.

Claudia gasped, flinching as Brishan appealed to people far less worthy then he. His eyes skimmed the ground again, and his hands clasped in front of him. *What must it cost him to behave so?* She couldn't imagine — and she wouldn't allow it.

"I am pleased to see you, Mother, Edward." She dipped her head towards them, using every drop of energy left in her. "However you have come at the most inopportune time, we're in the midst of a crisis. Perhaps you should stay in the village, until such time as these unfortunate people have had a chance to collect themselves and recover." She breathed deeply and stood straight, with poise, as Mr Campbell had taught her.

"Well, I never," Grace Spencer said, royal blue eyes widening. "At least I see you've been well schooled, child, but this situation is, well, disappointing to say the least. As for your obvious association with these people…" She scanned Brishan from head to toe, then dismissed him with the flick of a hand.

Claudia stood tall, directly facing her mother. "These *people* are my friends and I *will* help them. Please be so kind as to return in a few days, when we've had sufficient time to be useful to them." *Where did that come from?* Brishan gawked at her as though she was an alien.

She couldn't explain the jolts of power zapping through her, as they had the night of the gatekeeper's downfall, filling her with a sense of strength she'd only known since she'd met the gypsies.

"You are making a fool of yourself, my dear, despite your eloquent words. We will not stand for it, do you hear?" Edward said, eyes glinting in their black circled sockets. He strode into the house, arms swinging wildly and head pushed forward like an angry bull about to go into the ring.

Claudia glanced at Brishan as he wrapped his arm around her shoulders, green eyes searching her own. "No matter what happens, we'll get through this, I promise you, precious fairy. Always believe that," he whispered in her ear, stroking the soft skin of her neck as his warm breath caressed her cheek.

She shivered with the closeness of him. Despite all the chaos, she still felt awed by him, by his tenderness and strength and overpoweringly masculine smell. His black hair stood out from his tanned face, wildly framing his pointed eyebrows and she leaned into him, lifting her hand to smooth strands from his soot-covered cheeks.

"Move away from my daughter. This instant." Grace Spencer's voice, controlled and sharp, pierced through the calm Brishan had started to create within her.

Brishan turned and faced the woman, hands by his sides and eyebrows raised, a slight smile playing on his lips.

"As you wish. For now," he said, winking at Claudia and turning around, eyes already scanning the lines of people leaving the house.

"What on earth...?" Claudia ran inside, in time to see Edward standing in the middle of the entrance hall, barking orders left and right for the removal of suitcases, instruments and pieces of cloth holding their precious, hidden treasures — along with the people who owned them.

Claudia stood, eyes closed, trying to breathe normally. Brief gusts of wind whooshed by her cheeks as the gypsies ran outside, eager to escape the wrath of Edward, scared for their children, running for the safety of the hills and villages beyond.

Snow-White and Rose-Red hovered close by her head, swirling around and around until she was dizzy with their movement. But she would not send them out, searching for Dane's spirit, begging for his help. Oriana's need was greater than hers, perhaps greater than everyone's. She turned to stare at the stout English man as his voice boomed throughout the hall.

"Please, Edward, I only ask for your charity. These people have suffered enough." She spoke quietly and prayed the sincerity she felt would penetrate the man's cold heart.

Edward turned to look straight at Claudia. Stared as if he was seeing her for the first time. "I see you've grown into quite a beauty, like your mother. What a shame," he sneered, "you have that unfortunate, dark colouring." His face was impossibly ugly to her. "Why do you call me Edward?"

"Because...that's your name." Claudia floundered, her face burning under the scrutiny.

"I am your father and I will be addressed as such."

"All right then, Father." The word caught in her throat. "Please extend your sympathy to my friends." She grabbed her thighs to steady herself and looked him directly in the eyes.

"Your friends?" Edwards raised his eyebrows. "These people are constantly purged from society for their bohemian, thieving ways. Last night was no accident, my dear. Vigilante groups, though I don't condone such illegal pursuits, actually do us all a favour you know! And the police would have moved them on in any case." Edward drew his last words out through smirking, twisted his lips.

Grace moved to stand by her side. "Claudia, surely you know it's illegal what they do, going from town to town tricking innocent people with their pathetic, pretend magic. They are not your friends, however they may act. The law would have most certainly dealt..." Grace paused, her white hand fluttering to her neck as she turned to look at the door.

Eamon stood there, covering his mouth, stifling the cough that betrayed his presence. Selina was beside him, her back ramrod straight and her eyes fixed on Grace.

"Be off with you then," Edward barked.

"We simply want to thank the lady of the house, Claudia, for her unrelenting kindness. We will be forever in her debt. You should be proud of her." Selina remained poised and unflinching, now gazing directly at Edward.

"You are not permitted to tell me what I should or should not be proud of. Leave." Edward didn't look at them.

Selina took a step forward, but Eamon stretched a protective arm across his wife, pushing her behind him.

Claudia felt her bottom lip tremble as the tears came. Shame burned its way down her throat, her chest, her stomach. Selina smiled at her, the gesture reaching her warm, dark eyes and piercing Claudia's aching heart. Eamon raised his hand to his heart, then to his lips, blowing her a kiss.

Then, the gypsies were gone. All of them. Gone.

Great, rasping sobs escaped, the force of the emotion buckling her knees.

"Good Lord, child, it can't be that bad. I understand you've had a remarkable night, however, please, control yourself." Grace Spencer...*what a cold, brittle name*...knelt in front of her, placing a cool hand on the top of her head. The woman's voice was shrill and her touch unsettling in its lightness.

Margaret rushed in from the kitchen, flour coating her cheeks and grey hair standing up in odd, curling strands around her face without the headscarf. She was twisting her voluminous apron around her hands. "Excuse me, Mr and Mrs Spencer, it's my greatest pleasure to welcome you to the house. Please do accept my apologies for the sorry state you find us in."

She bustled behind Claudia and caught her beneath the arms, giving her a secret, sympathetic squeeze on the shoulder before pushing her towards the stairs. "You must understand that the girl has had no sleep and must go to bed at once. I'll see to it, then I'll prepare dinner for you both. Please, if you may, retire to the library and I'll be there promptly." Margaret pushed Claudia up the grand staircase before any objections could be made.

"Now, now, dear, I will admit, our circumstances could not be more awful at present, but we must make the best of it. No good can come of vexing your…your parents," she said in a dramatic stage whisper as they reached the top. "Go to bed, I promise I'll not abandon you, nor will Lenny, but we must ensure Mr and Mrs Spencer are consoled, or it will be worse for all of us." The housekeeper patted her on the back, ushering her towards her door.

Claudia's eyes were so swollen she could only stumble blindly into her room, half-registering Margaret's words.

She peeled back the covers and enfolded herself in their depths. The knot in her throat wouldn't subside as the tears continued. Still, she closed her eyes, incapable of further thought, and tried to breathe through the pain.

She awoke to find herself at the top of a tree, legs dangling from a branch and hands grabbing precariously to the sturdy trunk. Her white nightgown blew about in the gentle breeze. *How did I get here?*

"Sweet one, how are you? I hope you don't suffer as badly as I." Dane sat beside her, black clad legs wrapped around the branch, hands free as he balanced unaided.

"Dane?" She stared at him for long moments, drinking in his familiar, dark eyes. His brown hands reached out to smooth the wisps of her hair curling around her temples.

The sky glowed pale pink with streaks of orange branching out towards the horizon. Jasmine perfumed the air and Claudia pushed her nose towards the smell, careful not to lose her hold on the branch at the same time.

"Where are we?"

"We're safe, my dear daughter. We're astral travelling, in a different dimension. In a world vastly different to the one we live in most of the time. I don't know the address." He laughed, a soft, sad laugh. "I only know I've been able to speak to people of my blood through my dreams, since I can remember. That is where we are." He smiled and his face was so beautiful, so achingly familiar.

"Bad times are ahead, my daughter, I won't lie to you." His face was serious now, but his eyes spoke of courage.

"Bad times have already been."

"Ah yes, I know, my poor child, I know how you suffer."

"Have you found her?" She searched his face, the lines etched deeper now than ever before.

"Yes. But she's in danger still. Her beauty is…well…a curse sometimes. Men wish to own such passion as she has. But, for now it's saved her from death."

"You can't save her?" Claudia held her breath.

"I can. But I fear the damage has already been done, and I must bide my time…to ensure safety for all of us."

Claudia felt her face crumple. *Why is the world falling to pieces?*

"I tell you this because you've been sheltered from the world for too long — not to scare you. Sometimes fate grips us and won't let us go, other times we can control it." He looked down at his bare hands and shook his head. When he looked back up his eyes burned with fierce intensity.

"Claudia, you must not tell Edward what you know. He'll

only be worse for it. At least he's bound by societal rules dictating how fathers should behave. I will not have his hate for me affect you more than it already has. Go along with their ruse, for now."

"But I'm not staying here, I'll go with Brishan, he'll keep me safe, he…" She looked down. "He loves me…I think."

Dane chuckled, the sound drifting musically on the warm air. "Oh yes, he loved you the first time he saw you, my sweet one." He touched her gently on her nose. "But he, also, is on a path to hard times. He has responsibilities he must face." Dane put his hands over his face, briefly, and sighed.

"Brishan has a fire burning within. He's been that way since birth — running headlong into trouble, not caring if he puts himself in danger. You see, the adventurer in him clashes with the healer. And the healer is his destiny, whether he likes it or not. What this means for you, Claudia, for now, is simple. I won't let you be with someone who'll put you in the path of their own demons."

Claudia nodded, beginning to understand Dane's warning. The pulsating twitch above Brishan's mouth, the reckless way he rode his horse, the slow, burning anger that raged beneath the surface of his beautiful face whenever danger was near, or whenever he felt he'd upset her. All of it contrasted dramatically with the gentle, emerald-eyed Brishan she loved and knew so well.

"Precious Claudia, always remember, nothing is permanent, life is transient. Hold this knowledge close when you're scared and know that you're safe and looked after by the spirits of our ancestors."

"When will I see you again?" Claudia whispered, inching forward on the branch towards the promise of a hug.

"You will always see me, if you concentrate, if you believe, even if I'm across seas and over mountains. As you're seeing me now." He smiled and bent forward to cradle her in his arms.

"Claudia, I'm here for you forever and I'll always return when you call. Your pretty little Snow-White and Rose Red will ensure this." Again, he laughed, as he always laughed. And the music returned to his eyes.

"Miss Claudia, wake up, child, wake up, you must." The frantic shaking rattled her bones as she fought to stay with Dane.

Margaret, eyes wide and hair dishevelled without her curlers, stood above her, sharp hands gripping her shoulders.

"Margaret, no, Dane..." Claudia scanned the bedroom, searching for her father's face, only inches from hers mere seconds ago.

"He's not here, Claudia. But Brishan is outside, waiting for you."

"Oh." Claudia sat up, fighting through disorientation.

"Come now, your parents are asleep in the guest wing, they'll not hear us now. You must dress." Margaret held out her jeans and a jacket and helped her out of the nightgown she didn't remember changing in to.

"The gypsies have all gone into the hills, to take shelter there with the local villagers, but Brishan has returned to speak with you. Lenny and I will help you, Miss, but you must be inside and back in your bed by sunrise, do you understand? I don't fancy being on the end of one of Mr Spencer's temper tantrums again."

"Of course, Margaret." Claudia slipped into the clothes, her heart now beating faster than it should.

With Margaret behind her, full of silent warning, she crept through the back door. The night slapped her face with cold and frost covered the grass. She peered into the all-encompassing dark.

"Claudia." The whisper came from behind and the hairs on the back of her neck prickled. She turned, her gaze falling straight into Brishan's green, black fringed eyes, twinkling in a sliver of light from the kitchen window.

She stifled a sob and ran into open arms, feeling the deep thud of his heart as she moulded her body into his. "Are you real? I mean, am I dreaming?"

He laughed, the sound raspy and low. "I'm real, my fairy. I take it you've been talking to Dane this night, too?"

She nodded.

"Don't be alarmed, it's a simple trick of mind projection, nothing magical or wizard-like about it. You too could do it of your own will, if you were taught."

She nodded again, her tongue sticking to the roof of her mouth.

He took a deep breath. "I've to come to say goodbye. I couldn't leave without seeing you again, no matter the risk of your...um...*parents* catching me. But I promise I'll return, we'll all return, we won't abandon you." His words tumbled out as his hand grasped the side of her face.

She wrenched his hand from her cheek. "What do you mean? Where will you go?" Her words sounded whispery, barely audible.

"Through the hills, into the villages we know will welcome us and shelter us from this...uprising. And then towards England, hopefully on to the festival circuit, until we can rebuild the community again." His words were clipped and his lips were drawn into a thin line, just visible in the pale light.

"We need to work to recover. I can't leave them, Claudia, not without Dane. They need me, for now at least. So many are old, or too young."

"But I—"

"Claudia, I know how awful your mother and her husband must seem to you, but they're just products of their society. The point is, they'll feed you and house you and keep you out of danger. That's something I can't do. Not now. I just want you safe and away from harm, until I can look after you, properly. Right now too many others need looking after."

"But, I thought…" Her throat dried up as his words began to sink in. Reasons for leaving her behind, excuses, all of them. "I don't need looking after." Even as she said it, she knew it wasn't true, knew she'd be a burden on him. But it didn't matter, not now, not when being with him meant everything. "Please don't leave me here." The words drizzled out in the company of a rasping sigh.

The frown between his eyebrows was far deeper than should be possible on such a young man. He stroked her nose, her hair, her collarbone and bent to kiss her lightly on the mouth. Salty liquid greeted her lips and she pulled back, stunned to see his face streaked with tears.

"I love you, Claudia. I should have captured you in a jar when I first met you, to keep you safe under my bed. A bed that I currently don't have." His voice broke mid-sentence and he lowered his face into his hands, quickly wiping away the evidence of his pain.

"And I know you don't *need* looking after. I *want* to look after you. And looking after you means making sure you're safe, not putting you in danger for my own selfish reasons. Just know, that the only way you can ever, *ever* get rid of me is if you order me away. It's an old gypsy curse. Pride." He smiled, ruefully. "I promise I'll be back. And a gypsy promise lasts many lifetimes."

"Brishan, I love you too," she whispered, forcing her freezing hand to touch his shoulder. She wanted to throw herself on him, to beg, to scream, to force him to take her with him.

Lips caressed her eyelids, moving slowly down her cheeks towards her mouth. His tongue pressed gently inside her mouth, moving ever so slowly as he pulled her close. A strong hand gripped her hips, forcing her into him, her pelvis against his, her breasts scraping his chest. He groaned into her mouth, hands moving in circles over her back as they swayed lightly side to side, in a desperate, sensual dance.

He hugged her to him, pulling her face down to his shoulder;

so tightly she felt all breath leave her body. Just as quickly, he let go, staring at her with tortured eyes as he edged away towards the hills. She cried, silently now, standing with her arms by her sides, watching as he moved into the blackness.

Chapter Eight

The Butterfly Queen

Claudia stared at the wooden panelling on the walls of the formal dining room. The pretty dust particles she loved were nowhere to be seen today. Edward, with his dislike of open windows, had robbed her of even that. He preferred to eat under the glow of the chandeliers.

Is it dinner or tea time?

Days had turned into nights and nights into days. It'd made no difference to Claudia as she'd drifted around the chateau, eating, sleeping and talking to her captors, when she absolutely had to. She was worrying, for the gypsies safety, waiting, for her family to return. She knew they would.

Wouldn't they?

Margaret had moved back to her rooms in the servant's quarters and Lenny back to the gardener's cottage. It pained Claudia to see their wistful glances towards each other as they went about the daily errands. Although, she'd often caught Lenny winking and slyly tapping the housekeeper on her ample backside.

The days inched by, with the same routine, leading her into boredom and lethargy. The gypsies had left her weeks or maybe months ago now — time held no meaning and she refused to keep count of the miserable seconds.

Each day, they ate breakfast early, followed by a walk around the grounds: Claudia trailing behind the usurpers as they discussed politics with much animation.

They'd resigned themselves to being called Grace and Edward. They'd had to. She'd simply refused anything else; could not even fathom calling them names indicating love and affection.

And refusing gave her a strange, new sense of confidence.

At midday, every midday, Margaret served dinner to the threesome in the formal dining room and Claudia stared at the walls rather than their faces, reliving endless days and nights sitting in the same chair, all alone but for Snow-White and Rose-Red. Now, she had company, she'd always wanted company.

And she hated it.

The afternoons were set aside for reading. Study books for Claudia. Edward worked on correspondence with his London office in a sitting room now strewn with computers, fax machines and all manner of equipment Claudia rapidly learned to use.

And Grace moaned about the absence of her social circle.

They were not cruel; these pretend parents who'd invaded and destroyed her life when it had only just begun. Edward was cold, but polite, very interested in her education and a constant presence while she completed her schoolwork by correspondence. He'd enrolled her with a school in London and she spoke with a teacher each day via the computer. It wasn't bad, at the very least it meant contact with the outside world.

Grace looked nervous whenever she spoke to Claudia; her eyes twitched and her fingers trailed over her neck, sometimes gliding over her red lips, drawing attention to their plump softness. When she was around Edward, Grace oozed confidence, complimenting him and tossing her hair, but turning away each time he reached for her. Edward stared at her mother like a puppy stares at its owner.

No explanations of the past were given, nor were they asked for. Claudia no longer cared. Besides, Grace's old letters to Dane had explained enough. She didn't want to revisit any of those feelings. *Didn't need to.* Not now that she belonged to a family of her own. A family that would return soon.

Yes, soon.

A rush of blood flooded her face and tears pricked her eyes. It didn't matter how many times she told herself, or Lenny told her, or Margaret told her, that the gypsies *needed* to leave that night, that they'd had no choice. It didn't stop the clenching of her heart, the aching in her stomach. *It was leave or die,* Lenny said. But the gut-wrenching feeling that she'd been abandoned, yet again, lingered on every minute of every day.

That feeling ate at her stomach now as she sat at the dining table, picking at roast vegetables and letting Edward's words wash over her.

"Claudia, are you listening? Your mother and I are most happy with the decision and you'll meet him this week."

She looked up at her pretend father, frowning as she tried to replay what he'd been saying. "Meet who?"

Edward stared at her, as he often did, with raised eyebrows and a tight-lipped smile. Claudia was used to it. Mr Campbell had often looked at her in much the same way. She tried very hard to focus on his face; helped by looking at a small bit of food stuck at the corner of his mouth.

"Preston Myers."

Claudia glanced at her mother. Grace nibbled on a small piece of pumpkin like a nervous rabbit. She smiled as she chewed, the expression never reaching her eyes, and put her fork down neatly by the plate.

"Claudia, Edward has been trying to explain that we feel you'd make a fine match with Preston. He's the son of one of London's best architects, Ralph Myers, an old family friend." Grace cocked her head to one side and smiled at Edward. "It seems like only yesterday that we went to Preston's christening."

The words sank in. Claudia's cutlery clattered onto the plate. "A fine match? You mean as a husband?"

"Why, yes. We understand you'll need to enter society first and find your feet. But, Claudia, you're not in such an unusual position, many children of wealthy families are sent abroad to live, study and the like, especially over the last few years, considering the economic turmoil."

Edward shook his head and smiled at Grace. Yes, he seemed to be saying, your mother's right, it *is* the overriding factor of life.

She felt laughter rise in her throat and welcomed the relief from her recent lethargy. The thought became almost unbearably funny and she felt as if she were floating above the table, looking down at these absurd adults with their plans to take over her life after mere weeks of being in it. Claudia clutched her napkin, pressing her quivering lips into it.

"It's no reason to cry, I assure you. He's a very presentable man with lovely manners." Grace moved her head, making the blonde waves fluff about her face. "After those ruffians you were housing, I'm quite sure you think all young men are hideous, but that is not the case."

Claudia dabbed at her eyes, pleased with her mother's poor perception. Mr Campbell had never approved of her sudden giggling fits, Edward and Grace would no doubt feel the same way. She was learning to lie, but…why, when she'd so recently learnt of truth and justice and love? She carefully formulated her next words.

"Well, it would be nice to make a friend, I haven't had many opportunities to do so, as you can imagine." She watched closely for a reaction, but the finely veiled accusation was lost on Grace and Edward. "But as I'm not even seventeen yet, I don't think a husband would be appropriate." This time she did laugh, unable to stop herself.

Grace and Edward smiled now; no shock, no disgust registering on their faces.

"Yes," said Edward, his head cocked to look at Claudia. "We forget you've had little interaction with people your own age and I must say, despite your advanced education and obvious intelligence, you're still child-like in your outlook." Edward looked to Grace and they shared a brief smile. "That will all be rectified when we return to London. If you're a good girl, you'll find that many opportunities await you," Edward said, wiping breadcrumbs from his chin.

Claudia remembered Dane's delight in her child-like enthusiasm. *Edward wants to smother it. If I'm a good girl? What does that even mean? I don't want their stupid help. Just say it to them, just say it.* The sharp twinge of resentment felt good, she began to feel alive, as though she could fight off everything they wanted to throw at her.

Grace and Edward still smiled, as if they offered her the world's greatest gift and she should drop to the floor and kiss their feet in thanks.

She almost laughed again at the dramatic scenes playing out in her head. King Edward and Queen Grace, offering their leftover crumbs to the peasant Claudia. But, instead, she lowered her eyes to the table. "I would love to go to London, but this is my home and I would prefer to stay with Margaret."

Grace laughed, a dry, cackling sound that echoed through the room. "That is out of the question, Claudia. I know that woman must seem like a mother figure to you, but surely you'd prefer to be with your own parents? She is only an employee, after all."

Claudia pushed down on her knees. Her legs twitched with a need to escape Grace's mocking smile. *Or wipe it off her face.* "There was a time, yes, when I would have given anything to see you, even for a day, but that was before."

"Before what?" Edward's eyes narrowed and Claudia felt her cheeks burn.

Must be more careful. Neither adult seemed to suspect that Dane had been among the fleeing gypsies, nor had they ever broached the subject with her. *But…could they know?* She thought carefully before she spoke again, cursing her habitual honesty.

"Before," Claudia paused, staring at Grace and fidgeting with the edge of the tablecloth, "before I grew up and realised I didn't need parents as much as I thought I did."

Grace raised her eyebrows and pouted. "We expected you would feel"—she glanced at Edward—"dissatisfied with our decision. But, as we've explained, it's normal for children of wealth and high standing in society to be in your position and I do believe it's been of benefit to you. You may not realise it, but your education is quite superior to many other young women your age who attend school with all its distractions."

"And what will I do with it?" Claudia gripped the chair with her hands and fought the urge to throw her mother's red wine in her face.

"Make an advantageous match for your family, of course, or gain excellent employment," Edward said, his eyes staring unblinkingly into hers.

A coldness settled about the room and Claudia imagined icy tentacles clawing her neck and holding her, trapped forever under the gaze of a constant stream of jailers.

"Snap out of it, girl," barked Edward. "I see how you keep drifting off like that in company. Well, people will think you're mad if you keep doing it. Now, you must listen, carefully, there is something of great importance that you must comply with."

Claudia nodded at Edward, itching to peel the tentacles from her throat. Snow-White and Rose-Red had settled on the seat with her and she soaked in the rays of comfort radiating from their smiles.

Edward looked towards Grace and she returned his glance, batting her eyelashes. In that moment, her mother's behaviour reminded her of a butterfly's wing; thin and papery and flitting about in the breeze; completely without substance.

"Your mother and I were unwed when you were conceived. Therefore, as far as society is aware, we are childless."

Ahh. More confusion. More secrets. More lies. *Why are they admitting it now?* Neither of them met her eye.

"To avoid any public scandals, which would be detrimental to my political career, we'll return to London with you in our care, but as a distant cousin of Grace's family. You'll need to pretend your own family has died, Claudia. That we are your guardians until such time as you marry or — when you turn eighteen — find employment." The clipped, significant words rolled from his tongue without emotion.

What a blessing, really, that she could continue to ignore her parentage, and that she was even being asked to ignore it. But still, her stomach clenched, thinking about the lengths Edward had gone to, to keep the beautiful, but reckless wife that was her mother.

The butterfly queen who'd given birth to her now tore at her napkin, a delicate sigh escaping her lips. "In private though, Claudia, we still want you to view us as your parents, as it should be," Grace said, smiling and nodding as if the act of doing this would justify all the pretence.

"You understand what this means, don't you? It shouldn't be too hard, you barely know us, after all, and despite our efforts to offer you…affection, you don't seem to want to return it. A good thing, really." Edward mumbled his last words, nodding to himself.

Claudia could barely bother to feel anger about the revelations pouring down on her. The desire to laugh again was stronger than anything and Snow-White and Rose-Red were already giggling in anticipation of it. Especially when she looked at her mother's made-up face: a picture of sympathetic motherliness with Edward's thunderous frown serving as a backdrop.

"I understand and you're right, it won't be hard. I've never felt like I had parents anyway." *Until Dane and Oriana.* She paused, thinking of Oriana and the trouble she might be in. Her hands trembled and she caught them together in her lap. "And it won't really matter if I'm here and you're in London, in any case." She stared at them both.

Grace turned to Edward and put a finger to her lips.

"We'll talk about that another time, Claudia. For now you may take time to adjust to what we've told you. We only want to pave the way for a successful life for you. Our intentions are for the best."

"You're excused to do your afternoon study," Edward said, attempting a smile as he helped Grace up from her chair. "I look forward to seeing the results of that history project I helped you with. I'm sure you'll receive top marks. Could be a lawyer in the family, what do you think, Grace? Useful to have around." Edward chuckled and clenched the back of the butterfly queen's neck with one, square hand, steering her towards the stairs.

In the following two days, a team of cleaners swept in from neighbouring towns to put the chateau in order: dusting the candelabras and polishing the fine silver in preparation for Preston Myers' arrival.

Poor Margaret moaned rather than talked, running around breathless and sweaty trying to supervise the chaos. Lenny barely left the gardens, telling Claudia he was scared to run into the housekeeper's sharp tongue. The cleaners were like a cast of colourful characters to Claudia. Whenever she could, she stopped to talk to one or other of them; it helped her forget, helped her sidestep the problems filling her mind. Grace and Edward would look on with horror.

For days, Claudia had called these pretend parents Aunty Gracey and Uncle Eddie. She enjoyed watching the horrified expressions on their faces, knowing that Grace and Edward would put up with much to maintain the image they cultivated – and it served only to teach her lessons of deceit and mistrust, so different from those the gypsies had given with love, and Mr Campbell had driven into her with dreariness.

"Claudia, come and get dressed please, Preston's plane arrives any minute now and a driver has been sent to collect him from the airport," Grace called out to her from the top of the grand staircase.

Claudia, already clothed in a simple, brown shift dress, held her fingers mid-air above the piano keys and cocked her head to the side as Grace's voice echoed around the parlour. She scanned the brown the dress and shrugged. *No reason to look pretty when I'm surrounded by ugliness.*

"I'm dressed, thank you, Grace." She threw her head back and yelled towards the stairs.

Quick footsteps announced the arrival of her mother in the parlour, hair still in curlers and cheeks flushed red. Claudia scanned the butterfly queen from head to foot. She *was* lovely to look at, with her wide blue eyes and the skin of her long neck glowing flawlessly.

It would be so soft to touch. Someone so pretty can't be all bad.

But then, Grace looked at her with the signature expression Claudia now knew was filled with disdain and disappointment.

"What about the dress I left on your bed?" Grace asked, eyes flicking away from Claudia's.

"Oh," said Claudia. "Did you? I haven't been in my room since breakfast."

Grace sighed. "Well run along and put it on, Margaret is waiting to help you."

Claudia smiled, stood and dipped into a mock curtsy, before running towards the stairs.

"I didn't mean, literally, run," Grace said, her tone razor sharp.

Claudia smiled again and slowed down to a deliberate walk, enjoying her mother's frustration.

Margaret frowned as Claudia entered the bedroom. A blue dress hung over one of the housekeeper's shoulders, jostling up and down as her foot tapped on the wooden floorboards.

"Where did you learn to act like such a spoilt brat, Miss? I saw what you just did. Out and out misbehaving that is."

Claudia laughed. "I don't know where it came from. I just

know I can't help it."

Margaret seemed to struggle to stop the smile stretching her cheeks. "Those gypsies have a lot to answer for, giving you all this confidence, young lady."

"It was there, woman, the little lass just didn't know how to use it." Lenny stuck his head around the corner of the door, winking as he spoke.

"Get away from here, man, before you're caught." Margaret shooed Lenny out into the corridor.

Lenny raised his greying eyebrows. "Just supervising the rubbish collection from all the rooms, as instructed by Mr Spencer."

"You're the rubbish that needs collecting! Off with you now," Margaret said, a twinkle in her eyes as they crinkled at the corners.

The royal blue dress had a tight bodice, spaghetti straps and a slim-line skirt that skimmed her calves. A wide, brown belt with a gold buckle completed the outfit. Grace had installed a brand new, full-length mirror on the wall opposite her bed and Claudia looked at her own reflection. She neither smiled nor frowned.

Her breasts had continued to grow and now swelled over the top of the v-neck dress, making her waist look tiny. Her black hair sat in shiny waves behind her shoulders and her naturally red lips looked as full and pouting as her mother's. Soon, a small crease appeared between her dark, straight eyebrows.

""How could you possibly frown at that reflection, Claudia? You may be a brat, but you're certainly a decent looking one. That gypsy of yours must be suffering from an awful broken heart," Margaret said, almost panting in her hurry to arrange the errant wisps of hair around her face.

Claudia hugged Margaret who blushed bright red and fussed with even more enthusiasm over the erratic stray curls.

"Ah, that's much better. Surely you enjoy dressing up,

Claudia?" Grace glided into the room, her blonde beauty highlighted by a red, ankle length dress. An elaborate gold necklace with a diamond studded, lopsided heart, adorned her neck.

"Sometimes," Claudia said, throwing Margaret a sly smile.

Grace caught the exchange and stepped in between them. "Thank you, Margaret, I can take over from here."

"Of course." Margaret lowered her eyes to the floor and tugged at one of Claudia's curls in a secret, cheeky goodbye gesture. She made a great show of tidying up after Claudia, testing Grace's patience as far as she could. The housekeeper left only after Grace sighed loudly, tapping her red nails, at great speed, over the dressing table.

"This necklace is from Tiffany's, Claudia. Have you heard of them? They're just about the most famous jewellery designers in the world. Would you like one? I can take you there, when we go back to London." The butterfly queen waited until the door closed, then turned to Claudia with a sparkling smile.

"I don't really like jewellery, but thank you anyway."

Grace's eyes narrowed and her thinly plucked eyebrows drew together.

Claudia, I know how well read you are, but how much do you know of…male and female interactions?" The red nails began to shape one of Claudia's curls.

Claudia gazed in the mirror, taking in the unfamiliar sight of her own mother touching her, doing her hair, standing next to her. Like a dream, a dream she'd had thousands of times before. *With none of the happiness.*

Claudia steadied herself. "If you're asking if I know about procreating and the workings of the male and female anatomy, of course, I'm informed."

Grace's eyes grew wide. "You're so blunt, Claudia; you must learn some guile and tact." Her lips curved in a smile that didn't show her teeth. "I simply meant there are acceptable ways in which to act around men, now that you're nearly of a marriageable age. Surely you've observed me with your father?

Claudia ignored the question. "How would you like me to behave then?" Small talk held no appeal for her and the butterfly queen's liking of polite, superficial discussions made her want to stuff a sock into the delicate mouth.

"Well, be yourself, of course. You have delightful manners, when you choose, and your speech is articulate. But, perhaps you could smile more, ensure you listen intently to everything Preston says. Compliment him. These things, you have no experience with. You'd do well to watch and learn from me." Grace looked at herself in the mirror, fluffing her hair with her perfectly white hand, running her tongue over perfectly white teeth.

Claudia stopped herself from smirking. Her mother also taught her how to disregard loyalty and love and family while facing the world and pretending to be an upstanding, morally fit citizen.

"Of course," Claudia replied.

Grace smiled.

"Excellent. You look lovely, by the way, Preston will be very pleased." Grace looked her up and down, tapping a finger on her cheek. "You know, Claudia, I've imagined doing this with you. You know, the mother and daughter thing." She lowered her eyes and giggled, almost like a child.

Heat rolled over Claudia's face. "Well you could have, and you didn't." She knew her eyes flashed with quick anger, but she couldn't stand the sudden kindness, couldn't deal with the nauseating doubt over her mother's sincerity.

Grace tried to smile, but covered her mouth with her hand instead. She nodded, once, and turned to leave the room. At the door, she scanned Claudia's face, hair and body, one more time, and her eyes glistened with unshed tears. She turned and clicked clacked away up the hall on her six-inch heels.

Claudia let go of the breath she'd been holding.

Chapter Nine

The Gatekeeper in the Guise of a God

Preston Myers sauntered into the hallway, blond hair styled back from his face in thick, straight strands to his collar, dimples appearing when he smiled and a chin pointed high in the air above an impossibly smooth, blemish free neck. Edward walked beside him. Together they looked like a well-dressed giraffe and a fat wart hog, straight from one of the cartoons she'd so recently discovered on Edward's plasma TV. Claudia clenched her stomach to stop the gurgling laughter.

The giraffe's lean limbs were draped in an elegant black suit and a black and gold watch peeped out from under the sleeve of his jacket. The scent of oranges and cinnamon followed him as he strode towards Grace.

"Darling Preston, how lovely to see you. Did you have a good journey?" Grace hugged him and kissed both of his cheeks as he bent down to her.

"Yes, thank you, Grace. You look absolutely stunning, as always. Quite a property you have here." Preston clasped his hands together behind his back and turned in a circle, admiring the grand staircase. "Been in the family for three generations, you say?"

"Yes, a family heirloom, so to speak."

"Lovely, I am most impressed." The giraffe's eyes came to rest on Claudia. "And this, I take it, is the lovely Claudia, your second cousin."

"It is. Claudia, this is Preston, our much adored family friend." Grace presented Preston to Claudia with an elegant sweep of her arm.

"It's nice to meet you," Claudia said, stepping forward with her hand outstretched.

He took her hand and stared into her eyes, lowering his chin to do so. His eyes were the colour of frost on the lake, the lightest of blues, startling in their iridescence, especially when they settled on her lips for a few uncomfortable seconds. He lowered his eyes only to kiss the back of her hand, grazing his lips over her middle knuckle.

"Enchanted, Claudia. Please accept my apologies for your misfortune. One as young as you should not be left alone in the world. You're very lucky to have such generous, caring relatives as the Spencers."

"Yes. Thank you for your kind words." Involuntarily, she stepped back. There was something familiar, predatory even, in his intense stare. But, strangely, as soon as he looked away, she wanted him to look back at her.

"You must be tired, Preston, I'll show you to your room so you can freshen up. Tea will be served in two hours." Grace put her hand on Preston's elbow and steered him towards the guest wing.

As Grace led him to the second floor, he turned back, his body following his head at a slow, languid pace. He stared into Claudia's eyes once again. "I look forward to seeing you at tea, Claudia." His chiselled cheekbones and elegant, aquiline nose looked too pretty under the impact of his full, beaming grin, and the white teeth beneath the full lips almost blinded her with their brightness.

Ridiculous. He looks exactly like Prince Charming.

Claudia smiled and turned away, but not before she recognised the light that glimmered in the icy blue depths. Despite the handsome face, impeccable manners and smooth words, Preston stared at her as if he'd like to devour her.

Like the gatekeeper in the guise of a god.

"Claudia, that will never do. Your position's all wrong. Archery is an age-old tradition in our family you know, you must try harder," Grace yelled, shading her eyes with her hand as she looked up from her book.

Claudia put the bow down, planted her hands on her hips and turned to frown at her mother...second cousin...*whatever.*

"I think she looks fantastic with the bow, just like a little Celtic warrior," Preston called back to Grace, nudging Claudia with his elbow.

Claudia stifled a smile and tried to stop staring at the blue eyes focused on her.

Grace pulled herself up from the day bed and walked down the valley towards them. "She is *not* a Celt and that's not the correct posture. She's not training to be a fighter, Preston."

"Ah, but she could."

This time, Claudia couldn't help but return his gaze, her cheeks growing warm as she replayed his compliment in her mind.

Preston cocked a brow as his eyes travelled over her face. He bent to pick up the bow and pulled an arrow from the quiver on his hip. His fingers twirled the arrow back and forth as he pulled the string taut. Claudia's eyes flicked to his biceps, outlined beneath his white shirt as his arm stretched straight, ready to aim at the target.

The arrow whooshed through the air. Bullseye.

"That's amazing," Claudia said, clamping her hand over her mouth as soon as she spoke.

"Why, thank you, m'lady. Next I'll don my armour and take you for a ride on my black stallion." Preston laughed, pulling his stomach in and pushing his chest out.

"Oh, stop it, silly boy," Grace said, putting a hand on Preston's arm and smiling up at him.

In just one week, Preston had breathed life into the chateau; arranging horse rides in the valley, visits to museums and wineries, picnics by the lake...archery lessons.

No...won't fall for it. Stupid parents trying to make stupid fake marriages.

"Come, Claudia, that's enough for today. You're so much improved, I'm almost feeling a tad jealous." Preston caught her elbow, steering her around Grace, up the hill and over the gravel towards the kitchen.

"Don't worry about Grace," he whispered in her ear, "she just wants the best for you. The Spencers have…very high standards. Do you like archery, Claudia?"

"Well, yes, I guess so. If I was a bit better at it."

"Oh, but you're getting better every day, before you know it, that bullseye will be your best friend." He squeezed her arm, leading her over to the fridge. "Now, what can I get for you? How about Caprese? Have you heard of it? Delicious Italian dish with buffalo mozzarella and tomatoes and basil…let's see if Margaret's got what we need in here."

"You cook?" *Surely not. Prince Charming? In the kitchen?*

"A bit, I know how to rustle up enough to feed myself…and a hungry archer in the making."

Preston gathered supplies from the fridge, every movement slow and casual, occasionally stopping to brush a blond wave from his eyes. He chopped the tomatoes with easy skill, layering them with cheese and swirling balsamic vinegar over the top like the chefs Claudia had seen on television.

"*Voila!*" He put the plate in the middle of the table, handing her a fork and watching her closely.

Claudia stabbed her fork into a single tomato, bringing it to her mouth carefully, suddenly conscious of what she looked like when she ate. She nibbled a corner of cheese, holding the fork away from her mouth so the vinegar dripped on the plate, rather than down her chin.

"And?" His own fork paused mid-air.

"Delicious." She giggled. It was — sweet and salty and squishy.

"Good. Don't be shy, tuck in." Preston smiled, shovelling

three pieces into his mouth at once.

And she did, returning his smiles between every mouthful.

That night, Claudia huddled under the covers in bed. How changed life was. No fear of the gatekeeper, no breathless anticipation of a visit to the gypsy camp. Still, her stomach churned and her eyes stayed resolutely open.

Someone rapped on the door. Preston's smiling face poked through the opening.

"Want to come and watch a movie?" He pushed the door open further, standing very still in black, silk pyjamas.

"Um, I guess, Edward doesn't like me to watch anything without his approval though." Claudia sat up, holding the sheet under her chin.

"Oh, don't worry about Edward, he'll never know. You can trust me, Claudia, really." Preston walked over to the bed, holding his hand out to help her up.

Claudia reached for the hand, feeling the warmth as his fingers closed over hers.

In the guest wing, Preston patted the bed, lifting the covers so she could slide in. He sat on the other side, resting his head against the wall, tucking the covers around them both.

"Now, crime, romance or adventure? No, don't answer, I know already. Romance. Yes?"

Claudia nodded, her spine tingling in the dark room, lit only by the blue glow on the television screen.

"Right, Miss Claudia, say hello to Julia Roberts and Richard Gere. I think you're going to like them."

Pretty Woman started, and Claudia forgot who she was, and where she was, right up until the credits rolled. Her eyes drooped and her limbs felt heavy against the mattress. Oh, but what a story, and how many stories were there, that she'd never seen, never been allowed to see?

"Thank you," she whispered.

"You're most welcome. Any time. Now, shall I give you a lift home?" Preston laughed and scooped her up, to carry her down the empty hallways, to place her on her own bed as if she was made of precious porcelain.

And his smile was the last thing she remembered, before sleep took it away.

"Good Lord, girl, to look at you now, no one would ever guess the trouble I used to have trying to get you out of those night-gowns every day." Margaret turned the tap off and put one hand on the edge of the bathtub to help herself stand. An emerald green dress, knee length with embroidered white daisies, rested on the housekeeper's shoulder, ready for Claudia to slip into.

Claudia giggled. "I know. How quickly things change." She hesitated for a moment, gazing at Margaret.

"Margaret, please don't feel like you have to keep looking after me this way, I can run the bath and dress myself and I know you could do with the time to go and see Lenny." *And you shouldn't have to be in pain anymore from stupid chores and stupid rules.*

"Don't be silly, I'm still your housekeeper and I'll keep doing my job, thank you very much." Margaret put her hands on her hips and stopped to glare at Claudia, before taking a few deep breaths and straightening the bed sheets, but Claudia caught the smile tugging at the housekeeper's lips.

Claudia bent to help her, lifting the mattress so Margaret could tuck the corners under. "I don't understand the concept of servants. I mean…not that…I don't think you're my servant, Margaret, you know that, but I think it's selfish and ridiculous to have others do all your chores for you."

Margaret blushed red and her bottom lip twitched. "Well, happy I am to hear you say that, in any case, Miss. Dane would be right proud of you. But it doesn't mean we can ignore convention, you understand? There're certain obligations for a young woman like you."

"Living here, yes. But not for long." Claudia glanced at Margaret, stifling her nerves. *It's now or never.*

"Have you been having those dreams again?" asked Margaret. "Are the gypsies coming back?"

Claudia's throat tightened at the thought. "No. Truly Margaret...I've been desperate to dream of them, but, well, it's only a blank space when I search." Claudia lowered her voice and leaned in towards the older woman. "I want to leave here, and search for them myself."

Margaret clasped her hands, bringing them in close to her chest. "You're a brave little thing, I'll give you that. Who would have thought it, after we kept you so contained all these years!" She paused and looked towards the window, obviously lost in the regret Claudia often saw flitting over her face, adding to the patchwork of wrinkles. "But you absolutely can't, I won't allow it."

"Margaret..."

"I won't allow it," Margaret said, now grinning, "unless, young lady, you take me and Lenny with you! Goodness knows I owe you that much."

"Of course." Claudia reached for Margaret, pulling her into a tight hug. "I couldn't ask for anything more."

Margaret broke away, holding her at arm's length. "I must confess, Miss, it's been awfully boring here with your mother and Edward, I miss those mischievous gypsies more than I could have imagined and...well...I've been a bit worried about the influence that handsome Preston is having on you."

"Oh, him. Well...I admit he's made an impression on me." Claudia tipped her head to the side and stroked her cheek with her hand.

Like yesterday, when he'd helped her with a maths exam. He didn't give her the answers, he'd never do that, Claudia was sure, but he'd explained everything, just right, so that she somehow understood what had seemed like a foreign language. And he always smelled so good... *Oh stop it...*Claudia cleared her throat.

"Well...anyway...it's been fascinating to make a new friend and pretend that I belong in that life. But, Margaret, I don't! I ache every day for Brishan and Dane and Oriana." She paused for a moment, as she did every hour of every day. *Please be safe, Oriana.* "I don't want to wait any more. I'm tired of pretending my life, I want to start living it. Now. I can't wait any longer for them to return for me, they need to know I have the strength to look after myself. And I need...I need to see Brishan."

Margaret's eyes searched her own. "All right, we must be smart about it though." Margaret rubbed her chin. "I'll talk to Lenny and see what he thinks. We'll need enough money...it's not going to be a short journey, you know. They could be in another country by now, you do realise that?"

"Yes, of course, but they wouldn't have had the money to take trains, or anything. We...well, we can do that. We have a head start. Margaret, we can even get on a plane, can't we?" Claudia clapped her hands together. *This is what all that money can buy. This is what it's for.*

"Oh, Margaret, I understand so much more, now, than when my...when the gypsies were here. I can help them, I know it." Claudia moved closer to the window and looked out. "Dane could be anywhere, he'll be searching for Oriana, I know. But the others...they'll surely have settled somewhere we can find them. Brishan said they would follow the festival route in England. We'll do that! We'll go on the same gypsy trail."

"Hold your horses, Miss, it won't be that easy. You can't think you can just...well, your mother and Edward will look for you if you go away. With all their connections. I'm sorry to say it, as it's my own fault as much as anyone's, but you're still very new to the ways of the world."

Who cares what Grace and Edward do? But she'd have to care; it wasn't going to be easy to escape them, they would cling to the façade they were creating of her life. The one they'd always created.

"I know, Margaret. People do it though. Girls are out there travelling the world on their own!" *Bless the television, and Preston for introducing it to me like I'm an adult.* "I have to do this. I'm desperate to do it. I'm supposed to do it. I just know it's right."

But even as she spoke, Claudia's words didn't quite feel right. *Is it just fear? Just fear. Nothing unusual.*

Margaret's eyes crinkled as she smiled. "Well, I wasn't expecting adventure at my ripe old age, but adventure is what we're going to get."

And that was enough to get Claudia through. *Wasn't it?*

"You're obviously looking forward to today's picnic, Claudia?" Edward asked, mouth dripping with the runny yoke of his egg. Claudia felt exhilarated by her decision and Margaret's quick approval of it. Grace and Edward seemed delighted by her mood and Preston kept glancing at her from underneath his long, black eyelashes.

"Yes, of course, anything to get me out of this house, as you know." Claudia couldn't help the retort, though she smiled as she spoke.

"You don't like the chateau, Claudia? With due respect to your dear, departed parents, how long have you been here? Please don't think me rude, but when was their passing, exactly?" Preston raised an exquisite, ash-blond eyebrow.

"Claudia's parents died quite a few years ago now, Preston, but as they lived in the area, we felt it best she remain here, at least until we could offer her sufficient guidance," Edward rushed in, his words quick and purposeful. "Plus, we had the benefit of this property. You know the world of politics, no time to sleep, let alone organise your own affairs." He went on. "She's been fully schooled and governed on the property, away from the considerable temptations of the city."

"Ah, I understand." Preston faced Edward, then turned to Claudia. "But away from the fun also. Besides, she's a mature young lady now, I'm sure she'll do you proud when you return to the city." His eyes remained on Claudia, though he spoke to Edward.

Claudia wanted to poke her tongue out at Edward, to act like the child his words made her out to be. But, at the same time, Preston's quick defence of her stifled the urge, replacing it with an odd fluttering in her stomach. She crossed her arms, pressing them into her abdomen and leaning back in her chair.

She felt like a cheeky elf, dangerously careless, now she knew she'd soon be gone. And nothing was going to change that. "Perhaps I would make you proud. But perhaps we will never know."

"Oh?" Preston's fork paused mid-air and she watched as a thick wave of blond hair fell over his chiselled cheekbone and into the sauce-covered sausage he ate. He raised an elegant finger and pushed it neatly back behind his ear.

"I want to stay here. I like it and I feel at home. Especially now that I've met some of the local people, thanks to you." She nodded at Preston and he smiled, his dimples deep and enchanting. A piece of bread was stuck between his startling white teeth and she giggled.

"What?" he asked, turning to Grace and Edward. Grace raised a subtle hand towards her own teeth and made a rubbing motion.

"Food in my teeth? Oh, the shame!" He winked at Claudia, dropping his fork on the plate and placing one arm dramatically across his forehead as the other covered his mouth. Claudia laughed, feeling Snow-White and Rose-Red flitting about her head, their chime-like giggles adding to her own. Preston's ice blue eyes twinkled as he stared at her across the table. Another large smile as he deliberately ignored the food.

This is fun, Preston is fun. Nothing like Grace or Edward. Claudia was truly enjoying herself, now that it didn't matter. Nothing mattered except the journey she was about to make. In that second, she made a firm decision to enjoy the life her mother, Edward and Preston had to offer — before she left them. For good.

The lake glistened in the late morning sun, its frost covered surface reflecting the spindly branches of the winter trees. Voices carried on the cool air and Claudia buzzed with nerves. *Everyone will stare, they always do.* Perched on the dewy grass, the white marquee looked ostentatious and overly large for forty or so people. At least it hadn't snowed for a few days, she'd be able to take her shoes off later, feel the earth pulse beneath her feet. A familiar hollow ache joined her nerves. How differently she'd feel if she were walking down the valley to join the gypsies.

Badminton nets swung between the trees and fires warmed the guests inside the marquee: lounging on fur rugs and snacking on delicacies offered by waiters in black suits. Czech accents mixed with English, mixed with French. Anyone with any money in the nearby region — expats, holidaymakers, local businessmen — were invited to the Spencers' regular soirées.

Well, more like Grace's thinly veiled attempts at introducing Claudia to society. A society, thought Claudia, that was solely focused on money and power. One that she swore she would never join.

As she entered the marquee, Pavle, the horse trainer, and his family smiled up at her from their prime space near the fire. Thank goodness for the neighbours. Although, Pavle *did* look at her rather guiltily, no doubt still befuddled by the odd disappearance of the great Kladruber. Mr and Mrs Kadlec from the nearby winery and the Maseks, who owned the bakery in Lednice, all waved, their faces warm and welcoming. Many of the locals had spent years idly curious about the folk of the chateau. Now, thanks to Preston's social nature, Claudia finally basked on the fringes of their lives, like a normal person in a normal community, as they welcomed her as one of them. One of them — a local. Well, a local, but temporarily orphaned gypsy.

She couldn't catch the sigh before it escaped her lips.

"What are you thinking about, if I may?" Preston's breath warmed the back of her neck and goose bumps trickled down her arms.

Claudia turned to face him. "To be honest, I was just thinking how nice it would've been growing up with these people, having a more normal life."

"This is anything but normal, Claudia. I'm afraid you've been far too sheltered till now. Not everyone lives in such wealth, with a chateau all to themselves and servants do their every bidding."

Claudia's face flushed red. "I'm not so naïve as to think so, I just meant the social aspect would have been nice."

He rubbed his chin with a long, elegant finger. "Yes, odd that Grace and Edward wanted you housebound. Still, saves problems for them I imagine, nothing worse than unruly teenagers." Preston chuckled. "But, if I have anything to do with it, you'll be allowed your fun. Well, as long as I get to watch." He smiled.

What do you mean, watch?" Claudia frowned up him, her neck bending back as far as it would go.

"Watch, as you're unleashed into the world, of course. Someone like you will make quite a splash, no matter if you stay here or go to London."

Claudia shook her head and stared down at his long feet encased in black leather shoes. "I don't even know what I want to do, or what kind of a job I could get. I can't see how I'd make a 'splash' as you say." *And all that matters is finding the gypsies, anyway.* She shrugged.

"You're so unaware of yourself, Claudia." He gazed down at her. "It's endearing, in a quaint way, but frustrating. Look around! Do you see how people admire you?" Preston swept an arm out towards the picnickers.

Yes, she knew they looked, of course. She felt them at every party, every dinner, every picnic. They did look at her, and they spoke in soft tones and seemed to want to be introduced to her. *But admire? Not likely.* At first, she hadn't realised people didn't always get treated this way. And now she thought it might be because she had dollar signs floating over her head — and that it made people blind with greed.

"It's because you're beautiful, astoundingly beautiful, Claudia. You're almost ethereal," Preston said and caught both her hands in his own. "You have such strange, intense expressions and well, you use such old-fashioned words."

Claudia looked away.

"The men want you and the women want to look like you. And the money...well, that makes people want to be around you. You know that, don't you?"

Heat crawled over Claudia's body, starting at her neck and covering every inch of her. She stared down at the manicured hands entwined with her own. Preston's compliments didn't ring true. *Couldn't be true.* Except the part about the money.

"I was intrigued just hearing of you, alone in the world out here in a foreign country and Grace said you were beautiful, but I had no idea how beautiful and innocent and sweet." His hands moved so his thumbs could rub the insides of her palms.

A compliment? From the perfect butterfly queen? Unbelievable.

"Hello? Claudia, are you listening? Where do you go? It's like you disappear into a world of your own." He laughed again, releasing her hands.

If only you knew. Claudia realised her palms were sweating.

"Sorry, Preston, I'm just embarrassed, actually." She needed to reply before he thought she was rude, or even insane. She tucked her chin in towards her neck.

"Why, that's part of the appeal of you, your honesty, the way you don't seem to know how to use people. No doubt you'll learn to hide those good qualities quick enough." He smirked and held out his elbow for her to take.

Claudia smiled and let him lead. He moved towards the largest group lounging on the plush rugs. The women glanced at her from under their eyelashes, quickly turning away and whispering to their friends as Claudia approached. She clenched Preston's arm, digging her nails into his jacket. His eyes settled on her for a moment, then he moved to circle her waist, his hand resting firmly on her lower back.

It felt comforting to have him here. Especially now that she could see the picnickers were not as charming as she'd once thought; more like groups of circling sharks, each waiting to take a bite. *Of what though?* What on earth did she have to offer such well-established, intelligent, socially brilliant people?

Claudia sank into the soft depths of a rug, eager to hide from the attention as Preston mingled. He was so confident, like he belonged no matter where he was, like he already knew everyone would like him. She felt like he'd always lived at the chateau, the way he'd blended so effortlessly into her life.

But she missed rolling in the leaves and running without a care and laughing with the gypsies as they romped around the vans. She missed Brishan chasing her through the valley, and the children with dirt on their cheeks and bruises on their naked legs climbing the trees to watch the fun.

"Claudia, snap out of it please, dear." Grace loomed above. "I want you to meet the Seymours." She gestured towards a couple, two teenage girls and a boy of around eight.

Claudia stood up too quickly and her head spun in dizzying circles — but Preston's hands were there, gripping her shoulders, steadying her from behind, catching her before she had a chance to give in to her wobbling legs. She leaned back into him, breathing deeply and turning to smile her thanks. One dimple appeared as he smiled back and, for a moment, his smile made her feel like they were the only two people in the marquee.

"Mr and Mrs Seymour, Courtney, Tara and Jack, this is my cousin, Claudia." Grace directed an elegant hand as she introduced each one. "The Seymour family are old friends from America, dear." With that she departed the group with nothing more than an airy wave.

Thank God Preston is here. Grace had, as usual, thrown her to the sharks without a raft.

"Nice to meet you," Claudia said, shaking each outstretched hand, making sure she made eye contact with each person.

"And you," Mrs Seymour said, eyeing Claudia up and down, once, before turning towards Preston, her eyes wide and her cheeks flushed. "Preston, lovely to see you again, what brings you here for such an extended visit?"

Preston bent to kiss the heavily rouged cheek Mrs Seymour offered. "The Spencers are old friends of the family and I'm on a break from College, so thought I'd make the most of their generous offer to spend time here." Preston's voice sounded clipped, matching Mrs Seymour's pompous tone. It jarred Claudia's ears.

"So, what music do you like? Do you even get any new music out here in the middle of nowhere?" Tara, the taller of the two blonde girls, spoke to Claudia in a high-pitched voice, giggling and leaning on her sister as if she was a lamppost.

"I'm not familiar yet with all the American artists, if that's what you mean by new music, but I'm sure I'd like all of it." Claudia smiled, wishing she didn't feel like she needed these girls to like her.

The sisters looked at each other and laughed.

"Oh, that's cute, but no one likes all of it. You couldn't possibly like country music and heavy metal and still be into classical and hip hop. That'd be stupid." Courtney tossed her white-blonde hair over her shoulder and folded her arms under large breasts, pushing them up until the zip on her jacket strained to contain them.

Claudia's lips trembled as she tried to smile. She looked at the girl's parents instead, hoping to escape the conversation. The couple stood still, backs straight and hands clasped before them, silently observing the uncomfortable conversation. They looked like replica parent dolls in a doll's house, ready at the door to greet their guests. A giggle bubbled in her throat and Claudia almost choked trying to suppress it.

"Claudia has been classically trained on the piano and knows all about the local folk music. Television and pop culture isn't as popular here, although the country is quickly catching up. A pity really," Preston jumped in, words perfectly pronounced with a touch of sarcasm — an emotion Claudia had only recently learnt to recognise.

"Oh come on, Preston, you don't believe that!" Tara touched Preston on the arm, just above his elbow. "If there was no pop culture, as you put it, you wouldn't have had so much fun out clubbing with us."

Preston grinned, both dimples now in full view. "Right you are, but it's not the be all and end all of entertainment."

"How do you all know each other?" Claudia asked, wondering if her lips were ever going to stop twitching.

"We travel in the same circles, dear, spent quite a few lovely summer holidays in the Mediterranean with the Myers." Mrs Seymour turned towards her husband and nodded as she spoke. He mirrored her actions.

"Plus, Pres and I had a little fling last year, didn't we hon?" Tara leant into Preston, grabbing his hand and putting it very deliberately on her waist.

Preston cleared his throat and discreetly moved his hand back to his own hip. "If you call hanging out in nightclubs, getting drunk and occasionally kissing, a *fling*, I guess so." There was a dangerous undertone to his voice now; yet another voice she'd never heard.

Come now, you two, it's...well...we don't speak of such things in company," Mrs Seymour said, her voice cool and crisp. "Lovely to meet you, Claudia. Preston, we'll be seeing you in Prague, I take it? We're in the villa at Mala Strana for two months."

"Of course." Preston bowed his head and Claudia watched with relief as the group walked away. Mr Seymour and the young boy, Jack, followed the chatting women in silence. *Do the males in the family ever get a word in?*

Claudia slumped back on the rug. "Is that how all girls my age talk?"

Preston laughed and eased his long legs down beside her. "Many, yes, you'll find yourself an oddity among teenage girls, if only for their complete lack of interest in anything other than boys, clothes and what the celebrities are doing."

"I'm sure I would like to find out about those things. Not that I want to be anything like those two." *Listening to Snow-White and Rose-Red's gibberish is better than talking with girls like Tara and Courtney.*

"You never could be, Claudia. It's like you're from another time. I almost want to hide you from it all...you know, to preserve what you are."

"And what is that?" Claudia's coy and flirtatious tone was something new to her; it was just like the butterfly queen, she thought. She blushed.

Preston leaned in close towards her face. "A charming, beautiful young lady, unspoilt by the stupidity of the world."

"You don't know everything about me," she snapped. She was starting to resent his constant references to her quaint charms, but she knew it worked in her favour to pander to it. She wanted him, wanted everyone, to see her as an equal, an adult.

As Brishan and Dane had.

"Oh? So you have secrets? All women must have an ounce of mystery, after all." He tweaked her nose and jumped up to get them some food.

Preston was confusing her. He treated her like a child and then admired her as a woman — often during the very same conversation. He was so different to Brishan, who'd always been straightforward. She'd intuitively trusted everything Brishan had said and he had treated her just as herself. Being with Preston felt like being in the middle of a guessing game, never quite knowing how he'd make her feel next. It was frustrating. *But exciting.*

Preston came back with a plate full of ham off the bone, sauerkraut and fresh bread, soft on the inside, crunchy on the outside and layered with a creamy egg mixture. Putting it down in front of her, he turned to another table and poured two glasses of red wine.

"I thought we might start the fun now." He winked as he handed her a glass.

"I have tasted wine before, you know." Claudia twirled the wine around the glass as she'd seen Grace do

"I know, but a taste is different to a drink. You'll see."

Claudia gulped the deep, red liquid, something she'd been introduced to, admittedly with only small mouthfuls at a time, during meals with Grace and Edward. She wanted to show Preston she wasn't such an innocent after all. In three more gulps, she finished off the glass and pushed it in front of his nose, her eyebrows raised and her head tilted slightly to one side.

"Well done," he whispered, as if she'd completed some great conquest. "Let's see how you go with two glasses. But, eat first."

She was up for the challenge. Occasionally, in the gypsy camp, she'd seen the dancers and musicians come home from a night of shows, bottles swaying dangerously in their hands as they stumbled through the trees, laughing, crying and yelling into the early hours of the morning. If anything, it had looked like fun. Hardly the big deal Preston was making it out to be.

The second glass went down easily; the smooth, syrupy liquid feeling good on the back of her throat. She looked around at everyone, eating and trying to outdo each other with clever, sparkling conversation. *Just like a beautiful Renoir painting, come to life.*

She giggled at the 'subjects', in all their fine attire, lying about on fur rugs, crumbs falling from their chins and mayonnaise smudged on their top lips. The cursed giggling could not be stifled and she turned towards Preston, hiding her face in his arm as her body started to shake.

He bent his long neck down to look at her, lifting her chin up with one finger. Ice blue eyes sparkled as they scanned her face and his dimples appeared as a low laugh escaped his lips. She continued to giggle, her stomach clenching and tears rolling down her cheeks.

"I think it's a good time to go for a stroll, don't you?" he asked, pointing towards Grace. Her mother stood at the other end of the tent, glaring at them and raising a finger to her lips.

"I'm just laughing, silly. It's not illegal. She can't tell me to stop." She slapped him playfully on the arm, feeling the ground spin as she moved.

"Actually, drinking is illegal, at your age. So let's go where nobody cares." He stood to help her up and she leaned heavily on his arm.

"I would love to climb a tree right now." Claudia gazed ahead at the trees, as Preston made vague comments to the people they passed about needing to walk off all the food.

"That might be fun, Claudia, but I don't believe you are appropriately dressed."

"Oh. I've never liked dresses for precisely that reason. So impractical." Claudia stared down at her green winter dress, watching as the fringing on her matching poncho bounced as she walked. She lifted the skirt up past her knees, trying to twist the material in between her legs to make pants, all the better to climb in.

Preston laughed as he took a bottle of wine out from under his jacket. "You don't want any more of this, do you?" He raised one eyebrow.

"Oh yes!" She could almost taste the sweet wine just looking at the bottle.

He took a long drink, licked his full lips and handed it to her. Claudia held the neck of the bottle and tipped it towards her mouth. As she drank, small drops of liquid landed on her chest and dripped down towards her new dress. She'd forgotten her jacket, she thought as she looked down at the sticky patterns on her chest. *But it isn't cold, is it?*

"Oh my, you seem to have misplaced some." Preston stared at her chest as he pulled her under a large tree, its roots twisting out of the ground like thick, wooden armchairs high above the dewy grass.

Stumbling over her own feet, Claudia plopped down on his lap and felt his strong arms wrap around her from behind. Preston pulled her into his chest, inside the warmth of his jacket. His long, smooth neck stretched forward, over her shoulder until his nose nuzzled the front of her neck. It felt ticklish and warm, like the times she'd sneaked Spotty into her bedroom and the cat had nuzzled into her to sleep.

"So, a woman of the world, are we? Tell me your secrets, I'm intrigued."

She began to talk, the words just spilling from her mouth like the wine from the bottle. She spoke a little of Brishan, in the same way she'd rehash a fairy story to Snow-White and Rose-Red in the middle of the night. He chuckled and continued to fondle her neck, making small sounds of disbelief. Why must he think of her as such a child? She'd show him. *Only...how?*

She shivered as she felt his tongue, warm and wet, flick at a sticky drop of wine near her collarbone.

"Does that tickle?" he asked, voice low and husky.

"Yes." She snuggled in closer to his jacket, warm and relaxed in its depths.

"What about this?" His fingers traced circles over her shoulders and trailed down her arms, the heat of his skin a sharp contrast to the outside air.

"Mmm." The slow movement of his hands lulled her into a blissful daze and she could barely bother to move her head: though she wanted to look at him to see if his dimples were there.

She liked his dimples...she liked to make him smile. She felt her arms drop backwards, landing on his hard thighs. She tried to lift them again, but the energy to keep them in her own lap ebbed away as the heat from Preston's hands centred on her waist, snaking over her hips in long, slow strokes. His warm breath tickled her ear as his lips trailed a path over her neck, her collarbone and all the way up over her cheek, very near the corner of her mouth.

Claudia glimpsed clouds floating by through the bare branches above her head. They moved slowly and everything blurred when she tried to follow them.

Preston held the bottle up to her lips and she opened her mouth to let the liquid trickle down her throat. She sighed — the smooth, red substance tasted heavenly — and pushed her neck into Preston's shoulder to find a comfortable nook, arching her back in a languid stretch as she moved. His hands moved over her rib cage, pressing and circling upwards until they cupped her breasts. Claudia glanced down, liking the way her breasts filled the large hands drifting ever closer towards her nipples, now tingling in anticipation of his touch.

She closed her eyes as whispery moans escaped her lips. Preston chuckled, low and soft, and she wondered what was so funny. But everything was funny — funny and blissful and dizzy. *Blissfully dizzy*. She smiled at her own thoughts as his hands slipped inside the neckline of her dress.

Chapter Ten

The Fallen

The girl's face flamed red and sweat pooled over her neck as she tried to contain her screams. Brishan held her shaking hand and concentrated on surrounding her with a white light of calm. He closed his eyes. *God, her pain is so intense.* He tried to pull it into himself to ease her struggle.

Slowly, the deep frown above her nose lessened and her breathing became steady. Her eyes fluttered closed and Brishan stroked her hair until sleep claimed her.

"You are becoming a master healer, son." Eamon stood above him, green eyes twinkling with his smile.

Brishan glanced at his father as he placed the girl's hand gently back on the bed. Beside them, the Indian doctor, a rare professional using Ayurvedic and conventional medicine, wrapped the girl's swollen ankle in a thick bandage. He looked at Brishan and, with a smile, nodded his head to the door, indicating they might both go outside.

Brishan blinked to clear his grainy eyes as he emerged from the first-aid tent. Cool, early evening air stung his face and he pulled his tattered coat around his body, exhausted and needing sleep. But, sleep was not for those on the festival circuit throughout England — up at dawn in readiness for the daytime crowds, struggling through to the early hours of the morning as they entertained the hardiest of revellers.

Not for much longer. They were a smaller group now, just himself and his parents, Cosima the healer and two other families. Two families who desperately needed the money and support that he, and only he, could give to them until they got back on their feet.

And Dane, when he made his secret visits, disguised though

he was, almost beyond recognition.

"Thank you again, Valentino," Doctor Amra said, reaching his hand out to shake Brishan's.

Brishan laughed, a much-needed relief from such exhausting work. "My ego will explode if you keep up with the comparisons."

"No chance. You are far too gifted. Much more so than that actor you so resemble." The doctor's orange turban bobbed up and down as he nodded.

Brishan laughed again. The joke had started weeks ago when Brishan had offered to volunteer at the festival clinic. Doctor Amra had mistaken him for the Hollywood actor, Valentino Valitutti, and they'd shared an instant rapport. Brishan gave a silent prayer of thanks. Finding a friend here lessened the hurt, the emptiness in his heart.

Not that life was all bad. Performing for happy crowds at folk festivals all over Europe was almost like living a long, extended dream. A much better life than the families they'd had to leave behind. Only a month ago, he'd stood in front of a public housing block in London, waving goodbye to people who'd nursed him as a baby and children he'd taught to ride horses and build fires. At least they had shelter, but what of jobs and schools and security? They needed security, none of them were willing to risk their lives again, for the sake of their wanderlust, though it would always pump through their veins.

Brishan would be their traveller. He had salvaged and lovingly rebuilt just two gypsy wagons from the fires at the chateau. Fires lit to get them all to move. And months ago, they'd sold the horses, most of the costumes and some of the instruments; anything that would give those families some help. But Brishan missed them so much, missed all the freedom they'd had, the fun of travelling with so many friends. He missed his childhood.

And Claudia. Missed her so much his heart exploded in his

chest every time her face appeared in his dreams. Missed the smell of grass that somehow lingered on her after a long day outdoors, her odd glances and the way her head tilted to the side when she was curious about something, which was almost all the time. He chuckled. He only had to think of her and his face broke into a smile, his stomach flipping with hope to see her again.

Soon.

Slowly, very slowly, money drizzled back in from the constant performing. He'd made good contacts and could find employment all year round, in hundreds of countries if he chose, performing on the festival route. They'd even managed to buy an old Renault to get around in, so they could settle the wagons in for at least a few weeks at a time.

Claudia would love this, he thought. She had told him of her dreams to travel, to leave the chateau, and he couldn't wait to help them come true. *Strange though, that I can't reach her.* Of course, she was untrained still and barely conscious of her own powers, but she'd reached Dane, once, with natural ability alone and Dane had found her on the astral plane. It was possible.

Pain could sometimes block the mind and make it incapable of anything but basic levels of thinking. Brishan closed his eyes, as he did so often when he tried to pick up her trail. Nothing but black greeted him; not even those two cheeky companions of hers made an appearance. If she were harmed, he would undoubtedly know, as would Dane, so she wasn't in any physical danger.

It must be emotional.

He made his way to the wagons, with Eamon following close behind. His father was used to Brishan's moments of solitude, when all Brishan knew was Claudia.

Almost show time. Tonight he was fire twirling with the African bongo drummers. Then, he would rush to help his parents set up the freak show stand and play the guitar for them at show time.

As he dressed, he thought about Claudia and how badly the gatekeeper had treated her for years. Would she be healed of that by now? His chest tightened and he clenched his fists. He couldn't believe Dane had managed to stop himself from killing the evil bastard that night.

Could I have been so controlled? Me, the so-called healer?

And, had he now added to her pain? Leaving her with those two false, fawning parents? Would she feel lost again without love and true family and guidance? But, if he'd taken her from the chateau that night, would she have made it? Perhaps, he was right. She may not have survived travelling on foot, having to scrounge, even beg for money for train fares, going without food for days. Worse, sometimes, was having to defend themselves against the thieves in all the towns and villages they'd been in. If she had come with him, he thought, he would've been useless to the group. He would never have left her side, even for a moment.

And she may not have survived Dane's transformation.

Am I just making excuses for leaving her?

"Brishan! Hurry up, it's time," his mother yelled from outside.

Waiting for him in the softening twilight, Selina almost looked like the youthful mother he remembered. But, worry had streaked her chocolate hair grey and the loneliness of being without Oriana, her life-long companion, had etched deep lines into the skin around her mouth. Her sister's kidnapping had knocked her badly. Knocked them all.

He twisted his long black hair into a knot on the back of his head and wrapped a red bandana around the front. Stubble covered his cheeks and chin and a thin smattering of hair ran down the length of his naked, richly tanned chest. He wore baggy hessian pants with a black sash tied around the waist, no shoes and plaited, leather bands tied around his left ankle. As he tightened the bands around his leg, a lingering, nagging sense of foreboding knocked on the walls of his stomach. *Hunger, must just be hunger.*

Ready, with a deliberate smile forcing his lips apart, he held his mother's elbow and steered her towards their freak show. With nothing more than a small, wooden hut, Eamon had masterfully created scary little nooks and crannies, dripping with cobwebs and slime and the decapitated limbs of mannequins. Red and purple globes bathed the hut in eerie light and sound effects of whistling wind and howling wolves echoed throughout the small space.

Brishan's father was a man of many talents; carpenter, showman, even once, back in Ireland, a master calligrapher at his grandfather's printing company. That was before the authorities uncovered their document forgery.

Eamon was not proud of his past. But he'd been given a new life; starting the day he'd met Selina. Brishan knew that Eamon had done the best he could for his family. He only hoped he could do the same for Claudia.

At the back of the hut, behind a red, velvet curtain, he knew Cosima waited. Soon enough, the guests who'd had enough of the spectacle in the hut, would come out for air. Usually, she simply glanced at the unsuspecting people and yelled out their age, or the names of their children or partners. Some screamed, others ran out, but most stayed and paid for a reading. And then, she would dazzle them with her fortune telling skills. Using tealeaves and a crystal ball, mainly for show, Cosima gave them snippets of the images that flashed through her mind...but only enough to thrill. It was not for her to direct the lives of others, and even small glimpses of the future could be dangerous to untrained minds.

Brishan grabbed his poi and prepared to light it, taking a deep breath in readiness for the long night ahead. Fire twirling was his best paid act — spectators usually threw tips — but it was also the most exhausting.

Night had fallen. As he made his way towards the bright lights of the tents, Brishan began to move his body in time with the sticks, in time with the bongo drummers emerging from back of house, ready to draw the crowds with him. He smiled at the two men; far from their native Africa but so much like the gypsies. Life working the festivals meant an ease of friendship, new friends becoming old friends as they followed each other all over the country.

A hush fell over the crowds as they parted at the mesmerising sound of beating drums and the light from the fire drew awed attention. Cheers and whistles followed as the beat grew faster, faster. Brishan threw the poi in the air, expertly catching them, his movements fast and fluid. He lost himself in the dance, focusing on the fire and letting the drums dictate his moves.

Within minutes, someone tapped him on the shoulder. It was light; but, always aware of the risks of people getting to close to the fire, he snapped his head around to see urgency in a man's eyes.

Doctor Amra peered at him beneath the glow of the flames. "Brishan, we need you. Now."

Brishan nodded, immediately slowing his movements. The drummers took his cue, matching his movements with the beat and standing to take centre stage as Brishan bowed, extinguished his poi and followed the doctor through the rows of people, oblivious to the cheers from the crowd.

"What is it?"

"A man. Horribly beaten. I'm astounded. This festival has never attracted violence." The doctor placed his hand on Brishan's back, pushing him forward as they gained momentum through the crowds.

The first-aid tent was flooded with harsh fluorescent light. Children waited on wooden stools as their cuts and bruises were tended to by volunteer nurses, the smell of antiseptic controlled the air and Vivaldi's 'Spring' violin concerto played quietly from a portable radio. A curtain hung near the corner at the back creating a space, with a bed and a sink, for those with more serious injuries.

Brishan followed Doctor Amra behind the curtain to find a man on his back, his left arm covered in blood with wounds deep and gaping. His forearm bone was visible through the torn flesh. Swollen eyelids fluttered above a broken nose and dots of blood seeped through a bandage on his cheek. One hand clawed at the edge of the bed, clenching and unclenching, the knuckles turning white against the dark brown skin.

Brishan swayed backwards, trying to settle himself with a supreme effort of will. He stepped up to the bed and caught the hand in his own.

Dane's hand.

Dane's face, Dane's head, so recently shaved of its thick, grey streaked curly hair. A face as dear to him as his own parents'.

Dane's broken body.

He inhaled deeply, a violent wave of pain whipping his body as his skin connected with Dane's. Doctor Amra had already begun to clean the wounds around Dane's head, and a nurse tended to the mangled arm.

"He'll need to go to hospital, but we'll do what we can now," Doctor Amra said to the nurse. "The ambulance will take at least thirty minutes." He bent to extract a piece of gravel from Dane's chin.

Brishan knew Dane could not be taken away in the ambulance. It would jeopardise everything his uncle had been working towards.

He closed his eyes and conjured a heavy, white mist, infused with healing spirals, and felt the heat as it radiated through his hands. He concentrated on circling Dane's body with the mist, glowing now with a pulsating, white light, tendrils of it seeping into the damaged body. He put his hands out in front of him and hovered over Dane's face, letting the heat escape in a soothing wave over his uncle's body.

In minutes, the fingers stopped clenching and drooped on the bed, relaxed and still. Doctor Amra paused, his stitching needle inches from Dane's chin. His brown eyes flicked to Brishan, then down to his calm patient, then back to Brishan again. The doctor stared at Brishan until the nurse tapped him on the arm, urging him to start stitching.

"You will put the drug companies out of business, Valentino," he said, his rhythmical voice a hoarse whisper.

Brishan ignored the doctor, laying his hand across his uncle's again. A weak squeeze reassured Brishan that Dane knew he was there, knew he was safe.

Brishan allowed himself a deep breath and lowered his head towards Dane's chest, squeezing his eyes shut to fight the oncoming tears. Dane's breath moved slowly, heavily and Brishan knew that despite his best efforts, Dane was in deep pain. But now, at least, it seemed bearable. Time slowed as the medical team worked in silence.

Cosima was on her way. Brishan could feel her coming closer, and so he waited.

Moments later the master healer, dressed in her fortune-teller garb, crashed through the door of the clinic, screaming loudly about pains in her heart and sucking her breath in and out in huge gulps as if it pained her to do so.

Doctor Amra and the nurse looked at each other, eyes wide with alarm. "Brishan, stay here will you, while we go and see what's wrong?" The doctor ordered, shaking his head as he washed his hands in the small basin.

"Of course." Brishan inclined his head.

As soon as the curtain closed behind him, Brishan lifted Dane's head from the bed, slowly helping him to sit. Dane's one strong hand strained on the mattress to keep balance. Brishan could hear the chaos Cosima created outside and waited patiently for the help he knew would come. He held his uncle upright, murmuring calming chants into the bloodied ear.

"Quickly, Brishan, help me put this on him." Suddenly his

mother was there, inside the curtain, holding a black cloak.

Selina moved the coat gently beneath her sister's lover, slipping it over his good arm and hanging the other side from his shoulder. She slipped the zombie-like mask attached to the hood over the front of the bruised and battered face. Brishan could hear his father now, adding to the commotion outside as he fussed over Cosima and yelled at the medical team. Selina held up her hand, motioning silence as they stood with Dane in between them, covered now from head to foot, leaning on them heavily.

Brishan heard Selina's voice as quiet tones: as an echo inside his head. She would be taking Dane from here alone. Brishan was to stay, to continue the ruse. They must not create suspicion. Brishan nodded. Then, he let go of Dane and watched his uncle's weight transfer to his mother's small frame. She strained but stayed upright and walked slowly towards the curtain.

Brishan went ahead of her, rushing over to Doctor Amra and his father. Eamon looked up at him, face as red as his hair and green eyes sparking fire. A group of teenagers, one with a swollen, black eye, had gathered around Cosima, staring at the drama unfolding

"What's the matter, Dad?"

"For heaven's sake, Brishan," Doctor Amra shouted. "Take him away and calm him down will you? He's not doing the woman any favours with all the yelling." He was pushing Eamon away with one arm and holding Cosima's arm to take her blood pressure with the other. She lay slumped against a wall, arm over her head, wailing.

From the corner of his eye, Brishan saw Selina slip outside, Dane shuffling slowly at her side. "Dad, just leave, I'll make sure the doctor takes good care of her."

Eamon simply shrugged and rushed outside, his eyes tracking Selina's progress.

Doctor Amra's mouth fell open. "Surely your healing skills

don't extend to mind control? The man was a raving lunatic before you came out. You show biz types are so...passionate."

Brishan attempted a laugh and knelt beside Cosima, whose breathing deepened as the wailing and moaning came to a stop. He pretended to offer healing until she sighed, calling out, "It's a miracle! It's a miracle!"

On her command, Brishan helped her to her feet and she smiled, her knotted, long grey hair flowing wildly around her head.

"Thank you. I am feeling much better. Indigestion or something I'm sure. Peace be with you," she said to Doctor Amra. "Help me home, boy." She turned to Brishan, pushing her arm though his.

"I'll be back," Brishan said to the doctor, before leading Cosima towards the door.

They had only just escaped into the dark of night before the Doctor rushed out after them, frantically looking left and right

"He's gone. The patient...he's gone."

Brishan tried to register shock and surprise on his face — not hard considering the night he'd had. "What do you mean he's gone?"

"He's not in the bed. How on earth could he have walked out of there on his own? Did he resume consciousness while you were with him?"

"No, if anything I think he was asleep."

"Unbelievable. Truly unbelievable."

"Get me home to my bed, will you, boy?" Cosima snapped, tugging on his arm.

"You go, Brishan, I'll call the police. He can't have gotten too far. The man needs a hospital." With that, Doctor Amra turned, mumbling, "Must be in some kind of trouble, that fellow."

Brishan grabbed Cosima's hand and they sprinted towards the camp, the cool air rushing through their ears with the speed.

Dane lay, still and quiet, on the bed of Cosima's van,

surrounded by strong smelling potions. Selina and Eamon bent over his motionless form.

"Sit outside, everyone. Give me peace to work." Cosima threw her hands in the air, shooing them out with her long, curling fingernails.

They left without words, huddling on the stairs in front of the caravan. Worrying and waiting.

"Cosima had a vision of him walking for miles, trying to reach us, but she couldn't work out where he was coming from. Hours later, while she was doing a reading with a client, she saw him stumble into the clinic, just moments before he actually did." Eamon looked pale and his voice cracked as he spoke.

"What do you think happened?" Selina turned to her husband.

"My guess is someone caught him trying to smuggle Oriana out."

"I don't think so," Brishan said. "He'd be dead. International prostitution rackets don't normally leave people alive with their secrets." He heard a muffled gasp, and turned towards his mother. Her trembling hand covered her mouth and tears trailed over her cheeks.

I'm an idiot.

He put his arm around her shoulders, hugging her into him. "I'm sorry, Mum, I didn't mean for that to sound so harsh."

She lifted her face from her hands and looked at him; a lifetime's sadness poured from her large, chocolate brown eyes. "I just want her back, and if Dane's here, it means she's in there all alone."

"I know."

"Dane will pull through. I know it. He's so close to getting her back, he won't give in now, or ever," Eamon said, picking at the spiky grass poking through the stairs.

"He's right, Mum. Infiltrating a racket like that is no easy feat. This setback means nothing. Dane will bring her back." *Or I will.*

Footsteps approached and torchlight wove through the trees, landing squarely in Brishan's eyes.

"Police." A badge flashed in their faces. Two men in uniform blocked the light from the full moon. "We're looking for a missing person. Injured severely and a suspected criminal. He could be hiding in one of these vans. Are you just getting home, folks? We need to take a look inside before you go in. He could be dangerous."

Chapter Eleven

Smoke and Mirrors

The Czech countryside whizzed by the train window, a blur of orange and blue lines. A blur, just like the jumbled thoughts in her mind.

Preston sat beside her, his thumb and pointer finger cupping his chin as he read a business journal. Grace and Edward sat opposite, sorting the daily newspapers into different sections: the social pages for her and the finance news for him.

Claudia picked the skin around her thumbnail until small beads of blood formed. She strained to hear the shouts of '*čaj*' and '*pivo*' and '*kafe*' from the waiters outside. *Perhaps a beer would be nice.* Not that she'd ever tasted it. She imagined asking Preston to get her one.

But the smiles she'd inspired from Preston at the chateau hadn't come with them on their journey to Prague. Absently, she rubbed her cheek, fighting memories of that night under the tree. Memories, acutely sharp still, of a chateau picnic. How could she have been so drunk? So drunk that Preston's kisses had made her breathless and spellbound, leaving her aching for his touch.

Would it have happened anyway, without the wine? Maybe. Too hard to resist. Margaret had been right to worry about his unrelenting charm.

Her fingers pressed into her temples. *Oh God, the thought of his hands...down there. If only those hands had been Brishan's.*

Cringing, she remembered the sudden nausea in her stomach, the violent spinning in her head, the stream of vomit in the grass and the look of disgust on Preston's face. He still made jokes about it, cruel jokes that held enough power to make her cry and feel ashamed.

Why? Dane would have laughed, held her hair back from her

face and educated her on the effects of too much alcohol. Brishan…well…she pictured him enfolding her in his arms, healing her, loving her with an amused, emerald gaze. *But they hudn't been there, or here, or anywhere. They were a dream.*

Ignore it. She smiled at Preston's serious face. It was still important that he liked her. If he stopped, he'd leave, like Grace so long ago, like Brishan, like Dane. *And it hurt all the same, whatever their reasons.*

Just forget. Forget and live in the present. Lenny and Margaret, shedding awkward tears as she'd left for Prague, had warned her of wallowing in the past. Lenny always said that the present was all they had, so chin up and get on with it. Claudia smiled at the thought of the housekeeper and the gardener, her 'adoptive grandparents', so they said. Three weeks without them would be a long time.

She tapped her foot. Her eyes darted around the cabin in a way she couldn't control. She looked at her watch. Fifteen minutes before they reached Prague. Fifteen minutes before she stepped foot in the city for the first time. Fifteen minutes…

Crack.

Claudia gasped and gripped the edge of the seat as her body jolted forward. The deafening wail of metal on metal ripped through her ears and smoke coated the window. The green paddocks they had just passed were gone.

Preston fell off his seat, long legs tangling beneath him. "Fuck."

"There is no need for such language Preston." Grace whispered, one hand fluttering over her chest as she looked towards Edward.

"What on earth is wrong with the train driver, braking like that? Preston, come with me, I want to speak with management. Bloody negligent." Edward jumped to his feet, helping Preston up and pushing him out the door.

Grace hurried to follow. "You stay here, Claudia. Look after the luggage. No doubt every low life at the back of the train will try to take advantage of this situation."

Claudia nodded, still staring at the smoke billowing outside. It was heavier now and changing from white, to grey to black. There was no sound other than the wind whistling through the window seals and she concentrated on this, unnerved by the oppressive clouds of smoke and silence.

Where are all the people? She slid over to the other side of the seat, peering around the door into the aisle. Empty of life, in both directions. The train moved, almost imperceptibly, from side to side, creaking and groaning, groaning and creaking. Claudia wiped her forehead and slid back to the window. She cupped her hands on the glass to see, but there was only blackness. Her heart thudded, faster and faster and she matched her breathing to it, conscious of the panic edging up from her stomach.

Like a living creature, the train groaned louder and more often, as if it were in deep pain. Claudia closed her eyes and crossed her hands over her chest, trying to calm the thudding. Something was very, very wrong. Every cell in her body knew it. *Dane, please come.*

No, the gypsies were gone; she would not call for them. They were right to abandon her. Once again, she'd proven she couldn't look after herself.

She was disgusted by her own weakness.

Why is it so quiet? Surely others from the back of the train want to see what's happening up front?

She looked towards the corridor again. Not one person walked by.

Claudia glanced at the luggage sitting neatly above the chairs in racks. What a stupid notion from Grace. How would people steal them? *Where, after all, would they go?* She almost giggled at the thought of strange men running away into the fields with Grace's giant, Versace suitcases full of clothes. Grace could yell all she wanted.

She would get up and see what was happening. She could not stay a moment longer.

She stepped outside and waited for the door at the end of the aisle to open automatically. She walked into the next carriage. Empty. Completely empty and the door leading to the front of the train remained resolutely closed. She paused, trying to ignore the tingles racing up her spine.

Bang.

She jumped back as the door to her left slammed open hitting the wall. A woman, with wildly matted, red hair, stood in her path. A tiny baby sat on her hip, its fists balled and pushing into its screaming mouth. "Oh, thank God, please, please come in and help me, no one will answer my calls anymore."

Claudia's eyes flicked to the emergency intercom phone, dangling from a hook on the wall inside the compartment. A man, his face coated in sweat and deathly pale, lay on his back on the floor.

Her legs itched and she turned to run for help. "I'll be back as soon as I find help, I promise." She swallowed hard against her dry throat.

"No! They said not to go out there!"

"Who said not to go out there?" Claudia looked down at her feet, willing them to stay firmly planted.

"The staff, when they called about the crash, they told us all to stay inside the compartments. What's wrong with you, wandering around a disaster zone? I need help and that damn intercom won't work anymore. Can't reach anyone."

"Oh." Claudia felt all blood drain from her face. She didn't even remember seeing a phone in her own compartment...so lost in her thoughts...had she missed the call when she went outside?

"I need help with the baby so I can help my husband. Please." The red-haired lady stared right into her eyes, one hand reaching out to grab Claudia's.

Claudia breathed deeply. *Think, just think.* Surely Grace and

Preston were all right, after all, they hadn't been in the front of the train when it crashed. *Perhaps they're helping others.* Claudia swallowed, painfully, and reached out to take the screaming baby.

"Bless you," the woman said as she knelt to the ground near her husband.

Claudia bit her bottom lip; she'd never held one. *Holding a baby can't be that hard. Nothing to be scared of.* She bounced the baby on her hip and walked round and round the small space. She cupped the back of its soft head and whispered, "shhh," into a perfectly oval shaped ear. Commercials with smiling mothers and rosy-cheeked children flashed through her mind. Nothing to be scared of here.

"Her name is Jasmine," the woman said, as she took her husband's tie off and moved his head into her lap.

Claudia looked down at little Jasmine's face, watching as the fists slowly uncurled. Her pink mouth rested in a thin line and her blue eyes focused on Claudia's own. She made a soft sound, a gurgling that made Claudia smile. One chubby hand grasped a strand of Claudia's hair and the other one tapped her on the mouth. Claudia instinctively kissed the wrinkly fingers.

She dragged her eyes away to look at the man on the ground. He still breathed, but his skin was so white he blended in with the clinically bare floor. "Where's he hurt?" Claudia looked back at Jasmine, avoiding the woman's anguished gaze

"I don't know, exactly. He fell pretty hard when the train stopped. I think he might have hit his head, but I can't see a bump or anything." The woman's voice trembled.

"You should really let me go and find help for you. There might be a first-aid kit on board, at least, or a nurse." *Please let there be someone, out there in the silence.*

"No, don't leave me. Please. I can't cope with both of them on my own. I need to be able to help him when he wakes up." Tears dripped down her nose and trickled onto the man's neck.

Okay, it's fine. Everything's fine. Just help them. Claudia knelt on the floor by the man's feet, carefully cradling the baby on her lap. "Did they give you any information, on the phone I mean, about the crash?"

The woman shook her head in one, quick movement and sighed. "No, just to wait here for help. Not go to the front of the train."

Claudia swallowed hard again. "My family went to the front of the train, to talk to the driver."

The woman's mouth set in a grim, straight line. "You can't go there. Don't go and look for them. Please, not for my sake, for yours."

"I don't understand."

"I know you're...listen, I've seen train crashes before, right near our old house in Leeds. It's not a pretty sight."

"But," Claudia's voice dropped to a whisper. "They may need help. Others might need help."

"You might not make it far enough to help them, can't you here the creaking? The train is unstable. We can only wait for help to come to us."

"You can help, Claudia. You can make a difference. Right in front of you."

Claudia gasped and looked at the unconscious man. "How does he know my name?"

"What?"

"Your husband, he just spoke."

"What do you mean? He's out cold." The woman leant close to her husband's face.

Claudia could see that, without any doubt: he was grey and dribble shone on the corner of his mouth. He wasn't moving.

The woman looked at her closely, her eyes darting over the baby and back up to the open cabin door.

"S-sorry, I must be hearing things," Claudia said.

Oh my God. She realised she knew the voice, so familiar, so calm. So *not* real.

Claudia stared at the man's motionless body, focusing on one part at a time: the sweaty brow, the wide, slumped shoulders and the chest, still moving in and out. A green, slightly hazy mist floated above his chest, centring over his heart. The longer she stared, the thicker the substance became, swirling over him in quick circles, clumping and thickening around his neck.

"I think there's something wrong with his heart." The words flew out of her mouth before she could think.

"What makes you say that?"

"I...I don't know." Claudia glanced down at the baby, watching the blue eyes droop into sleep.

"Oh...dear...God, he could have had a heart attack!" The woman shrieked as she wrenched open her husband's shirt, uselessly, as if releasing his chest would fix the problem.

Claudia crouched next to her and put a firm hand on her shoulder. The woman's eyes widened and she instinctively stretched her arms out to take the baby.

Claudia splayed both hands and placed them above the man's chest, in the thick of the darkening mist. "Aaah!" Pain shot through her body — a deep, stabbing pain near her heart.

"What, what for heaven's sake?" The woman's voice sounded like an echo.

Claudia opened her eyes again and stared into the mist. It wove around her fingers, coating them in green, slithering towards her face. Automatically, she pulled her hands upwards, away from his body. She continued until her arms were high above her own head, the mist following her movements and drawing slowly from his heaving chest.

The pain near her heart intensified, stabbing and clenching until she could bare it no more. Her hands, paralysed now, fought to close, to release the tension. *Go, go, go. Leave me.*

"John? Oh John! That's it, honey, sit up, I've got you. Here, here, drink some water."

As if from afar, Claudia heard the ecstatic voice as the red-haired woman spoke to her awakening husband. The baby cooed in her own language and the energy she'd felt from the man's body seemed to dissipate, leaving Claudia with a light-headed, drowsy feeling.

"Good Lord, girl, I don't mind telling you, I've been thinking you're half out of your wits, what with hearing voices and flinging your arms all over my husband. But whatever you did, it worked."

Claudia looked up to see a blinding smile beneath the knotty red hair as the woman held the baby in one arm and a water bottle to her husband's lips with the other. John's eyes were bloodshot and his skin was still tinged with grey, but he was awake and sipping the water.

"Oh." No more words formulated in her brain. *What on earth just happened?*

Claudia stretched her arms signalling she would take the baby, allowing the woman to help her husband up onto the chair.

Little Jasmine was barely awake, but her mouth made circles as her thumbs pressed around chubby cheeks to find an opening. A white haze surrounded the baby and Claudia rubbed her eyes with her free hand. It made no difference; the haze shimmered and moved about the baby. Not in dramatic, swirling patterns like the thick substance over John's heart, but calmly, in one, thin sheath of fluid movement.

Her eyes moved to the woman again and now she noticed a red haze, spinning around the feet, making dramatic patterns and clinging on to the calves. Claudia shut her eyes against dizziness and backed towards a seat, holding the baby more carefully in two arms.

"Pop her down in the bassinet over there if you like, love, she'll go off to sleep now."

Claudia tried to smile and placed Jasmine gently in the portable cradle, careful to wrap the baby in a pink cloth she found scrunched on the mattress.

"He's going to need a doctor, and soon, but it's a blessing that he's awake. Thank you, for staying." Tears still glistened on the woman's cheeks and John, unable to talk yet, nodded in agreement.

Claudia just smiled. Words, again, escaped her despite the warm glow she felt as she looked at the little family in front of her, safe at least, for now. "I'm just going to go up the aisle and see if anyone's come back yet."

"No, love, that's not smart."

"I won't go to the front of the train; I just need to have a look."

The woman sighed, twirling her silver necklace around her fingers. Claudia felt a pang of longing for Margaret. *Need you, Margaret. More than ever.*

"If you must, but come right back, okay? Someone will come soon…truly…and I don't fancy seeing you, or anyone, hurt," she said.

Claudia nodded and walked on before her nerve caved to the strong fear. She shut the door behind her in case the baby stirred with any sudden noise. *If only there was noise, any noise other than the creaking train*

The door to the next carriage remained closed. Claudia waved her hand in front of the automatic sensor. Nothing. Reaching out, she touched the steel. The metal felt cold and hard as her fingers gripped the edge. She tugged, hard. Harder and harder until her knuckles turned white and jolts of pain ran down her fingers. Still nothing.

"Come on," she mumbled under her breath, throwing her whole body into it. A gap appeared and a sliver of smoke shot up her nose. She sneezed and pulled harder. Finally, with an ear-piercing screech, the door opened.

She fell backwards onto the carriage floor, landing on her thigh with a sharp thud.

Smoke now billowed from the opening, catching in her throat

before she had time to close her mouth. She blinked as streaming tears blinded her vision. Rolling onto all fours, she stretched one arm in front of her face and tried to make her way forward. The acrid smell of burnt hair controlled the air and low groans — human groans — mixed with the wailing wind as it rushed around her head. *Are all the windows broken?*

As soon as the thought occurred, her knee jerked upwards as something sharp pushed into her flesh, stopping only when it reached the bone. She paused, inhaling in one, swift breath. Her eyes, slowly adjusting to the pain and the smoke, flicked to the shards of glass scattered over the ground. Most stood straight up and down, their pointed edges like swords waiting to impale unwitting victims.

Victims…

Oh my God. No…

She screamed, her throat burning with the effort.

Like a macabre pile of misshapen mannequins, bodies lined the path ahead. Twisted legs, impossibly angled arms and eyes as dead as the stag heads at the chateau.

Bile rose in her throat and her whole body convulsed as it released the contents of her stomach. Vomit slipped into spaces between the broken glass and splintered chairs. She struggled to hold her head up, the bitter taste in her mouth making her throat close up. Finally, she had heaved enough and dropped her forehead to the ground, reaching for the silence within.

Snow-White and Rose-Red were there, behind her closed eyes, smiling and beckoning to her with rhythmical fingers. But she didn't have the strength to summon them out.

Don't deserve them anymore.

A tight, strangled squeal, more animal than human, interrupted the speed of her panic. Her head felt like a rock resting on a pin, but it lifted automatically so her gaze could settle on the source of the horrifying sound. Red-streaked, blonde hair at the far end of the corridor moved, falling over a face coated in blood.

Claudia's body froze; she could not move further through the gauntlet of glass and terror ahead.

"Help me, please," she whispered into the ground, trying to settle her panic and focus her energy.

The squeal grew louder — a long, shaking sound of anguish as the blonde head turned to face her. One bright, blue eye shone through the matted strands of hair.

Claudia felt all breath leave her body.

Grace. The beautiful butterfly queen. Trapped under a massive pile of rubble. It was her mother's life that Claudia watched, ebbing towards a slow, painful death. It was Grace's squeal, that sound of pure terror.

Whoosh.

Adrenalin rushed through her veins, physically pulling her up, killing her own fear with it. "Grace, it's okay, I'm coming." Her hands pressed into the floor, ripping and tearing as they pushed towards Grace.

An explosion of dust, mixed with clothing and deadly glass, rained down on her head and she sneezed, mucus and blood combining to coat her hands.

A blackened face emerged from the dust, followed by a tall, willowy body, heaving its limbs over broken, vinyl seats. Ice-blue eyes burned bright in the charred face.

"Preston!" Claudia rasped through the smoke, stretching her arm to point towards Grace; her mother's head lolling at an angle, her mouth open in a perfect circle to release harsh, quick puffs of air. Preston looked back at Claudia, slowly and method-ically wiping remnants of debris from his body. With a slow shake of his head, he peered down at a deep slash on his arm, before his eyes darted to the shattered window closest to him.

The train moved, swayed, almost gently in time to the constant creaking. A sound escaped Preston's lips — half sigh, half gasp — as his legs carried him to the window. In a display of surprising agility, one long, lean leg lifted and kicked the jagged glass from the opening.

Claudia sobbed with relief. *Preston will save us. We're safe.* She tried to stand up, careful to keep her weight off her torn knee, wiping her eyes and her mouth with the back of her hand.

She looked back at Grace. Her mother stared at her, eyes like swollen, red slits as she tried to form words from dry, bloodied lips. The hoarse whisper reached Claudia over the sound of smashing glass. "I'm sorry, my daughter. So sorry. For it all."

No, no Grace, you'll be okay now, you're not leaving me again. Did the words come out? All she heard was a strange, strangled cry. Her own cry.

Preston was halfway out the window now, legs straddling the ledge as he bent his head to avoid remnants of glass. Glancing at her again, he opened and closed his mouth, over and over. *Just like the fish in the aquarium at the chateau, the stupid, brainless fish.* He shook his head back and forth as the train lurched sideways, his face crumpling along with his body.

With one, giant leap, he jumped from the train.

Claudia felt nothing.

No time, no time for hurt. Move. Besides, maybe he was just going to get help. *Yes, that's what he's doing, helping us. Not leaving. Not abandoning me.* She looked quickly at Grace and back again to the shards of glass between them. Her stomach churned, pain ripped through her knee and dizziness attacked her head. *Just move.* In one swift motion, she tore a piece of wood from beneath a broken chair and started to push the shards to the side, creating a path to her mother.

She realised, as if she were watching someone else, that sobs tore from her throat as she pushed with the makeshift stick. Glass crunched beneath her and small particles of debris rained down on her face as she moved forward.

The train lurched, angrily protesting its dying form.

Hinges, above her head, sighed as they snapped. Her eyes widened as a baggage shelf swung, like a guillotine, towards her face. Steel blocked all else as it landed in front of her eyes, pinning her between it and the side of the train. She tried to stand but the cold, impenetrable racks blocked her.

She tried to push forward, but her waning strength and the weight of the shelves made it impossible to move. Smoke filled her lungs, tightening her chest with its hideous potency.

She closed her eyes against her fear...and allowed the dark to come.

Chapter Twelve

Paralysis

"My mother is ill, officers. I've been tending to her all day and I don't want her disturbed." Selina's voice embodied command as she stood to face the policemen. Brishan breathed a silent sigh of relief for his mother's quick thinking. Scarier men than they had backed down from one of Selina's withering looks.

"All the same, Mrs...?" The officer raised one, bushy eyebrow.

Eamon stood beside her. "My name is Eamon O'Flannery, this is my wife Selina and our son, Brishan." He proclaimed, with a flourishing sweep of the arm. "You must understand that my mother-in-law is not...shall we say...in her right mind." Eamon threw an exaggerated look of apology towards Selina.

"If she wakes up, we're in for hours of trouble. We just don't want to risk it. Of course, we'll report any...what did you say was wrong with this man? Badly beaten? A criminal? Should I be concerned for our safety?" Eamon's voice took on a higher pitch and his cheeks flamed bright red.

"No need for concern just yet, but for your own good, we do need to take a look inside. A badly beaten man wandering around a festival speaks only of trouble to us. We won't make any noise." His bushy eyebrow stayed raised.

Eamon cleared his throat and stood aside to let them up the stairs. Both men covered their noses and frowned as they opened the door. Moments later, a vile stench gushed from the wagon — ointment, blood and vomit blending with the sickly sweet smell of tea-tree oil.

"What the hell..." the officers cursed at the same time.

There, at the end of the bed, hair knotted around her face, was wild Cosima. She rocked back and forth as a long, slow chant vibrated from her thin lips. The officers walked in, tentative but determined. She pushed one gnarled hand through her hair to uncover her eyes and stared at them with piercing intensity. The other hand rose slowly from her lap, spindly fingers swirling slowly to point at them.

She spat viciously at their feet.

"Excuse us, mam." The policemen backed down the stairs, both stumbling and falling over each other, landing with small thuds on the grass. As they scrambled to stand, Cosima hissed and left her bed, emitting a frightening wail as she slammed the wagon door closed on their reddening faces.

"Our apologies for disturbing you, and for your...unfortunate situation." Mr Bushy Eyebrows wiped sweat from his neck. His fellow officer stood and stared at the ground, shaking his head and blowing out through his nose as if to rid himself of the stench.

"I did try to warn you," Eamon said with a sheepish smile.

"We'll be off then. Please report to the festival organisers if you come across any persons of interest."

"Will do." Eamon waved as the officers rushed to the next van.

Brishan shared a look of relief with his parents and, at Cosima's call, went inside.

"I must be losing my gift in my old age, I only saw them coming minutes before they did, it used to be hours," the master healer said, as she took the rugs and pillows from Dane's battered body.

Dane's one good eye sparkled with life in its red-rimmed depths. He was covered in green ointment and bandages, but the blood that had coloured his body was gone. Angry purple and yellow bruises scarred the small amount of skin not wrapped in gauze.

"Dane," Selina whispered, sitting beside him on the bed and soothing his forehead. Tears dripped down her face and Dane turned to look at her, a small smile cracking his swollen lips.

"I'll be all right. I promise." His voice was hoarse but his tone rang with the confidence of old. "Brishan."

"I am here."

"I need your help now."

"I'll do anything."

Selina gasped. "No, Dane, you must not put him in danger, not even for Oriana."

"Selina." Eamon put a warning hand on her shoulder.

"I would not give him a task he wasn't ready for. Sit down, everyone, please. First, I have to tell you everything, so we can prepare. The ground work is done, but one step remains." Dane stifled a groan as he pushed his head forward.

Brishan was quick to catch his uncle's hand in his own. Selina and Cosima settled on the bed beside him and Eamon stood at the foot, arms crossed and eyes blinking furiously to contain tears.

"It's hard for me to start, and I want you to know, all of you, before I tell this story, that I leave some...some parts out for my own soul to endure, not yours." Dane's eyes closed and his breathing deepened.

"You need not protect us from what you've been through Dane," Selina whispered.

Brishan glanced at his mother and back to Dane. "No, don't...please...we can't help you if you don't tell us the truth."

"Ah, Brishan, always rushing towards the fire. I thought I might find you softened with the ache you must feel for Claudia, and the healing you've accomplished here."

"I've accepted my path, Dane, it doesn't mean I've turned into a monk."

Dane laughed, holding his side with his good hand as if the very movement hurt him. "I would never expect so. Have you managed to contact her?"

Brishan studied his hands, a pang of guilt turning to white-hot anger. "No. I've tried. Over and over. I can only imagine what's going on inside her is blocking…I can't get through."

"Yes, that may be so. But she'll return to us. I know it."

"And Oriana?" Selina's voice cracked as she spoke.

"Selina. My love's beautiful sister, it hurts me to look at you right now, you're so like her." Dane took a deep, rattling breath. "That night, after the fire at the chateau, I followed them, to Mikulov. I could see her, through the windows of an old farm house, tied to a chair, blindfolded and…"

Selina gasped.

"Hush, Selina, we need to know," Eamon said, his tone gentle despite his words. Selina bowed her head.

Dane's eyes fluttered closed, then opened again with startling clarity. "Outside, ten or more men, I can't remember, stood around, smoking, talking," he sighed. "I felt like I could take them all on — smash their heads together and rid the world of their useless energy."

"If I'd been there I'd…" Brishan felt the words escape through clenched teeth.

"Brishan, shh." Again, Eamon strived to maintain quiet.

"Yes. I know what you would have done. And, for that, you would now be dead." Dane's good eye focused on him and Brishan lowered his head, shame burning his cheeks.

"I followed them here; to their headquarters, right near the Tower of London. My disguise, this revolting body I now reside in with muscles I don't need, the shaved head, the beard — I did so I could infiltrate. And I have."

"Who are *they*, exactly?" Selina's eyes widened as her hand agitated her thick, brown hair.

Dane winced, as if the very thought of what he was about to say pained him more than his physical wounds. "It is as I thought. An underground prostitution racket, hidden beneath Seething Lane. They call it 'The Lair' and you can only get there through the bowels of London's streets. Its…its prime function is to sell women, women from all over the world, to the wealthiest of men. They're held in rooms and drugged, then dressed and put on display for an...auction of sorts."

A deep sob from Selina tugged at Brishan's heart.

"You mean my sister is one of these gilded birds? Waiting to be sold to the highest bidder?" Selina's voice was barely audible.

"Yes. And I am now a security guard. I'm there to make sure their venture remains secret and protected from the eyes of the law. Not only me, and a team of thugs, but some of the city's politicians, highest ranking police officers...these lauded citizens are some of the Lair's best clients, in fact."

"So, tell us of the first time you saw her in there." Cosima spoke, her voice calm and clipped.

"You have seen some of this?" Dane asked, his eye flicking to the master healer.

"Yes, but only flashes. You are too clever at masking yourself."

"I've tried to, yes, but only to save you all pain."

"We know, Dane, please, go on. I'm sorry," Selina said.

"I attend the auctions, standing in the shadows as the clients view the women. Oriana is among ten women they keep for the highest possible bidder. The others are rented out, by the hour sometimes — so she's lucky in that. She's not aware of me, or anyone, she is...her mind is..." Dane's voice broke and a single tear escaped, running down his battered cheek.

Brishan stood and squeezed his uncle's hand. "She's only drugged, Dane, she can overcome that. She's still there, inside. She can't be broken that easily."

Dane squeezed Brishan's hand. There was strength there still and Brishan felt hope...hope for Dane's recovery.

"You have a plan, yes?" Cosima moved around the van, whipping up a new, foul smelling potion to ease Dane's suffering.

"The mastermind of the ring goes by a different name while he's at the Lair, though I know he's well known and in the public eye. I can't get any more information from the scum I work with, they're nothing but hired thugs. But, yes, I have a plan...for him."

The fire returned to his eye. "First, though, we get Oriana out. Every day, I get closer to the staff who look after the women — the housekeepers, the cooks. The first step is to—"

"Ahhh…" Brishan clutched his stomach as searing pain ripped through his body.

"Brishan, what is it? Where's the pain?" Selina rushed to his side.

"Clau…" He ran out of breath as an imaginary knife attacked his knee. "Claudia."

"Yes. I am seeing it too. She is rushing towards — death." Cosima's voice, vague and monotone, broke through the roaring in his ears.

Selina moaned and dug her fingers into Brishan's shoulders. Brishan shook his head and clawed at his mother's arms, desperate to pull himself upright. *Get up, get up. Must help her.*

"No, it hasn't happened yet, Brishan. She is not dead. I can also feel the pain that's coming… I think perhaps I have all day, but it's been numbed by my broken body. I can't reach her as I am." Dane pulled his bruised head up from the pillow.

"She is rushing. Moving ever closer. To the crash." Cosima stared at the wall, unblinking.

"What did you say?" Brishan rasped.

"A crash. A train."

"Where? Where do you see the train, Cosima?" Eamon caught the fortune-teller by her shoulders, adding his energy to hers to help maintain her vision.

"Very close to the turrets."

"Turrets? There are castles all over Europe, she could be anywhere! Spain! Italy!" Eamon's face turned a deep shade of purple.

"No. She's not that far away. I feel her close still," Dane said, his voice unwavering in the midst of Eamon's panic.

"Where then?" Selina whispered.

Brishan's hands stiffened, almost paralysed. He tried to

clench his fingers, but the movement was impossible. A lump filled his throat and when he opened his mouth to speak, no sound escaped.

"Oh God, Cosima, help him," Selina cried as she took the weight of his falling body to the floor.

"He's too connected with Claudia, he needs to fight the paralysis, so he can help her," Dane said. Lifting himself to the edge of the bed, he bent down, "Do you hear me Brishan? You must fight it. It's Claudia's panic you feel, not your own. You are calm. You are taking control of your body." Dane's voice, as melodious as Brishan had always known it.

But the pain, it's so deep…in your eyes. Don't hurt yourself further, Uncle. I'll deal with this. Why won't my tongue move? Claudia, Claudia, I'm coming. Reach out. Tell me how to find you.

"Cosima. We will all concentrate with you. Hone in on your vision. We must know where the crash takes place," Dane spoke to the master healer, keeping his unwavering gaze on Brishan.

"The countryside is flat and orange. She is with many people. I can feel she dislikes them. Well, all except one. He has eyes like ice and his grip on her mind is strong."

An image flashed through Brishan's mind — a tall, blond man, handsome, jumping from a train, staring at Claudia as he left. For a quick, painful moment a jolt of jealous anger whipped him senseless. *I cannot waste time on that now.* In the vision, the crooked, broken glass of a window shattered as the man jumped. Outside, the horizon gleamed with pointed turrets. Spires.

The City of Spires. Of course! Prague. She was on a train to Prague. She was going to the capital. He flung himself forward, violently straining against the paralysis. His parents stared at him, tears streaming down their faces, eyes searching his own for clues.

It took all he had to focus on Dane's brown eyes, searching for the calm he knew would be there, desperate for help. The gypsy gazed back at him, his uninjured eye opening more as the energy flowed between them. Brishan tensed, trying to make a sound. His hands remained stiff and open. *Can't...even...write it down.* His eyeballs strained against their sockets with the effort.

"I've never seen this before," Brishan heard his father mumble to Cosima, as they all leaned in towards him.

Cosima's vision had faded entirely. She nodded at Eamon. "I have. It's one thing to have visions of strangers in trouble, it's quite another to feel your beloved in such pain. He can't cope because he's never known such a feeling. It's debilitating. But he's strong. He'll overcome it. I know."

Brishan took some comfort in the words; Cosima was not the type to pretend for the sake of other's feelings. Dane pulled him close. *How is Dane so strong, even as his own daughter faces...God...what?*

He opened his mouth again, but only a rasping sigh came out of his dry lips. Selina put a glass of water to his mouth and he drank as if he'd thirsted for days.

"Just use your mind. One word, Brishan, concentrate on one word. Give it to us," Dane said, closing his eyes as if ready to go into deep meditation.

Brishan closed his own eyes. *Prague. Prague. Prague.* He chanted over and over and prayed that their combined psychic connection was enough to force its way through the pain barrier. His eyes opened and he tasted the salt of a single tear, making its way down his cheek.

And his family stared back at him – their faces blank as they fought his emotions...emotions blocking the path to Claudia.

Chapter Thirteen

Lost

A tranquil breeze caressed Claudia's cheeks and the lake shone with pink-tinged twilight. Jasmine vines crept up the old oak trees, filling the air with their sweet smell and fluffy, white seeds floated on the breeze like tiny parachutes, landing softly on her arms and in her hair.

Dane sat in the grass beside her, one leg crossed over the other, drawing patterns in the dirt beneath the largest oak tree she'd ever seen. She could feel the presence of the chateau — looming like a giant shadow blocking the sun — so she knew they were in the valley somewhere below her childhood home. *But how did we get here?*

Still, it was hard to care about the whys and the hows, with Dane so close and nature stirring all her senses.

"Did you know, those seeds that look like miniature clouds are colonising that mountain slope in the distance?" Dane pointed towards the horizon. "See how they all travel in the one direction? They instinctively know when the breeze is blowing towards their destination and they detach from their pods, ready for the journey."

Claudia looked harder at the seeds. They were all on the same path, rising higher and higher as they drifted further away. "Yes, I see now."

"Today, Claudia, when you helped that man with his heart, you followed your own instinctive path. You knew what to do, even without training. You knew, because it is in your blood…to heal, to help, to do great things."

Claudia rubbed her temples. She didn't want to remember what Dane was talking about. She could sense…danger, somewhere in her mind, pushing forward and trying to puncture her thoughts. But she wasn't going back there. Not now.

Then, Dane smiled at her, his glorious, brown eyes twinkling through the laugh lines. His head was shaved, which was strange. Claudia wanted to ask why. But the temperature was so mild, the air so soft and scented, the grass so cushioning beneath her that questions, talking even, seemed ridiculously irrelevant.

Besides, it looked good; his scalp was brown and perfectly shaped and his hairlessness highlighted the strong contours of his face. Her father's face.

"You're studying me." He chuckled and placed his thumb and forefinger under her chin.

"Do you think we look alike?"

"Hmm, let me see." He stared at her mouth, her eyebrows, her cheeks and her chin. "Our eyes are the same colour. Your mouth is always ready to smile and your eyebrows make you look strong, they're dark and straight like mine."

Claudia smiled, outrageously happy with the resemblances.

"But we are most alike through our souls. The vehicle that carries us is not so important, not in the long run. You'll come to know this too."

Claudia swallowed, consumed by an insurmountable lump in her throat. "Dane?"

"Yes, precious one."

"I…" The words stuck in her throat and tears flowed unchecked down her cheeks.

"It's all right, darling, everything will be fine. Just speak."

"Dad, I…"

A flush of colour swept over Dane's neck and before she could speak, Claudia was caught in a tight hug, her tears disappearing onto his chest. She started to sob, gripping his shoulders and resting her cheek on his muscular arm. She had never felt so safe and so miserable at the same time.

"I can't tell you how it feels to hear you say that," Dane whispered in her ear. "I feel like I've been given the most amazing gift in the world."

Claudia pulled back from his chest and tried to smile. "Something is very, very wrong with my vehicle now, isn't it? I can feel it, somewhere in the distance, but it's tugging me closer."

"I know. Claudia, sweetheart, I know, but hold on here with me, for a little bit longer. I know you can do it."

Claudia pressed her palm against her forehead, pushing against the current inside: the force that was determined to sweep her back. "Tell me more about where we are and how we got here."

"Good girl." Dane smiled. "We're in the astral plane, you and I. You've managed this, you know. Your soul has travelled here, to meet me."

"How?"

"You're asleep, my precious. And I'm meditating on meeting you in the astral plane. Think of it as a long rope that connects us always. Not only us, but Brishan and Oriana and Cosima, all those with gypsy blood."

"Brishan…" Claudia sighed as her hand involuntarily drifted over her heart.

Dane brushed the hair from her forehead. "Brishan's connection to you is strong, stronger even than mine. Now, as we speak, he fights for you."

"I don't understand."

"You will. Without our spiritual self, we are nothing but a vessel. It's like we're…well like a car and the car's engine is the most important part." Dane cocked his head to the side and smiled without showing his teeth. "But, I know…it's hard to think about it like that. Your body feels so important when you're young; there are so many things to discover about it."

Claudia felt the blush creep up her cheeks, instantly remembering the day Brishan had first touched her while they'd swam in the lake. She'd come a long way from the screaming, frightened child she'd been then, physical intimacy didn't only mean the gatekeeper's vile touch.

Fresh tears coated her cheeks as she reached out to hug him again. "I have to tell you something...but you'll hate me," she whispered in his ear.

"Not possible."

"I don't know how to begin." Claudia took a deep breath. "I was...I became...so hurt and angry that you'd all left me."

Dane opened his mouth to speak, his eyebrows tugging inward.

"I know, more than anything, I know, why you had to, especially you," she jumped in before he spoke, looking up at him from underneath her eyelashes. "I'm not brave enough to ask about Oriana. I guess you would have told me if she was...safe."

Dane simply rubbed her shoulder and nodded encouragingly for her to go on.

"Grace and Edward..."

"Ah, yes. Grace." Dane bent his head and stared at the ground for a long time.

"She's arranged my marriage."

Dane looked up and chuckled, softly, under his breath.

Claudia cringed, her shoulders rising upwards, as she mentally arranged her next words. "I fought the whole idea, of course. But, then *he* came. Preston, that is. At first, I hated him. So suave and polished, so...well...from Grace and Edward's world." Claudia held her face in her hands. "There's so much to tell."

"I know, I too, have much to tell. But I sense there's one thing you want to get off your chest. You're brave, I know you are. Tell me."

She took a deep breath. "I started to like him. He was so attentive and polite and, well, fun and...handsome."

"I understand. You were intrigued."

Claudia sighed. "Yes, so much so. Not in the same way I was

— as I am — with Brishan. It doesn't feel like love, or belonging, or trust. All the things I discovered when I met you." She smiled at Dane and he smiled back in a way that tugged on her heart. She didn't want to cry again, but emotion pooled in her stomach. It came bursting out, unheeded.

"But I kissed him," she gulped in air. "And I got drunk and I let him touch me…and I liked it." She hung her head, waiting for his shock and disappointment.

"Oh, Claudia."

She rushed in before he could speak. "Worse than that, I almost wished that Brishan knew, wished that I could hurt him like he'd hurt me. I thought, if he was jealous, he'd come back for me and I thought this, so stupidly, just as I'd decided to come and find you all, to be with you."

"Sweetheart…"

"I know! You think I'm shallow and weak. Maybe I am. I don't want to feel like I do, but I was going to keep doing it anyway. I was going to Prague with Preston and maybe I was even going to marry him. It all seemed like a fairy tale and so, so easy and it felt like you were never coming back. Were you?" She sobbed, a great, heaving sound that ripped from her chest.

"Claudia. Stop." Dane grabbed her shoulders, roughly, and turned her to face him. "This is the last time you berate yourself for something that's simply a part of growing and learning, do you understand?"

"You're…you're not angry?" Claudia's mouth dropped open.

"I can guarantee that Brishan will be mad enough for both of us." He smiled and it took the sting out of his words, a little. "You need to experience life, Claudia. No one would have been happy if you'd stayed in the chateau instead of having adventures, least of all me." He still held her shoulders, though his grip softened.

"As much as I disagree with Grace and all she stands for, I knew you'd be safe and that she'd introduce you to a different side of life, which is what living is about! You needed to have the choice between that life and ours. To do that, you had to experience it. And, my beautiful daughter, of course we were coming back for you. Don't ever doubt us again, we're yours for life."

Claudia crossed her hands over her heart, love for him filling her completely. "I choose you."

"I was hoping you would. But, Claudia, you must understand that even without the vigilante attack at the chateau and Oriana's kidnapping." He grimaced and paused for a moment. "I still would have made sure you spent time with your mother. You needed to be able to make an informed decision about how to live your own life. She is your mother, right or wrong."

Claudia felt a strong pull at the back of her head; white spots dashed in front of her eyes. A slight tingling ran up her leg and continued throughout the whole left side of her body. She reached out to Dane and he engulfed her hand with his own.

"I can't fight this anymore," she whispered.

"I know. It's time. I love you. Brishan loves you. We all do."

"I love you too."

Dane squeezed her hand and kissed her palm, letting her see the tears shining in his eyes. The image of him was fading and black shadows etched shapes over his body until all she could see were the laugh lines on his face and the shimmering water on his cheeks.

Thunderous cracking exploded in her head. She blinked furiously to loosen the dirt and ash coating her lashes and clenched her teeth when sharp specks scratched her eyes. One side of her body was trapped under the fallen baggage shelf and severe, shooting pain pulsed up and down her leg.

The salty tears cleared the dirt and she saw a bright light. *Sunlight? In the train?* It blurred her vision and she remained still, focusing ahead for long seconds as her mind struggled to register anything but pain. Cool air circulated, moving the dust in small patterns in front of her nose. She sneezed, wincing as the movement caught her rib cage.

Outside, grass came into focus and beyond was a hill, dotted with houses. A gaping, jagged hole in the side of the train served as her window and precious sunlight streamed through it, warming her face and distracting her, briefly, from her battered limbs. Voices, echoing in the distance, reached her ears. She opened her mouth to scream. Nothing but a rattling moan came out. She closed her eyes for relief from the sharp stinging. Only now, under darkness, did she feel the motion of the train, a slow rocking, and the occasional roar of a power tool, suffocating the distant yelling.

Where is Grace? Alive or dead? Claudia couldn't sense any life nearby, only her own terror as it gnawed at her stomach. The voices sounded so far away, maybe at the very front of the train.

A numbing sensation invaded her legs, spreading over her trapped toes to her calves and thighs. *Like severe pins and needles, it's killing the pain as it comes.* Claudia stretched her neck to try to see outside. *Please, someone walk by, please.*

But the small movement of her head put too much pressure on her trapped arm. As her shoulder popped out of its socket a silent scream tore at her throat. Her eyes shut against the white-hot pain.

It was almost unbearable. She was dizzy, desperate to give herself up to the pain. But, one more time, she opened her eyes and relished the rays of sunlight, with the dust particles shimmering as they floated. *Amazing, nature can turn even the most horrific things into something beautiful.*

She sighed at the thought and the sound of her own voice reached her ears. *Ah — too late to scream now.* Surely such pain meant her body was broken beyond repair. She didn't panic, there was only an overwhelming calm that threaded through her, infusing her with white light. And this was to her a place of no return...*bliss*

And there they were, Snow-White and Rose-Red, returned to her in her moment of need, floating above the grass outside.

Someone else was there too, running towards the makeshift window. His black hair streamed behind him in the wind and he ran like an athlete, arms pumping strongly, consistently at his sides.

"This is it then," she whispered into the dirt on the floor, waiting to take her last breath, ready to greet whichever gypsy relative came fast to take her to the afterlife.

The runner was so close she could hear his heavy breathing. In an instant, the sun blacked out and the heavy breathing consumed her — and the smell, the smell so familiar; like sandalwood and rain.

"Claudia."

And that voice. So cherished, so soothing, something out of a dream.

"Claudia, open your eyes. Please, my fairy, look at me."

Dare she open her eyes and view the afterlife? Her head felt so fuzzy and light, like it would float off her neck any moment. *But that voice...*

Something warm touched her forehead. It was a hand. The gentle movement, back and forth, making waves of pleasure cascade down her body, infiltrating and relaxing her muscles, cooling the flames of pain licking at her bones.

"That's it, my fairy, let yourself relax, accept the pain, don't fight it. It will fade, I promise you."

Claudia's eyes snapped open. There, above her, Brishan's bright, green jewels gazed at her, glistening and soft, imparting all the love and healing from his body into her own.

"You came for me," she whispered, her stomach clenching.

"I never left you, not really, not in here." Brishan pointed to his heart and smiled his lopsided, beautiful smile.

This can't be real. I'm dead. Surely he's not really here, leaning over my broken body, healing my pain and staring at me with such... love.

"Are we... Where are we? Am I dead?"

"No, beautiful, you're not. I'm here, with you. You're fully conscious. Can you hear that noise?"

She'd been blocking out the harsh sounds of screams and power tools, but now her ears rang with the sound of drills and sharp hammering.

"That's the rescue team. They're coming in through the carriage in front of this one." He tensed, clutching her one good arm. He did not take his eyes off hers.

Claudia breathed deep to allow words to come through the limited air in her lungs. "Tell them to be careful! Grace is over there, right near the door, but she's trapped..." And the hoarse sound that was her voice stopped abruptly.

Brishan's lips tightened into a pale, straight line and he bent down, so that his nose touched hers, his hand still stroking her face. "Claudia. Grace can never be hurt again."

As his words started to make sense, Claudia watched him pull a bottle of water out of a bag on his back and tip it up so tiny droplets dribbled into her mouth. His eyes flicked over her trapped body and his chest rose and fell too quickly.

"How do you know, did you see her?"

"No." He shook his head and kissed the tip of her nose. "The rescue team told me they'd found you, both of you, earlier. They thought you were dead, Claudia, and they couldn't reach you... They helped others while they called for equipment to come and cut you out. Grace, well, she'd fallen out of the train, probably at the same time you got trapped." He dipped the edge of his shirt in the water and softly wiped her face. "My fairy. Brace yourself. They've taken her body away."

Claudia sighed and inhaled Brishan's smell. "And Preston could have saved her," she whispered to herself.

Brishan paused, then began to wipe away the blood and dirt, now from her neck and arm. Gently, he touched her knee, staring at the wound left by the glass shard. His face paled.

"I'm sorry about your mother, Claudia," he whispered as his

eyes came back to rest on her face.

"I hardly knew her."

"I know."

Deep understanding passed between them. *He knows. He knows what I feel.*

"Ahoj," a deep voice bellowed. It belonged to a dirty face, suddenly peering at them through the hole.

"Er…can you speak English?" Brishan turned to face him.

"Yes." The man scratched his beard as he looked at Claudia. "Now, we will lift the rack from your feet. Up and up, okay? Pain, yes, but the ambulance is outside and we will stretcher you out. Okay?" He frowned, as if concentrating hard on speaking perfect English.

Claudia nodded, reaching out to grip Brishan's hand.

"Focus your eyes on mine, Claudia," Brishan said, crossing his legs under him and leaning in close to her face.

She held his gaze and took a deep breath as more men moved into the carriage, carefully moving debris and luggage and positioning themselves around the metal frame.

"Okay, we will try to move this now; we hope we won't need the saws," the man said. He flexed his muscles, glancing at his team of rescuers. "On three. Ready?" He waited until each of the six men nodded. "One, two, three."

A dull, loud groan filled the air. The men heaved the rack upwards, lifting it off her feet first, then her legs, before pushing it over the demolished seats. Excruciating pain. Claudia's head fell backwards, her eyes involuntarily closing. She bit her lip to stop the scream, but it came out anyway, shattering the sudden silence that followed the extreme effort.

"Claudia, come back to me, look at me. Now." Brishan held the back of her neck and rubbed her check, coaxing her eyes open. She tried, she tried so hard but her eyelids fluttered and the darkness beckoned. Her head swam in circles and bile rose in her throat as her stomach churned.

Two fingers now rested in the middle of her eyebrows, the 'third eye' Dane had called it. The pressure calmed her fluttering lids and she was able to hold them open, long enough to see Brishan's face, so tender and so pained. She felt like a fragile, baby bird as he cradled her head in both arms now and continued pressing her forehead.

"Everything's going to be fine, Claudia, the medics are bringing pain killers. They'll be here any moment. I...promise." His voice broke and faded into a whisper.

A rabble of voices descended and suddenly, Claudia saw a woman standing over her. *Where had she come from?* Brishan gently lifted her arm towards the woman. She felt a sharp jab, then Brishan placed her arm back in his lap, pressing points in her hand. She relaxed into the calming pressure.

The dark behind her eyes became even harder to resist. So cool and quiet and pain free. The emerald eyes she loved so much held her gaze, and she wanted to keep his gaze, but it was too late to fight anymore, even with him alongside her, giving her every ounce of his soul to lean on.

"Claudia, please, please stay with me, my fairy. We're nearly there, the stretcher's coming and we'll be in the hospital before you know it." His voice was so distant now and his face, that gorgeous face — winged eyebrows bent inwards and jaw clenched and pulsating — was disappearing. She tried to smile, really concentrated on it, just to show she'd heard him, knew she loved him. Tears rolled down his cheeks, and as they landed on her chest, she remembered the story he'd told her when they'd first met, about tears making dreams come true, and as she prayed that the story was real, she managed to smile, just a little, before all noise, all light, all pain, disappeared.

Why is the world so white? Her nose refused to take in air and a slow, methodical *beep, beep, beep* rang through her head. She scanned the room with her eyes only, while her head remained immobile and trapped in the white. A face smiled above her, its startling, white teeth blending with the surroundings.

"Claudia! Oh, my darling, how very thrilling to see you open your eyes. I'll call for the doctor." The shiny, white teeth glared at her as the lips moved.

Rushing feet announced a new, smiling face. "Hello, Claudia, my name is Doctor Novákový. Do you know where you are?" The man in a white coat fussed over her, fiddling with a machine at her side and adjusting a tube in her arm. *Why are those in my arm?*

"No," she said. She recognised the kind of place, but the actual word just wouldn't come to her.

"You're in the hospital. You were in a train accident. You have a broken leg, wrist and a fractured pelvis. Your shoulder was dislocated. All in all, after a period of recovery, you will be completely back to normal." Doctor Novákový's voice was monotonous and clipped, but kind. "Really, you are a very lucky girl, to be alive."

An accident? Only blank space greeted her when she tried to understand him. For the first time she noticed her leg; encased in an ugly, large metal brace.

The doctor turned to the sparkling white teeth. "She is going to be very confused for some time, weeks maybe, she has concussion and shock. Just gently release information as needed and she will slowly return to normal."

The handsome face peered down at her again with a smile. "Claudia, do you recognise me?"

Yes! The dimples and the teeth and the blond, blond hair. "Preston, of course, silly!" *Why would he ask something so absurd?*

"Good girl. Edward is here too and you needn't concern yourself with the secret you've kept for so long. I know all about it and I think it's wonderful! You must not concern yourself with anything, dear girl, but recovering."

Secret? Nothing like a secret came to mind. In fact, she understood *absolutely nothing.*

"Your father is understandably eager to help you, and it will be so much easier for you, not having to pretend he's *only* your distant cousin. No one cares about children being born out of wedlock these days anyway. Aren't you relieved, darling? I'm sure Grace would have been."

"Where is Grace?" Last time Claudia recalled seeing her mother was right before dinner, on the eve of a trip of some sort, as Margaret had bustled around them, packing suitcases and warning her of 'earthly pleasures'.

"Oh, Claudia, I'm so sorry, my darling," said Preston taking her hand. "Grace…she died, in the accident. You don't remember anything, at all?"

Claudia gasped. "No. She's dead?"

"Yes. I'm so very sorry. We will all miss her dearly." Preston's lips curved downward. "There was a terribly bad train crash. Hundreds dead, darling. You are very lucky to be alive, and Edward and I, would you believe, escaped with barely a scratch. Blessed, I tell you. We are all blessed."

Grace. Gone? No… She'd been gone before, but now, in the last few months, she'd come back. She'd returned, eventually, to claim what was hers. *Surely that meant something.*

"You mustn't worry, I'll look after you. Edward will too. Of course he shares your grief." Preston stared at her, his face a study of exaggerated sadness.

The words were like a life raft just as she began to flounder. "Thank you."

"Oh, silly Claudia, you don't have to thank me. It's my duty… I mean, well it's the least I can do for the woman who will soon be my wife!" He laughed, too loudly for the quiet room. "Now, darling, as you're awake…there is one more matter we should discuss. It's rather urgent."

"Claudia!" A cool breeze swept over her face as she saw a figure running to her side from the open doorway.

"Speak of the devil," Preston said, folding his arms and glaring at the intruder.

"You're awake, my precious fairy."

"Brishan?" She stared, unable to believe he was here, in front of her, after all this time.

"Just give me the word, Claudia, and I will have him removed. He has refused to budge from your side all night, despite Edward and I being quite firm with him. Cursed public hospitals…if only we were back in England, where riff-raff like this are kept out of such places. Unfortunately we could not stop him from coming to the hospital. Godforsaken boy won't even speak to us, but I imagine he was on the same train, worst luck." Preston's fists curled at his sides.

Brishan did not glance at Preston, or show signs he had heard anything. He reached out to stroke her cheek, but Claudia flinched. Hurt came like a torrential downpour, flooding her body. *Why now? After he abandoned me so long ago?*

She lifted her hand and tried to rip out the pipes blocking her nose. Her chest heaved and adrenalin rushed through her veins so fast it felt like she was sprinting as fast as her legs would carry her. *Move. Escape.* But her broken body lay limp, helplessly trapped on the bed.

"Claudia, what is it? Are you in pain? You might need more morphine." Brishan's eyes darted to the machines controlling her world. His hands raised high above his head, splaying out and descending over her body.

Love for him exploded through her, mixing with the uncontrollable hurt. The emotions swirled and battled against each other, neither winning. But both serving to build a tension so fierce it blinded any thought.

There was now a loud, rapid beeping from the machines and she could hear feet rushing, coming closer and closer. She gasped and clawed at her throat, pushing his hands away and staring as white-coated men invaded the room.

"See what you've done? Leave, now!" Preston shouted, his voice almost a growl.

Claudia looked from one to the other as she was moved and prodded by the doctors. The beeping pierced her ears, drowning the sound of her thudding heart. As an oxygen mask was pushed onto her face, she took a deep breath, desperate for air.

"Claudia, he needs to leave, he should never have been here. Goddamn gypsies, as if they haven't caused you enough trouble. Just nod, darling, and I'll have him removed." Preston caught her hand in his own, squeezing it until she looked at him.

But she could not look away from Brishan's gaze, a gaze that never wavered from her face. Yet, his eyes were wild and confused as he raked a hand through his dark hair. She'd started to feel so safe, just moments ago, calm even, in the circle of Preston's care.

And this beautiful gypsy brought chaos, and she couldn't stand the feelings building, building, threatening to destroy her sanity.

She looked at Preston, closed her eyes — and nodded.

Chapter Fourteen

A Wash of Red

The cigarette smoke curled above his head, drifting in smooth arcs towards the trees. All was quiet inside the caravan and he knew his family sat in silence, waiting for him, sending their love out to cocoon his aching heart.

Finally, Dane emerged, his arm sitting at a stiff angle but almost mobile, his face still covered in yellow-tinged blotches. "You saved her, Brishan, that's all that matters for now."

"I know."

"I've tried to contact her again, but I can't. She's not...her mind isn't open to it in the state she's in."

"I know."

"Come inside, have some food. There's a lot to do — and plan."

Brishan stubbed his cigarette out on the step. He stared into Dane's eyes, for the first time since he'd returned in the early hours of the morning. What he saw, in those dark depths, the knowing soul of his uncle, tugged at the knots in his stomach.

He swallowed, the movement painful against his dry throat. "I saw an article, in the paper at the airport, about a human trafficking ring in Germany."

"Yes, I saw it too, and yes, it's linked. Next week, we finish this," Dane said.

"I thought as much. I'm ready."

Dane placed a strong hand on his shoulder. "I feel your pain, but you can't use this battle to hurt yourself any further. I see it on your face, your need for revenge. It's a crazy urge, Brishan and it makes us rush into the face of danger."

"Isn't that precisely what we're doing?"

"Not in that way, no. You must have full focus and that's

impossible if you're so affected…if you're so much under the influence of your emotions."

"I know."

"Brishan."

"Yes."

"I will not force you to do this; you know that, don't you?"

"Of course."

"Let Cosima help you, please. Oriana's life depends on all of us…our skill, our minds, we must be focused."

"No, I won't have this taken away from me."

"Holding on to your anger won't bring Claudia closer, but holding on to your love will."

A dull roar raged inside his head. Surging, banking, threatening to overflow. The raw, harsh reality of her rejection of him stabbed his heart; thinking of the blond man made him boil. His fear for her well-being consumed him.

"Her pain…her pain was so intense. But she was so brave, so strong, so much the image of you."

Dane's jaw clenched and he lowered his head, almost bowing to him. "My gratitude for you, for her life, is infinite."

"You would have gone, if you'd been able." Brishan cringed at Dane's obvious struggle, torn between lover and daughter and the injuries that had stopped him from helping them. "But it would have…she may have…if only you'd been there, instead of me."

"Her mind will clear, her soul will fight. And she loves you."

Brishan nodded, aching to believe it, even as the memory of her face, fearful and full of distrust at the hospital, scarred his soul. He stared at Dane's rapidly healing body.

"You haven't told me, the rest of the story…how you got hurt?

"Ah. Such are the tortures of the world you will enter, all too soon." Dane still stared at the ground, his face a closed, tight-lipped sculpture. "An angry client, who I was ordered to…remove…didn't like being ordered around. It's that simple."

He shrugged.

God, what he must have suffered. "I'll let Cosima help. Only because I'd die for you, for all of you."

Dane nodded, once. "As would I. This time, my boy, it won't be necessary. But thank you...thank you for the offer." Half a smile cracked the marble face as he walked back inside.

Only minutes later, Cosima emerged. She held out a glass filled with murky, green liquid. "Drink."

Brishan took it, swirling the gritty, thick relaxant around his tongue before swallowing in one gulp.

"Now. Relax until the morning. You must drink again when you wake, and twice every day after that. No more, you hear, or the valerian root will make you sleep for days."

Almost immediately, Brishan felt the potion warm his stomach, his eyelids becoming heavy with its potency. The danger from Cosima's potions was not to his health, but to his mind. Too much, and he could become numb and oblivious to all around him. He walked to the back of the caravan, to his single bed, squashed in its own compartment, and lay down. His arms crossed his chest, holding on to his love for Claudia as the anger and pain diminished with sleep.

Over and over again, Dane's plan replayed in his mind. Brishan wore a black suit, the most expensive cloth that had ever touched his skin, and his hair was pulled back into a sleek ponytail. The red shirt beneath his jacket gleamed in the sun and his shiny shoes rubbed blisters into the back of his feet.

Although it had only been hired for the day, the outfit cost more money than he'd ever seen. The fake business cards and passport, courtesy of his father's forgery skills, sat uncomfortably in his left pocket. He rubbed his finger over the new moustache and the hair round his chin, shaved so finely. He scanned the busy traffic as it raced by London's famous Harrods building — and he waited.

His heartbeat thudded, slow and steady, numbed by Cosima's drugs. He felt no panic, only mild discomfort in the heat of the sun in the thick, Armani suit.

Before it came to a complete stop, Brishan knew the black limousine, with dark tinted windows, would be for him. The back door opened and a pint-sized man, with brown, slanted eyes and a pointed goatee, stared at him from inside.

"Mr Valentino?" he asked, a smile stretching a pink scar on his left cheek.

"Yes," Brishan replied, nodding and forcing himself to grin.

"I am Mr Sidaki. Please, come." The man gestured for Brishan to enter the car, sliding over to create room for him on the seat.

"Before we can further conduct business, I'm sure you understand our need for complete privacy within our operations."

"Yes." Brishan nodded once.

"Please do not be alarmed, this is merely a precaution on our behalf and will be removed the moment we are on the premises. I assure you, once you arrive at our establishment, you will be amply rewarded." With that, Mr Sidaki pulled a black hood out from a brief case and placed it over Brishan's head, patting him down at the same time.

Brishan was not alarmed by the action, Dane had briefed him on all possibilities, but the black cloth made it hard to breathe and the loss of sight unnerved him, breaking through the numbness from Cosima's potion.

"May I check your identification?"

"Of course." Brishan tried to make his voice sound confident and calm through the material. He felt Mr Sidaki reach into his jacket pocket and pull out the cards and the passport. The long silence was only punctuated by the soft hum of the car's powerful engine. His own breath, slow and regular, grew loud in his ears.

"Very good. This is all in order. Thank you for your cooperation. We will arrive shortly." The Japanese accent was oddly comforting in its extreme politeness. His documents had passed the test. He felt a slight pressure on his chest as Mr Sidaki pushed them back into his pocket.

He didn't bother trying to calculate where they were taking him; he knew they entered the bowels of the city, far below the major tourist attractions and business hubs. An Italian accent, required for the ruse, played over and over in his head, along with visuals of a swaggering, self-absorbed celebrity. Dane had joked that it wasn't quite enough of a stretch.

It was now, faced with the reality of their plan.

The car came to a stop and he was led, by a hand placed coolly on his elbow, down a long straight path, then into an air-conditioned place where his feet landed on a thick, carpeted floor. The hood was removed and he breathed deeply; the air smelled of alcoholic spirits, fresh roses and leather.

"Welcome, Mr Valentino, to The Lair." A woman spoke, her white-blonde hair glowing in the light of an elaborate chandelier. A floor to ceiling mirror behind her showcased a slender, naked back in a red dress, hugging her hips and running the length of her long legs to the floor.

"It is an honour to be here," Brishan replied, bending to kiss both her cheeks.

Her soft, pillowy lips stretched in a dazzling smile and she hooked her arm through his, steering him towards another room.

"What may I get you to drink?"

"Cognac, on ice."

"Certainly. Please, take a seat." She gestured towards four black leather chairs, all facing a curtained stage. Soft candlelight illuminated black walls, adorned with statues of entwined, naked bodies and crystal vases brimming with blood red roses. A cigar cabinet overflowed with Cuba's finest and slow, rhythmical drumbeats filled the silence.

Brishan pulled an envelope from his pocket. A down payment of ten thousand dollars, cash. The money Dane had earned in this very establishment. Money they could have used to rebuild their life. Money that was about to slide down his throat in the form of expensive alcohol.

The blonde retrieved the envelope and ice-cubes clinked as she placed the drink in his hand. He turned to the back of the room, conscious of a new, barely noticeable presence. Two figures, blending seamlessly with the black walls, moved towards the shadows in the far corner. They were almost as silent as they were invisible. His breathing steadied with their arrival.

A soft hand ran the length of his arm. "Please relax, security is a necessity that I'm sure someone with your wealth can appreciate. You will soon forget they are here." The blonde knelt in front of him, her wide, blue eyes deceivingly innocent.

"Of course." Brishan tilted his head and winked.

"You are an actor, yes?"

Brishan feigned shock. "Yes, but how do you know that? It is of utmost importance that my visit here is…in secret."

She laughed, a low husky sound. "Everyone's visit here is secret. It is important we know who we are dealing with, though. As the madam, I'm made privy to the information."

"I understand."

"I saw your photo, recently, in a magazine. You are much better looking in real life."

"*Grazie* — and you, too, are beautiful."

"Ah, and the Italian accent, so sexy." She knelt further between his legs, pushing them apart to stroke his inner thighs. Brishan focused on the long, red fingernails instead of the fire starting in his groin. One finger ran over the zip of his expensive pants, up and down, up and down, until he felt them stretch and pull uncomfortably with his erection. He lay back into the soft leather, closing his eyes in an effort to coax his body back from its betrayal of him. She laughed again, softly.

"Not yet, gorgeous one, but soon. First, you must make your choice." She stood, elegant and tall, and swept her hand towards the stage. "There are ten women for you to choose from. The first five, you may have for your own personal use while in London. The last five are our most expensive acquisitions — they are for sale. As you'd appreciate, offers have already been made on them, so your price needs to be, shall we say…generous."

Brishan forced himself to smile as he sat straight in the chair. She gazed at him, gently biting her bottom lip. Then, she pointed a remote control towards the stage. A red curtain slid across a glass wall. Inside, gold tassels glimmered from hanging lanterns. They dangled from the roof, from the tops of a gold, ornate chair in the middle of the room, shooting sparks of light over red-velvet walls.

A girl sauntered in. No more than eighteen, her long, red hair tumbled below her hips in dramatic contrast to the white dress clinging to her slender form. The dress was transparent enough to see the outline of dark, erect nipples and the shadow of pubic hair between her thighs. She was breathtaking — and the defeated look on her face heartbreaking. Brishan breathed deeply, stilling the rage flaring within.

The blonde goddess looked at him, quirking a finely arched brow.

"She is lovely. But redheads are not for me."

"Certainly." She flicked another button and the curtain closed on the girl's silhouette.

"They can't see me?"

"No, they see only their own reflections."

"Lucky them," Brishan joked and felt bile rise in his throat.

He braced himself against the next, and the next and the next girl in the long line of women, more beautiful, more vulnerable each time the curtain parted. Finally, they came to the last two of the five most expensive women. His palms stuck to the leather armrest as his adrenalin peaked. He gestured to the blonde goddess to reveal the next woman.

"She is part Japanese, part German and part Hawaiian. A sensual cocktail, wouldn't you agree?"

Tall, with a mass of thick, raven hair, ivory skin and a face like a fine china doll. His soul ached for the woman, possibly in her late twenties. Her beauty, like Oriana's, had obviously only increased with age. She was almost certainly destined for a rich oil sheik or underground mafia boss. *Not if I have any breath left in my body.*

"I can see this one creates passion in you." The blonde goddess bent over his shoulder to whisper in his ear. Her red nail trailed from his cheekbone to his mouth.

"Yes, she is exquisite. They all are, but I'm a man who likes many choices." He caught her hand in his own, bringing it towards his mouth and running her fingers over his lips.

She smiled, tracing her hand down his neck and over his chest. "Of course."

When the curtain next opened, Brishan felt a small part of his heart die. *Oh God, precious Oriana, what have they done to you?* His aunt stood so still, gazing into the glass, her stare blank and listless when it should have been intense with the gypsy fire that coursed through her veins. Her wild beauty was perfectly framed by a scarlet dress, cut low at the front and slashed into strategically placed strips, seductively swirling around her lean legs.

The olive skin, so like his own, glowed with oil or something they'd rubbed over her bare shoulders and her chocolate brown hair flowed in perfect waves to the swell of her hips.

A sharp, muffled intake of breath reached his ears from the shadows in the corner, causing a wave of pain to roll over him – pain that was not his own. He tasted anger, regret, guilt, overwhelming love and sadness.

Dane's.

His eyes flicked to the blonde goddess and he noticed a small frown appear on the smooth forehead. She stood as if to walk towards the hidden security guards. Brishan clutched her arm.

"This is a hard choice. How will I make my mind up?" He ran his finger over the fine veins in her wrist. She was immediately distracted.

"Perhaps something to take your mind off it for a while? Then you can come back to them with fresh eyes." She curled her fingers around his cheek.

He smiled and stood to pull her into him, looking over her head, watching as his aunt swayed, unsteady on her feet. Oriana's eyes rolled back and the tassels above flickered as her arms reached out to no one.

She fell, noiselessly, to the ground.

"My God," Brishan said, pushing the blonde goddess away and staring, mouth open, at the stage.

The blonde's arms flew up in the air. "Men!"

Two black clad figures raced from their hiding spots, entering the stage from a door behind the curtains. She pointed the remote control at the glass, jabbing it over and over towards the curtains until they closed on Oriana's motionless form.

"What is wrong with her, do you think?" Brishan asked, eyes wide with feigned shock.

"Oh, nothing serious I'm sure, perhaps she just hasn't eaten today. They like to stay skinny, these beautiful women. Come, we will wait outside until she is...tended to." Her eyes darted from side to side as she pulled him towards the door.

Brishan scanned the room and noticed the cameras, small black objects secured into the ornate carvings on the roof, barely noticeable unless under close inspection. A phone rang, somewhere, and before he could speak further, his hostess picked up a small, silver object and murmured, "Yes," into it, three, four, five times.

"Mr Valentino," she said with a teeth-baring smile as she put the phone down. "Unfortunately, we must end today's viewing, but we will accommodate you for another appointment as soon as you wish."

"But, this is unacceptable!" Brishan waved his arms in the air, channelling an Italian in a fit of passion.

"I know and I do apologise. But Mr Sidaki is already on his way, to take you out. I'm afraid I cannot offer any further explanation. You will be suitably compensated, however, when you return." Her pink tongue ran over her teeth as she smiled, reaching her hand towards his crotch and pressing her whole body into his.

Brishan gripped her shoulders, kissing her, putting on a show for the cameras. She moaned into his mouth, her tongue circling his, her hands almost inside his pants.

Mr Sidaki cleared his throat as he approached. Brishan pulled back, wiped his mouth with the back of his hand and looked at the Japanese man. He held the black hood, a smirk playing on his thin lips as he twisted his goatee into a fine point with his thumb and forefinger.

"Nice to see you again, Mr Valentino. We will go, and I will bring you back when it is appropriate."

Brishan nodded, staring at the blonde goddess until the hood was placed, once again, over his eyes.

The potion had worn off; his heart raced as he left the limousine, thanked Mr Sidaki in a flourish of hand gestures and superfluous words, and hailed a taxi. *Fuck, so much traffic.* The Tower of London seemed hours away in the throng. Brishan drummed his fingers on the seat, closing his eyes to view the map in his mind. The map to Seething Lane. The image of skulls on an archway that lead to a church. The need for perfect timing with the corpse collector...

Don't think about where this is leading. Stay focused.

As the taxi slowed, gaping skulls came into view, guarding the entrance to secrets long held. Brishan breathed deep and removed his suit, rolling it up and squashing it under the passenger seat. *Some lucky bastard will find it and benefit from our lies.* Underneath, he wore a plain black jumper and skintight jeans. He pulled the hood down over his face. Spare notes were scrunched inside the pocket and he pushed a handful at the driver, his eyes already locked across the road on the deserted alleyway.

Where is my father? As the taxi motored away, leaving him alone in the street, Brishan's eyes searched the shadows for Eamon, hoping for a glimpse while the road stood empty between them. Rubbish bags lined the ancient walls and he covered his nose. *Dad definitely drew the short straw having to hide in that.*

Tyres screeched in the distance and Brishan lunged inside a red phone booth, his shoulder slamming into the glass. In seconds, a black van took the corner hard, the driver poised to turn down the alley.

Sweat prickled his forehead. Seconds ticked by.

Red hair flashed by his vision as Eamon leapt from a garbage pile, hurtling himself at the windscreen of the van. With a sickening thud, his father's body smashed into the bonnet. The van's breaks screeched to a stop and the driver flung the door open, his thick, muscular trunk coming in to view as he prepared to deal with the intruder stuck on his windscreen.

It's now or never. Brishan ignored the pain in his shoulder and surged forward, launching himself on the driver. He gripped the thick neck and sought the pressure point, just above the man's temple, with his fingers.

*One, two, three, four...this will break my hand...five, six...*the man slumped to the ground.

"Perfect...timing." Eamon pealed himself from the bonnet, breathless as he slid into the passenger seat and crouched low on the floor.

Brishan jumped behind the wheel, shoved the van into gear and turned it, with agonising control, into the alleyway. Minutes later, the security guards appeared, shielded behind giant garbage bins, one of which hid the entrance to Oriana's captive hell.

Brishan stared straight ahead, eyes unblinking. *Cameras, think of the cameras, don't move.* He visualised Oriana, bundled in a black bag between Dane and the other guard — her skin cold and lifeless from the opium potion Cosima had concocted and Dane had smuggled into her food. He tried to silence his thoughts, to send healing energy to her — for she had mere hours before the potion infiltrated her blood completely, stopping the flow to her heart.

Dane's face appeared at the window, his disguise so perfectly constructed Brishan barely recognised him. "Identification please."

Brishan mentally steadied his hands as he shoved the false documents towards his uncle.

Dane glanced at them and turned to nod at the other security guard — standing at the back of the van, the black bag drooping in his arms. His uncle nodded, again. With a click that echoed through the silent alley, the back door opened and the bag was dropped, unceremoniously, on the floor of the van. Brishan allowed himself a quick intake of breath, and Dane shot him a look of relief, as the door closed on Oriana's motionless form.

"Stop, motherfuckers."

Fuck. I didn't press hard enough, long enough. The thug driver he thought he'd immobilised stumbled towards them, thick veins throbbing in his neck as his hands fisted.

So. The ruse is over then. This thug made a living out of collecting the bodies of murdered women, butchered and battered women, lost to the world because of the insane desires of a few.

Brishan felt all the anger of the past days rush his body in a wave so strong he yelled with the pain of it. His body flew from the car before his mind registered its actions. He threw himself on the driver, slamming his fist into the side of the man's face. The thug collapsed forward, clutching his injured eye.

"Ahh." Brishan's knuckles were a mottled mass of blood and hanging flesh. The thug looked up, met his gaze, and roared like an injured animal.

Brishan was ready.

As Dane rushed at the security guard, Brishan leapt into the air and, with all his strength kicked the driver's head. The neck snapped backwards and, as the body stumbled in slow motion, the legs gave way. Brishan drew breath again only when the man fell, to the ground, now still and silent.

"Brishan, get in the car, now," Eamon hissed. Brishan heard the engine start.

Too late.

Move. Move. His legs froze. A heavy metal rod clamped over his throat, squeezing the air from his lungs. His throat burned and his eyes watered.

Dane was running towards him, face wild and violent, throwing punches over Brishan's head. The air rang with the crack of breaking bones.

The guard's blood spurted over his face. The metal rod dropped and Brishan leapt back, furiously swiping at his eyes.

Dane, fuck, Dane, get up. His uncle struggled with the security guard and blood coated them both in a wash of red.

Brishan anchored himself in his anger, summoning it, urging it to overflow. The metal rod rolled uselessly over the gravel, waiting for him, beckoning to his rage. Gripping it like a baseball bat, he smashed the weapon across the security guard's head. The man stilled, his mouth forming a silent scream.

Dane. We did it. I'm getting you out of here. Throwing the rod aside, he hooked Dane under one arm, hauling him towards the van.

"I'm okay, go, I'll follow," said Dane, blood spilling from his lips as he spoke. Brishan turned, let go for a second as he reached for the van, turning again to pull Dane to safety.

A shot rang out, echoing over the metal rubbish bins and rebounding off the narrow walls.

And then, he heard rushing feet.

Dane's mouth opened, and Brishan stared at his uncle's chest. A dark stain soaked through Dane's shirt.

Brishan propelled himself from the car, reaching for Dane, catching him as he fell to the ground.

"Go. Now. I know I can't be saved. I know Brishan, I feel it. Hurry," Dane rasped, a stream of blood chasing the words from his mouth.

The agonising pain stabbing his own chest proved Dane's words. The calm, beatific light pouring from his uncle's eyes asked to be obeyed. *But I will ignore it, I love you, you will not leave us.*

"My body...it's not important. Go...please. You only have seconds to save Oriana. I love you." Dane's words gurgled.

Then his body became a dead weight in Brishan's arms.

He felt pressure on the back of his shirt.

His father; grabbing his collar, pulling him into the van, slamming the door on Dane's body. Brishan gasped, fighting for air as Eamon shoved his head towards the floor of the passenger seat.

A voice echoed through the alleyway, reaching Brishan's ears with eerie clarity. The voice was familiar, rasping, mocking. "I hoped to prolong your torture, Dane."

Another shot blasted a hole in the back window. Eamon accelerated and the van shot forward. Glass shattered around them and shards pierced Brishan's skin.

He looked back, his heart leaping from his chest.

A familiar face hung over the top of a shotgun, the receding hairline shining in a sliver of light. The short, stout body heaved as he stared, smiling, at Dane's lifeless body beneath him. When recognition hit, a roar ripped from somewhere deep inside and Brishan slammed his fist into the dashboard.

That body, that head like a pit-bull. There was only one person it could be.

Claudia's stepfather. Edward.

Chapter Fifteen

Take it Back

Claudia moved her feet towards the room, guided by the lazy moan of a thin reed pipe. The room was hazy with smoke, the air inside rolled over her, its tendrils thick and musky. A woman beckoned, her eyes half-closed. Claudia watched, transfixed, as the woman tossed long, red hair over her shoulder and lifted a stiletto-clad foot. Her leg, impossibly long and slender, stretched over the lap of a man reclining in a black, leather chair. The redhead's mini-skirt slipped up to her waist as she eased her body forward. The man's fingers glistened with gold rings, as his arms circled her thighs, pulling her towards his grinding pelvis.

Why does she still stare at me?

Claudia dragged her eyes away, glancing around the unfamiliar room.

Men stood in all four corners, ramrod straight, guns held tight against their chests.

Her breath caught in her throat at their empty expressions. *Why am I here? Can't remember, but it feels...important.* Fingers grazed her arms, reaching out from the black walls. Someone breathed, too close to her ear, whispering, sliding moist lips over her neck. She shivered, turning to make it stop.

All eyes fixed on the doorway, focusing on a newcomer. One gun lifted, glinting in the candlelight, aimed at the door. The smell of rain and wet earth and sandalwood rushed over her. She inhaled deeply, pulling the scent into her lungs, tensing her body from the exquisite pleasure of it.

He's here, as always, he comes.

Brishan's eyes glowed, his winged brows drew together and his naked, upper torso gleamed with sweat. A thick vein, running the length of his neck, pulsed as he faced the gunman.

Her mouth opened to scream. *Run Brishan, run!* She walked but it was like moving through quicksand. She wanted to throw herself in front, to shield him. Die for him.

But her legs wouldn't cooperate.

Brishan moved to stand in front the gun, staring straight down the barrel. *No fear for his own life.*

Her scream escaped from deep within; a piercing arc of terror.

"Claudia! Wake up."

She gasped, opening one eye and squinting towards the sun streaming in the window. Preston bent over her, shaking her shoulder. He quirked a disapproving eyebrow.

"Why are you shaking me?" She rolled over to wipe her eyes and escape his hand.

"You were screaming! It sounded like you were being murdered."

"Oh." The dream flooded back, filling her with heavy dread.

Brishan again, Brishan, who only ever appeared in nightmares. Especially one. A recurring dream of him staring down at her at the site of the train crash. It was real, she could even smell him, hear his soothing voice, taste the salt from his tears as they dripped on her face — and it haunted her sleep most nights.

This dream, this night, was new. New and terrifying.

That and the image of the long, white hall of the hospital, the pain invading her body and the silence in between the beeping machines, the image that flashed through her mind each time she awoke.

And always Brishan, standing at the end of her bed, equal doses of love and anguish distorting his face.

"The gypsy again?" Preston rolled his eyes.

"Yes. It feels so real."

"Just nightmares, nothing more. I'm not surprised you have nightmares about those god-awful creatures. But they're gone now... You haven't seen them in over a year. Put them from your mind once and for all, then the nightmares will stop." Preston splayed his hands in front of her face, as if he'd stop the dreams with his own physical actions.

"That's just it, Brishan isn't on my mind and I barely even recall the others. I mean, only sometimes, when I think of the chateau. It's just my dreams that he's attacking, as if he was at the hospital, or in the train or...I don't know." *Why are the dreams so real?*

"He was your first, well, experiment, in love, darling. And you were, well, just a child. And...he left you. You've been damaged by that and by your parents leaving you at the chateau with only a housekeeper and an old man for company. We will find the best psychiatrist in the city, as soon as we return to London. I promise the nightmares will fade."

Every day, Preston helped her filled in the blanks of her life. Like piecing together a puzzle of familiar pictures that held no meaning. The doctors urged her to be patient and let her memory come back at its own pace.

But the confusion is killing me. Where do my memories stop and Preston's begin?

Her image of Margaret was strong. And of Lenny. Enough to feel a well of love and kindness. It seemed easy to imagine herself with them, growing up at the chateau. Preston painted a comforting picture of the estate. But, in the space between wakefulness and sleep, wild, passionate music filled her head, dancers swirled in rainbow clothes and beautiful, dark-haired people cherished her, but they disappeared with the sun; as her stomach clenched and bile rose in her throat with the force of lost emotions.

Just nightmares. Preston said so.

Snow-White and Rose-Red sat by her, as she somehow knew they always had, their laughter tinkling in her ears. Odd, that they brought her so much comfort, though they were only a figment of her imagination. She kept their presence to herself.

Can't have Preston thinking I'm that crazy. Except...maybe I am that crazy.

She did remember packing for their journey to Prague. Strange, but simple things shone among the confusion. She saw Preston holding her at the hospital, her smiling at the sweetness of his dimples as he led her outside after weeks of long, intense recovery. But blank space reigned for the time in between. *The doctors said something about traumatic experiences disappearing from memory? Told her not to worry.*

She sensed, in private, they thought it unlikely she'd ever remember it all.

But Preston had told her the story. Over and over; how he'd held her hand and waited while the emergency vehicles freed her broken body from the wreckage. How, together, they'd watched Grace's body as it was hauled from the train. How he'd bowed his head in prayer for them all.

And how she'd passed her seventeenth birthday in the hospital, barely awake. He'd brought a cake to her room anyway, and filled the stark whiteness with flowers.

She remembered the flowers.

Now, she languished, alone for most of the day in the plush bedroom of the Prague mansion they'd rented for her recovery; not just her memory but also still, her broken leg. Edward and Preston flew back and forth from London on business, leaving her with a nurse. Svetla was from Pilsen. Her accent made English sound like an entirely new language. But, she was kind and thoughtful and, sometimes, tried to make Claudia laugh. After a while, Claudia had started to relish the challenge of figuring out the warbled English.

*But once my leg is out of the cast...*Preston and Edward were in a great hurry to relocate back to London, once they'd sold chateau. *Why would they sell something so beautiful? Grace's house. And poor Margaret and Lenny, what will become of them?*

She sighed and tried to sit up, as Preston fluffed a pillow

behind her head.

"We have the will reading this afternoon, so the nurse will help you dress to meet the lawyer. He's agreed to come here, so we needn't move you unnecessarily."

"Okay." The will. *How awful, that in the end, life amounted to nothing but a piece of paper and material processions to be handed out to the ones left behind. And sold.*

Feet hurried up the hall and Edward popped his balding head around the door. Both men grinned at each other and Claudia felt the underlying sense of excitement running from one man to the other. *But we speak of sadness, not joy.*

Edward's face reconstructed itself into the more familiar one of serious, subdued grief as his eyes met hers. Claudia seemed to recall that she hated him.

"How are you feeling, Claudia? Hmm? Looking brighter, good girl. After the will reading today, we should be able to release some money to get you back to London. You'll travel in style, my dear. And you will be looked after...you can continue your recuperation there, until the wedding," Edward said.

Why is it necessary to use those funds? Isn't Preston wealthy in his own right?

She just nodded.

Preston looked at her intently. He seemed to read her mind. "Not that I wouldn't pay, darling, but we don't make money by wasting it now, do we? We need to find out what all our resources are and invest it immediately into the business. Edward's business that is, now that I've finished my studies and he's invited me to join him." Preston's chest swelled and he looped his fingers through the belt on his pants, thrusting his pelvis forward. "This afternoon, we'll know."

Claudia didn't care about money. At all. It seemed completely irrelevant. But she did care that Preston was here, now. And that she wasn't alone. Her eyelids drooped with heaviness. *Why can't I just stay awake? Need to.* But her eyes closed.

"This afternoon can't come too quickly I say, I only hope the girl manages to stay awake to sign everything. Tell the nurse to ease off on those pills, just for today." Edward's voice, gruff and quiet, faded slowly down the tunnel of sleep.

"Yes, she must be awake to hear how much she, or rather, we, will be gloriously swimming in. God rest her mother's soul, I shall never need to work again." Preston's voice had dropped to a whisper, but it still floated into her subconscious.

"One can never have enough, boy," Edward replied with a low chuckle. "In any case, I'll need a lot for the campaign. Can't take on the Prime Minister without funds."

"Can't afford me as your right-hand man without it either."

The men laughed and Claudia heard the sound echo in the hall as they walked away. The money banter should have meant something to her, but it didn't. Her mind was as empty as her heart had been before Preston filled the gap. Even if she'd wanted to, she couldn't come up with an emotional reaction. And she didn't want to.

Did my soul escape with my memory?

Weeks later, or maybe months — she had no indicator of time but for the sun rising and setting — Svetla helped her outside to the courtyard. Apparently, she had a visitor. *Who would visit me here?* She dared not hope for Margaret and Lenny, the only two people in the world she felt anything for, in the blank recesses of her heart. She almost walked normally now, her leg a little painful, but working, at least.

Not so, was her mind. *Filled with nothing but Preston's words.*

Perhaps it was the lawyer. *What was his name?* He said he'd return, and his eyes had been kind as he'd read Grace's will. Dark brown eyes, she recalled, because they'd moved something inside her, something hidden and out of reach. She hadn't yet signed the papers, declaring her the sole beneficiary of Grace's entire fortune — and Grace's father's and his father's before that — and now it would be Preston's to share. Perhaps that's why the lawyer had come.

The details escaped her, but she remembered the look of intense joy on Preston's face when the amount had been divulged. She sighed, reaching out to clasp Svetla's hand as they struggled down the stairs. Other than her signature, Preston and Edward could take care of it all. She simply didn't have the strength, or desire, to care.

Yet, a nagging memory tugged at the back of her mind. The acute gaze of sympathy from the lawyer when he'd learned she was about to be married. He'd stared at her long and hard, so much so that the spot between her eyebrows had throbbed and pulsed, reminding her of a happier time — a time of learning, of a dark-haired man speaking of mysteries. A time that the mere recollection of, caused her palms to sweat and her throat to constrict. She succumbed to the memories, as Svetla guided her down: down to the unknown person below the stairs.

That day, as soon as Preston and Edward had left the room to gather paper work, the lawyer had bent close to whisper in her ear. "Claudia, please listen, carefully. I know it's hard; I know you're in pain." She remembered the warmth of his hand grazing her arm. "But, have you considered a pre-nuptial agreement before your marriage? It's not that your fiancé isn't wealthy. I mean...well, yes. But this kind of money, your money, could last for generations. You might want to consider safeguarding the bulk of it. I can help you." His words sounded clipped, urgent.

"I don't really understand."

He'd frowned then, opening his mouth to speak.

But Preston and Edward had returned, and the moment was over.

Now, the thought of it gnawed at her. Perhaps she would have a second chance to speak with him; she hoped.

But the woman sitting in the courtyard, with the sun turning her chocolate brown hair into a halo of autumn highlights, was no lawyer. *A gypsy?* She gazed into Claudia's eyes with a familiar intensity. She wore a long, orange dress, the skirt flowing to her feet and trailing the courtyard pavements as she walked towards her. *Beautiful. She's so beautiful. Who...?*

For moments, she forgot to breathe. She pressed herself into Svetla, suddenly desperate to escape that gaze, to escape the feelings flooding her. Emotions she could feel would drown Preston's carefully formulated world; a world she had felt safe in.

The gypsy stood, holding her hand out towards Svetla's face, as if the nurse were an excited horse to be placated. "Go, now, all is well. Your charge is perfectly safe with me."

Svetla's body pulled back. *Leaving, she's leaving me.* Panic tingled her spine.

"Claudia, don't you recognise me?" The voice was low and smooth, as if coated in velvet.

"Yes. I think so." Her mouth was dry. Her knees trembled and she fought to stay standing. But...somewhere, she felt love. *Love and longing.*

"It's me, Oriana. It has not been so long, after all, barely a year." The gypsy's forehead crinkled. "Cosima knew...we knew you had memory loss, but we didn't know how bad it was." Her hand, still raised, waved back and forward before Claudia's face, hypnotising in its grace.

"I do remember...something...I..." Claudia lowered her eyes and cleared her throat. "I feel something for you." Peace, calm, love, joy. She tasted the emotions as they rolled over her.

The gypsy smiled. "Of course you do precious, we are family. You are of my heart. Here, come. Come." Oriana held out her arms.

Magnetised, Claudia stepped towards Oriana, sitting now, on the patio chair, arms open and welcoming. Claudia curled into her lap, laying her head on the tanned shoulder, breathing in the scent of roses from the silken hair.

"There, there, my sweet lost one. Let the memories come. They must; they will in time. You've been too long in the control of master manipulators. I came for you as soon as I could, you must believe me. You've not been abandoned, it just took time for your green-eyed guides to find us, to tell us where to find you." Oriana ran her fingers over Claudia's hair, her arms, her hands.

Her mind exploded with images. "I can't do this. It's too much." Claudia's hands quivered as she clawed at her own head.

"Don't be afraid, my sweet one. They've placed triggers in your mind to make you believe false memories, bad memories. Find your own, Claudia, they are your soul, your heart, your life. Embrace them and the false will separate from the truth. You will see clearly again." As she spoke, Oriana pressed her thumbs around Claudia's eyes, murmuring and chanting.

Claudia took a deep breath and let the war rage inside her head, trusting the woman who so lovingly held her. It would get clearer, she knew, somehow.

Then, she fazed into a trance, frozen within its spell.

"It is simple neuro-stress release, Claudia, not magic, relax and be calm."

And so she did. The memories came. Her deep love for Dane and Brishan. The gatekeeper's evilness, Spotty the cat, the lake, the terror of vigilantes at the chateau, Grace and Edward invading her life, and again, Brishan. Always Brishan.

Oh God, the train crash.

Now, she saw Brishan rushing towards her. Soothing her, calming her, loving her. Brishan, standing in the hospital, devastation killing him as she ordered him away, proving her dreams true.

And Preston, running from the train. Leaving her — and Grace — to die.

Not dreams, but truths, muddled and chaotic and confused, but penetrating the hard shell coating her soul.

Her mouth fell open as she squeezed Oriana's arms. "You're safe!"

Oriana smiled, a smile that did not reach her eyes. "Yes. My life is safe."

Claudia's stomach churned, her eyes watered with unshed tears and her chest heaved to contain her thudding heart.

Oriana clutched at her cheeks with sharp fingers. "We must leave here. Now. Your jailors return as we speak. Eamon is outside with a car, you don't have time to pack anything."

The last remains of an enforced fog lifted from Claudia's mind, reacting to Oriana's urgent tone. "You know they will search for me, they'll do anything to get Grace's money."

"We know." Oriana's arms were under her shoulders, helping her to stand.

They stepped onto the street. A street she barely knew.

A round face, engulfed by a shock red hair, appeared to her. The Irishman, Brishan's father, embraced her, cradling her like a broken dove, tears streaming down his freckled cheeks. "Brishan's little fairy. You're home now, sweetheart. Home with us. Forever."

Home. Yes, home, I feel it.

"Come now, we must leave," Eamon said, shuffling her into the back seat, his eyes glancing up and down the narrow, cobbled street. Oriana slid in beside her.

"What of Dane and Brishan?" Claudia caught Oriana's hand, lost in the anticipation of reuniting with her father and her precious, precious Brishan.

Oriana's eyes fluttered closed, hiding her thoughts. "You must trust me. No questions for now. Not now."

"Okay." Claudia held her breath.

"But an answer, please. Just then, when your memories returned in full, did you see yourself ordering Brishan away? At the hospital?" Oriana opened her eyes, and the intensity behind the brown forced a gasp from Claudia's throat.

"Yes."

"Sweetheart, there's no easy way to tell you this. He chooses death rather than life without you and…there's worse."

"How can it be worse?" Claudia whispered, chest tight as narrow walls closed in over her heart.

"This is where you must trust me and ask no questions. Brishan is in grave danger and only you can help him. His mind is full of nothing but revenge and death and we can't reach him, no matter what we do. Not even Cosima can help. We must focus on this. Now."

"I dreamt…" *Oh God, just breathe.*

Oriana clutched at her shoulders. "What? What did you dream?

"He was…about to be shot. And…" Claudia gulped in air. "He didn't care."

"Claudia. This is very important. You and he are intrinsically linked. Your dream could help us predict his movements. Where were you?"

Claudia thought back to the smoky room with the seductive, red-haired woman. "In a room, maybe some kind of brothel. There were beautiful women, leather chairs, smoke. And men with guns."

Eamon glanced back at Oriana from the driver's seat and the air grew thick with tension.

"Faster, Eamon. Straight to the airport," Oriana said.

Eamon accelerated the rental car through the winding streets of Prague. The city's black turrets whizzed by; gone before Claudia had even begun to explore.

"Nothing is important right now, except your concentration, Claudia. We're going straight to London on the first flight we can get. You must try to reach Brishan. It will be hard; he thinks you're lost to him and he's filled with pain, a pain even I can't penetrate. But I know you can." Oriana's eyes filled with tears and her sadness scared Claudia to the core.

"I don't know how to do that. The other times, like when I saw Dane, have been nothing but...accidents."

"I understand. I'll help you. We can meditate to a place where the outside world is irrelevant and you only speak to your inner being. This is the way you can reach him."

Claudia reached for Oriana's hand and nodded. All that mattered was Brishan and her life with him. With them all.

My family.

Under Oriana's skilful hypnosis, Claudia tried to make sense of the scene through the clouds. London's landmarks stood tall in the mist as the plane descended into the city, and she wished she'd been alert for her first ever plane trip.

I've failed. Brishan was still lost to her, even on the astral plane, even though she'd felt the thread of his love — somewhere. She'd tried searching for Dane also, even though it meant disobeying Oriana's instructions. But she couldn't help it; a void accompanied each thought of her father, unnerving her.

"Claudia, you've not failed. Every time you focus on Brishan, it brings us closer to him. You learn fast." Eamon winked at her "But you still might need help with this," he said and leant over to fasten her seatbelt.

Tired now, she smiled, no longer surprised at the perceptiveness of her new family. "I'm so sleepy."

"That's normal precious, close your eyes, rest a little, we'll take care of you," Oriana said, leaning over Eamon from the aisle seat to stroke Claudia's cheek as the plane dipped low through the clouds.

The carnival grounds exploded with noise. Festival goers, music and the mouth-watering smell of fried food assailed her senses and Claudia held fast to Eamon's hand. Lights flashed and bells rang as she was pulled through a maze of people. She realised she'd been holding her breath only when they ducked beneath a fence made of black, plastic tarps, to arrive at a small caravan park.

Cosima stood in the distance, a bright, solo figure in a purple and orange robe. "Hurry, there's no time to lose." The master healer's voice rose above the noise.

Claudia's heart thudded like the drums at the festival.

Standing in front of a large, bright caravan was Selina, arms open and tears flowing unchecked down her cheeks. Claudia ran to her and buried her face in the gypsy's chest, soaking the unfettered love into her own heart.

"Sit." Cosima commanded, pointing to a small footstool inside the caravan.

Selina looked at Claudia and nodded. "Sit here and close your eyes, my lovely one," she said, indicating to Cosima it was time. With that, a potion smelling of aniseed and peppermint was shoved under her nose. "Drink." She threw her head back to shot the black liquid. It warmed her throat, her stomach, her cheeks. *Am I drunk?*

"Claudia, close your eyes. Don't worry. Just relax with it and please…visualise yourself tied by a thread to Brishan, an unbreakable thread. Grasp the thread and follow it, keep following it and trust that you will reach him," Selina said, her tone low and melodic. "I know, we all know, you can reach my son. My only son."

Claudia closed her eyes and tried to focus on Selina's words.

She followed the long, thick thread, woven with gold, its end floating in front of her face and heading up into the sky, all the way to the horizon. She grasped it with both hands. One in front of the other, she climbed, higher and higher until the blue changed to rose pink. Scattered clouds moved through the twilight sky and within the clouds, images appeared.

There was a busy road, a wide building with a terracotta façade, a security guard standing beneath green awnings. *And…Brishan!* In front of the building. His hair gleamed, pulled back in a ponytail, and a grey suit hugged the rippling muscles of his lean body. The green eyes came closer into focus. *He sees me...* They narrowed as he watched her climb further up the thread towards him. She smiled and frantically pushed forward, groaning with the effort.

But the eyes turned away. Brishan turned so his back was to her, his fists balled and his shoulders rising and falling as if he struggled to breathe.

"Ahh..." she opened her eyes, shivering, crying, moaning into her hands.

"Are you all right, precious?" Oriana hugged her.

Claudia nodded, gasping as she tried to relay the vision to the anxious faces staring down at her.

"Harrods!" Eamon whooped, clapping his hand to his thigh.

"Yes, I see now, you have unmasked his emotional block. Clever girl, Claudia. But you have only minutes. Go," Cosima said.

Just go? What do we do when we get there? He turned away...he doesn't want me... She opened her mouth to speak.

"No, no questions. Not yet. Come." Oriana reached for her elbow.

Selina raised a hand, in goodbye or good luck, Claudia couldn't tell. "I would go with you, but I...I can't..."

"Your son comes back with us. Trust me." Oriana stared into her sister's eyes as she pulled Claudia from the van.

And then they were running again, through the festival, weaving in and out of lines of people, all the way to Eamon's old Renault parked on the street. Limping now, her leg aching in protest, Claudia slid into the car.

"Listen carefully." Oriana turned to face her in the back seat. "When we find Brishan, we'll stop the car as close as we can. You will have only a few seconds to stop him from getting into a black limousine. Do you understand?"

"This is crazy," Claudia whispered.

"Yes, it is." Oriana's hand lifted to graze Claudia's forehead, pressing her thumb over her third eye.

Calm. Important to stay calm. "Yes. I understand. But what if he refuses to listen to me, or even see me? He turned away from me only moments ago, yet, I know he saw me."

"If he gets into the limousine...as you saw in your dream, so it will happen. He must not attack because of revenge." Oriana paused, pushing her hair from her face, her trembling hand betraying her nerves. "He is a healer, foretold to be one of the greatest of our time, the act of it will kill him. But, right now, he has nothing in his heart but revenge."

Sweat trickled down the back of Claudia's neck. "Revenge for what? For..."

"I said no questions. Claudia, you must compose yourself." Claudia could barely keep looking at Oriana, so intense were her eyes right then.

"Okay." She steeled herself. She was on the verge of leaping headlong into a fire but it was one she didn't create and didn't know how to put out.

The car, under Eamon's deft hands, took a sharp corner and the busy street from her vision materialised. Her eyes flicked over the pavement, searching for Brishan. *Too many people, too many cars and motor bikes and buses. Don't panic.*

"There!" Oriana yelled.

Eamon cranked hard left on the steering wheel and the car screeched to a halt behind a bus. Claudia turned to look out the window.

Brishan.

He stood tall and rigid, one hand moving to open the back door of a sleek, black limousine. Claudia sensed his anger, his panic. His fearless resolve to die.

She flung the door open, hitting the pavement hard on the soles of her feet. She ran into the crowd surrounding Harrods, eyes glued on Brishan as he ducked his head to slide into the backseat of the limousine.

Her breathing deafened her. The light, the noise, the smell of fuel was ultra-sharp. Air whooshed by as she pushed arms and bags out of her way, weaving under elbows and dodging angry words blending together in a low drone.

So close now. His upper body disappeared inside the car.

She leapt forward, her arms reaching for his legs.

"Ahh..." Her knees smashed into the pavement as her hands caught Brishan's ankles, pulling them out from under him.

Concrete grazed her chin and pain exploded in her jaw as her face connected with the gutter, trapped under the weight of Brishan's falling body.

Her eyes filled with dirt as black tyres, inches from her nose, whirled to life, screeching away from the curb. She blinked furiously and tried to focus on Brishan as he sprang to his feet above her.

His mouth gaped and his arms reached out to block bystanders as they rushed to her aid. A man pushed Brishan from behind, ordering him to move, screaming, "Help the girl!"

Me, I'm the girl. Focus. Breathe. Stand up.

Brishan shoved the man back into the crowd with one hand, all the while staring at her with crazy, tear-filled eyes.

Claudia struggled to sit, watching blood drip from her chin to stain the grey gutter red. Her tears mixed with the red as she met Brishan's gaze, fighting her fear of what she'd find there.

Brishan knelt down to her, his hands lifting as if to cup her face.

"I'm not a ghost." Claudia smiled, cringing as the movement tore at her skin.

"You must be...an illusion." His voice cracked as he cradled the back of her head with one hand. The other gripped her elbow, helping her to stand, the strong fingers digging into her skin.

"I'm in too much pain to be an illusion."

A tortured groan followed his sharp intake of breath. He pulled her face towards his. Feather light, Brishan touched his mouth to hers: a kiss so tender, so *real*.

She swayed, falling back, trembling so much she feared her legs would give way.

"I've got you, my fairy." Brishan scooped her up in his arms, holding her against his chest as if she might break.

"And I've got you," she rasped through the sting of gravel lodged in her skin.

He smiled then, a radiant, beaming smile as he turned to carry her through the crowd gathered on the pavement. Strangers stared at them; excited onlookers whispering, pointing, stepping reluctantly aside to create a path.

Oriana and Eamon stood by the old Renault, beaming faces streaked with tears, arms held out to enfold them. This, thought Claudia, is love. This is home. She was bundled into the back seat, gentle hands cleaning her cuts, lips brushing her cheeks, cool touches soothing her brow.

Brishan's arms circled her waist in a grip that was a little too tight and his emerald gaze fixed, still and unwavering, on hers. "How? What are you doing here?" he asked, his voice little more than a whisper.

Claudia's eyes flicked from Oriana to Eamon and back again, nerves fluttering in her stomach.

"We're saving your life, my nephew," Oriana said. "But we didn't think we might have to be bowling you over in the street." She smiled, the cheeky twinkle of old returning to her eyes as she glanced at Claudia.

Like the sun peeping out from dark clouds, the corners of Brishan's mouth tugged upwards and slowly, delightfully, his lopsided grin transformed his face.

"Bowling me over was the best thing you could have done. I thought I'd died when I fell, and that smack on my head...well, I thought it was heaven when I opened my eyes and saw you. Apart from the blood on your chin." Brishan said, eyes wide with wonder, love.

Why can I feel his emotions? Almost taste them?

Claudia grazed his cheek with the back of her hand, trailing a path to his lips. One by one, he kissed her fingers, closing his eyes and inhaling deep through his nose.

Eamon stopped the car. They were in front of a row of public phone boxes.

"Hey! Can't we just get her back home?" Brishan tapped his father on the back.

Eamon stepped out of the car and bent down to look through the window. "Steady on there, Casanova. We've managed to save you from killing yourself, so, hopefully, your little fairy here will keep you too occupied to get into any more trouble. And now, we'll finish business my way." He winked, almost strutting as he walked to the nearest phone.

Claudia looked up, and felt Brishan's tears drop, one by one, onto her forehead.

No. No more. There's been enough sorrow. I can't take anymore. But her body tingled with the familiar foresight. Of danger. Of pain. *I don't want to know. Please.*

"You know what he's going to do, don't you?" said Oriana, her breathing quick and her voice low. "He's going to call the police. Every police station in the area and tell them about the secret entrance to the Lair. Not all of those officers can be corrupt. Someone will follow through. Someone has to."

Oriana turned to look at Brishan, speaking directly to him of things Claudia was yet to understand. "And they can't harm us now that he...now that we're both out of there. To them, I am dead and no threat, and they have no way of finding out who you are, Brishan, even after the ruse is discovered...which it surely will be. That actor, Valentino, will deny it, and let's just hope, for his sake, it doesn't go public." Oriana's words tripped over themselves in her race to say it all, her face stretched in a forced smile.

What is she hiding? Claudia's chest tightened as if she'd held her breath to long. "Where...where is Dane?" The question spilled from her mouth before fear froze her vocal cords.

Oriana's eyes shone with unshed tears. She sighed, turning to nod at Brishan.

Brishan's arms cradled her so tight that her ribs ached with the pressure. "I love you," he whispered, his eyes scanning her face.

"I love you too."

"I think, somewhere deep down, you already know what we have to tell you."

Claudia gasped for air, the weight of realisation bearing down on her with unrelenting force.

Tears pooled in Brishan's eyes as he stroked her cheek, her hair, murmuring her name over and over in a broken, grief stricken tone. "I'm so, so sorry...my beautiful girl...hold onto me, I've got you...Dane is...gone from this life."

Gone. No...he can't be...can't breathe.

Take the words back.

Take it back.

Chapter Sixteen

The Treasure Trove

Claudia swam to the centre of the lake, her arms slicing the surface in powerful, even strokes. There, Brishan waited, his skin glowing under the twilight sky. Water lapped at his shoulders and she noticed how strong he was, how alert, always there to protect her.

She smiled, knowing there was no need, not now, not when her body grew stronger and stronger as the months flew by. She pushed forward to swim into his arms, watching his biceps clench as he pulled her close.

Beautiful, he's so, so beautiful.

Her nose lifted to breathe in his scent. She let her hands graze his chest, loving the hard muscles beneath. "We should get back, *you know* how Margaret gets when we're late for tea." Claudia glanced over her shoulder towards the chateau, just visible in the dimming light.

"Hmm. No, I don't want to leave…not just yet." Brishan ran his fingers over her lips and she parted them, helpless under his gaze.

He sighed, lifting her chin to kiss her, feeding on her lips, her cheeks, her neck.

Her legs clenched his waist as he waded into the shallows. She laced her fingers through his dripping hair, sliding them over his ears, trailing a path from his nose to the edge of his jaw.

When her feet touched soft sand, she stood to face him. Brishan rubbed her shoulders, hooking his fingers under the straps of her swimsuit to slide them over her arms — so slowly that she ached for the moment the cloth left her body. Heavy with cool water, the swimsuit grazed her nipples as it fell away, leaving her bare under his gaze.

"You're..." He cleared his throat, one hand reaching for her face. "You're the most beautiful thing on earth." His chest rose and fell, faster and faster as his emerald eyes feasted on her body.

Soft kisses followed his fingers across her collarbone, between her breasts, teasing her tightening stomach. He moaned, his breath hot on her skin as he curled one hand around her side and wove the other into her hair, pulling her closer; closer into him.

I could drown in this.

She gasped; her mouth opening on his, her mind relishing his sharp intake of breath as their tongues connected.

Then, he was picking her up, carrying her to the grassy bank, pushing her with urgency against the ancient oak tree. Their fingers entwined as he raised her arms above her head and gazed down at her naked body.

Her eyes fluttered closed; she could taste his desire in the air. One hand clasped her wrists, holding her captive against the rough bark of the tree. The other trailed down her arm, his hot palm leaving mini fires in its wake as he cupped her breast. She swayed, squirming and twisting against the rising tension as he rubbed one finger down the centre of her, circling and probing until she arched against him, her blood roaring through her veins.

"I love you," he whispered, his voice husky in her ear.

She cried out; moaning as he pressed into her; changing her, claiming her as his own.

On this, her eighteenth birthday.

"Claudia!" Margaret's voice competed with the dusk loving crickets as it echoed over the valley.

Claudia shivered, her nerve endings still exquisitely sensitive. She sat up within the circle of Brishan's arms.

"I've wanted you, like that, for so long." His eyes flicked back and forth over hers, to her lips, and up again.

"I know," she whispered. "Me too."

"Was it…are you…are you all right?"

"I'm in love." *Melting. I'm melting in his eyes. Do I feel different?* She inspected her body, looking for physical marks of first time, passionate, all-encompassing sex. *Stupid.* There was only love.

"Oh no. Terrible infliction, being in love. But I know how you feel." Brishan winked, finding her clothes, helping her dress. He kissed the tip of her nose, lifting her in his arms to carry her home. *Home.*

Lights burned bright in the kitchen. Brishan lowered her to the step at the back door, putting one finger to his mouth. They rested their ears against the wood, laughing into their hands as they listened for Margaret. Claudia could hear footsteps in the kitchen, too many it seemed, but the sharp-tongued voice of the housekeeper was absent. She nodded, and Brishan turned the handle.

"Happy Birthday to you,
Happy Birthday to you,
Happy Birthday, dear Claudia,
Happy Birthday to you!"

Claudia's hands flew to her cheeks. Her eyes widened at the sight of Margaret and Lenny, Oriana, Selina and Eamon, even Cosima, all singing at the top of their lungs, clapping, smiling and reaching to hug her.

A cake took pride of place in the middle of the table; three layers of chocolate dotted with delicate icing roses. Eighteen candles glowed, one in the middle of each rose.

"Margaret, it's a masterpiece!" Claudia threw her arms around the housekeeper.

Margaret beamed. "You deserve a masterpiece for your special birthday, dear. Mind you, it took so long to make, I hardly want to eat it now."

Lenny chuckled, putting his arms around them both. "The little lass here and I'll be happy to eat it for you." He winked, a special wink just for her, and her stomach clenched with love for him.

Please let me keep this feeling forever.

"Come into the parlour, Claudia, while Margaret finishes the tea." Oriana caught her elbow, leaning in close to her ear. "You're positively glowing, precious."

Claudia blushed under Oriana's amused, sideways glance, ducking her head into the gypsy's arm.

"I...um..." Snow-White and Rose-Red fluttered about her head, beckoning with dancing hands. Claudia welcomed the distraction.

"It's okay, sweetheart. I promise I won't joke about it...much." Oriana laughed, pulling her in for a tight hug. "I'm just so thrilled for you both. But if you want to talk, you know you can tell me anything." Oriana smiled, pushing the parlour door open and presenting the room with a sweeping hand.

Flowers, vines and miniature fairy statues decorated the red velvet walls, swayed from the ceiling and glistened in the light of hundreds of candles. Oriana nudged her forward, into the centre, her smile so radiant it took Claudia's breath away.

A single, haunting note from a violin pierced her soul. She turned, gasping as Brishan stepped forward from the flickering shadows. The bow, in his hands, moved with heart-breaking grace as he teased Rimsky-Korsakov's '*Scheherazade*' from the strings. One by one, her loved ones drifted in to stand behind her, mesmerised by the music.

Above the sound, she heard Margaret sniffling and Lenny clearing his throat; embarrassed, no doubt, by the sentiment.

Then, only awed silence greeted Brishan as he lowered the bow, still gazing at her, the corners of his lips tugging upwards. Claudia cupped her hands over her mouth and blew him a kiss.

"Good heavens, Brishan, that is the most beautiful thing I've ever heard," Margaret gushed, wiping her eyes with the corner of her apron. "Well, almost as good as hearing the news that Edward Spencer was hauled off to jail last week."

"Shush, love, now's not the time to bring that up," Lenny covered Claudia's ears with his hands, eyebrows raised high at the housekeeper.

Cosima clapped her hands together, a rare smile lighting her face. "You're right, Lennard, let's not defile the moment." The master healer turned to Brishan. "Your talent defies even your own extraordinary heritage, my boy. Come, it is time." Her gaze fixed on Claudia, darting around as the witch caught sight of Snow-White and Rose-Red. "Off with you, girls, she needs to focus."

Margaret shuffled her feet. "Erm, I'll just go back to getting the tea. I'll be needing some help, please."

Poor Margaret, still scared of what she can't see — or understand. Claudia realised that maybe she was too.

Selina and Eamon hugged each other as they left with Margaret. Cosima and Lenny followed the couple, looking far too excited about the prospect of helping in the kitchen.

Claudia shivered with unexpected nerves.

"We have another gift for you, birthday fairy." Brishan caught both her hands in his, pulling her down to sit on the floor.

Oriana already sat, cross-legged, before them. "To receive this gift, you need do nothing but close your eyes and concentrate. Concentrate on the thread to the astral plane. Catch hold of it and climb towards the sky, thinking of nothing but love." Oriana placed her hands on top of theirs and closed her eyes.

Brishan swirled his fingers inside her palm. *Be still, calm, relaxed.* His voice filled her head. *But how?*

Silence arrived: warm, deep silence. The black behind her eyes soon filled with white and the gold thread dangled above, daring her to catch hold of it. Climbing was easy, she felt weightless, energetic, joyful. Higher and higher, one hand over the other, she moved towards the bright white.

Her fingers slipped from the end of the thread and her body relaxed into stillness. Thick tendrils of mist caressed her skin, bathed her body in gold and tickled her nose with the smell of spring. Her hands floated in the air of their own accord, stretching to wade through the mist.

The mist started to thin, to drift away, leaving in its wake a tranquillity that spread through her veins until she felt the subtle, golden glow transfuse with her blood.

Far in the distance, a man walked towards her: a black silhouette with greens and purples and yellows surrounding it like a rainbow halo. Threads curled from his body, reaching out to her, connecting her body to his. She squeezed her eyes shut tighter, trying to focus on his red shirt, black jeans and tanned, bare feet. Black curls bounced as he started to run and dark, dark eyes crinkled at the corners with his smile.

She stretched her hand out, incapable of speech or movement.

"Claudia, my daughter."

But...it's not possible.

Dane opened his arms, his laughter feeding her soul. "Oh, but it is. In this realm, almost anything is. Happy Birthday, little lady of the glass house."

She flew into his arms, grasping his back, smelling his shirt, resting her head against his chest to hear his heartbeat. *Real, he's real. I feel him. Am I dreaming?*

Again, he laughed. "Not quite, but soon you will understand. That's what I've come to tell you, my precious child, that your path, along the gypsy trail, has only just begun, and that's the greatest gift that I...that all of us...can give you."

The rush of love swelling her chest was too much to contain and Claudia opened her eyes. The vision was gone.

But Brishan's green gaze was there, holding hers, safe in their emerald glow.

She blinked, pushing her hair back from her face, looking towards the ceiling as if Dane would be there, floating above them. "What...how..." She swallowed, caught between fear and

---

awe.

"It's okay, Claudia, nothing to be scared of. Your world will soon open to these mysteries, as you learn, as you grow. Dane can't be with us…always…" Oriana glanced down at her own hands, a single tear tracing a path down her cheek. "But, he's not gone in the way that you think he is. Our spirits are eternal, and eternally connected. Brishan?" She quirked a brow at her nephew, and Brishan blushed.

He's blushing? Claudia sensed his discomfort, fear almost. She squeezed his hand and her spine tingled, sensing…*what? Danger?*

He took a deep breath, hiding his eyes beneath his black lashes. When he next looked up, the green burned with an unnatural, other-worldly glow. "Claudia, we…I…have something to tell you. Something you must know. It's time for you to know."

Claudia's eyes darted from Brishan, to Selina, and back again.

"My precious fairy. You know I love you. I have loved you forever, thousands of years, in fact."

A nervous giggle bubbled in her throat. "I feel like I've loved you forever too, maybe not thousands of years…" Her laugh erupted: a shallow, quivering mockery.

He gazed at her lips, then met her eyes with shocking intensity. "I speak the truth. I have loved you for thousands of years because…"

Sweat trickled a path down her spine.

"You are my twin flame. The other half of my soul. Our paths are intrinsically linked, and yours, my fairy, blends with mine as a healer. It has been foretold that…our child"—again, he blushed—"will be a guiding light for humanity towards peace. A great spiritual leader, but…you must begin extensive training. That's what Dane meant by the gypsy trail. It won't be easy Claudia…and you must first swear an oath to follow the path. Forever. Will you do this?"

Claudia closed her eyes. Tasted the challenge in the air…the secret treasure trove of endless mystery opening before her. And she knew she belonged in its depths.

"Yes."

And the wind whistled through the chateau's turrets, gaining force, trapped and swirling in narrow crevices. A storm, dense clouds still forming in the distance, rumbled as lightening pierced the dark. Perched high on their ledges, the shadows of gargoyles stretched their talons, inching towards the storm and beyond, to the new light of morning.

Inside, the candles flickered, as if in response to the chaos outside...brewing with the promise of fires lit in the wake of the past.

About the Author

Information about Nicole Leigh West can be found at the author's website, www.nicoleleighwest.com or www.facebook.com/nicoleleighwest

LODESTONE BOOKS

Lodestone Books is a new imprint, which offers a broad spectrum of subjects in YA/NA literature. Compelling reading, the Teen/Young/New Adult reader is sure to find something edgy, enticing and innovative. From dystopian societies, through a whole range of fantasy, horror, science fiction and paranormal fiction, all the way to the other end of the sphere, historical drama, steam-punk adventure, and everything in between. You'll find stories of crime, coming of age and contemporary romance. Whatever your preference you will discover it here.